Peter Xu

林苑『双龙』译丛

总主编◎许景城

英汉对照

爱德华·托马斯诗歌全集译介

基于道家生态诗学视角

[英] 爱德华·托马斯◎著

许景城◎译

知识产权出版社

全国百佳图书出版单位

—北京—

Endorsements

This bilingual edition of Edward Thomas's poetry is a remarkable feat of cultural translation. It also bridges poetry and metaphysics, and wonderfully illuminates poetry's contribution to ecological thinking.

—Edna Longley

An astonishing achievement. Dr Peter Jingcheng Xu's translations have made a valuable contribution to the global reception and recognition of Edward Thomas's poetry.

—Lucy Newlyn

The poems of Edward Thomas are the fruits of an intense and remarkable period of creative intensity. They speak in striking ways of landscape, Englishness, humanity, and an elemental nature. The impact of this work is still being registered a century later. Dr Peter Jingcheng Xu has the expertise and the passion to bring these poems to a wider audience in China. His academic research reveals new richness in Thomas's work, whilst his translations will share that bounty with new readers.

—Samuel Rogers

推荐语

爱德华·托马斯诗歌双语版堪称文化翻译之壮举，不仅搭建了诗歌与哲学的交流桥梁，而且巧妙地阐明了诗歌对生态思想的贡献。

——埃德娜·朗利

可谓惊人之举。许景城博士的译著在推动爱德华·托马斯诗歌的国际接受度进程上做出了极为重要的贡献。

——露西·纽琳

此诗集是爱德华·托马斯诗性才华横溢的结晶，以精巧别致的方式描绘了乡村风景、英格兰特色、人性和物质自然。100 年后，其影响力依旧无远弗届。许景城博士凭借专业的知识素养和热情将托马斯诗歌译介至中国。他的学术研究展示了托马斯作品内涵的新颖性，其中文译本将与新的读者分享那份匠心独妙。

——萨缪尔·罗杰斯

Dr Peter Jingcheng Xu adheres to the principle of "translating poetry with philosophy, interpreting philosophy with poetry, and integrating poetry and philosophy". He has been long engaged not only with the English translation of classical and contemporary Chinese poetry, but also with the Chinese translation of English poetry, the rich practices obtained that enable him to understand Chinese and English poetics, and their translation well. All this I believe without doubts ensures the quality of this book.

—Xiangzhan Cheng

This volume, translated by Dr Peter Jingcheng Xu and well grounded on his in-depth research of Edward Thomas's poetry, is of high poetic value as the first collection of Edward Thomas's poems in entire spectrum ever published in China. Dr Xu's thorough understanding of the source-language text enables him to offer a faithful, smooth and readable translation.

—Zhimin Li

Dr Peter Jingcheng Xu revives the poet's melancholic and romantic temperament in his dynamic, vigorous and scrutinous translation.

—Jia Cheng

许景城博士秉持“以哲译诗、以诗释哲、诗哲相融”的译诗之道，既从事中国古典和现代诗歌的英译，又从事英语诗歌的中译，对于中英诗歌的各自特点及其互译有着比较丰富的实践。这就保证了这本译著的质量。

——程相占

许景城博士对爱德华·托马斯诗歌颇有研究，并在此基础上翻译出版了爱德华·托马斯诗歌全集，这是在我国出版的第一部爱德华·托马斯诗歌全集及译文，具有很高的诗学价值。许景城博士对原文理解透彻，译文准确流畅，可读性很强。

——黎志敏

许景城博士这个译本生动而又细致地再现了诗人的沉郁浪漫气质。

——程佳

This work is supported by both the Excellent Young Talents Fund Program, the Institute of Hermeneutics (grant number CSY-2021-YA-07) and the Scientific Research Foundation for Returned Overseas Chinese Scholars and Early Career Researchers, Guangdong University of Foreign Studies (grant number 2021RC213).

本书获广东外语外贸大学阐释学研究院 2021 年度创新研究项目（编号：CSY–2021–YA–07）和广东外语外贸大学引进人才科研启动项目（编号：2021RC213）资助。

To every being that loves me and I love

谨以此书献给爱我和我爱的万物苍生

Preface for Chinese Translation of Edward Thomas

By Professor Edna Longley
(Queen's University Belfast, Northern Ireland)

Edward Thomas (1878—1917)

Edward Thomas was killed on 9 April, 1917 at the start of the Battle of Arras. A hundred years after his death, his reputation has never been higher. Thomas wrote his first poems in December 1914 when he was thirty-six. His late start as a poet, together with his early death, meant that appreciation of his poetry took time to widen and deepen. But Edward Thomas is now acknowledged to be one of the makers of modern poetry in the English language.

“爱德华·托马斯汉译集”序

埃德娜·朗利[1] 作

（北爱尔兰贝尔法斯特女王大学）

许景城 译

爱德华·托马斯（1878—1917）

1917年4月9日，爱德华·托马斯殁于阿拉斯战役之初。卒后百年，其声望极高。1914年12月，36岁的他，开始作诗。作为诗人的他，大器晚成，却英年早逝。这就意味着，无论在广度上还是在深度上，若深层次地欣赏其诗，皆需要时间。时至今日，托马斯已被公认为现代英语诗歌的奠基者之一。

[1] 北爱尔兰贝尔法斯特女王大学文艺批评教授，英国诗歌和爱尔兰文学批评家、著名的托马斯研究专家。——译者注

This is shown by the growth of Thomas studies, by recent publications such as *Now All Roads Lead to France* (2011), Matthew Hollis's account of Thomas's last years, and Jean Moorcroft Wilson's fuller biography *Edward Thomas: From Adlestrop to Arras* (2015). The very titles of two critical books—Andrew Webb's *Edward Thomas and World Literary Studies* (2013) and my own *Under the Same Moon: Edward Thomas and the English Lyric* (2017)—imply Thomas's importance to the history of poetry in English. Meanwhile, a six-volume Oxford Selected Edition of his prose-writings is underway. Again, as this splendid Chinese publication proves, translations of Thomas's poems are multiplying (an Italian translation has just been published). On a different front, Thomas has greatly influenced the so-called "new Nature-writing": books about the countryside, the natural world and the environment by Robert Macfarlane and others. He is seen as the first truly "ecological" poet. Above all, Thomas is one of those rare modern poets who is loved by "the common reader". And his poetry has been equally loved by poets—from W. H. Auden to Ted Hughes to Seamus Heaney. Thomas remains a live presence in the work of leading Anglophone poets today.

Edward Thomas was a prose writer before he was a poet. His output included country books, meditative essays, impressionistic sketches, and autobiography. But he was also a critic before he was a poet. Another reason why Thomas's

这一点可从托马斯研究不断成为显学得以印证。近些年来相关出版物如下：2011 年，马修·霍利斯出版了《如今条条道路通法国》，该书记录了托马斯生前最后几年的光景；2015 年，吉恩·穆尔克罗夫特·威尔逊出版了更为全面的托马斯传记《爱德华·托马斯：从艾德斯卓普到阿拉斯》。另外，还有两部学术专著分别于 2013 年和 2017 年问世，即安德鲁·韦伯的《爱德华·托马斯和世界文学研究》（2013）和拙作《明月共此时：爱德华·托马斯与英语抒情诗》（2017）。这两部作品暗示了托马斯在英语诗歌史上的重要地位。同时，由牛津大学出版社挑选的爱德华·托马斯散文选集（六卷本）正在筹划当中。此外，这本汉译双语诗集也表明了托马斯诗歌翻译正往多语化和多样化方向发展（意大利语翻译集刚出版不久）。另外，托马斯极大地影响了所谓的"新自然文学创作"，有关乡村、自然界和环境的文学作品，如罗伯特·麦克法兰等人的著作。托马斯被认为是第一位真正的"生态"诗人。最重要的是，他是现代诗人中难得的深受"大众读者"喜爱的诗人之一。他的诗歌同样深受其他诗人，如 W. H. 奥登、泰德·休斯、谢默斯·希尼的青睐。时至今日，在诸多一流英语国家诗人的作品中，托马斯的"身影"依然清晰可见。

托马斯在成为诗人之前是一名散文作家，其创作成果包括了乡村游记、沉思论文集、印象主义素描集、传记等。然而，成为诗人之前，他同时也是一名评论家。之所以成名晚，另一个原因在于其思辨论著还未公开于众。

reputation has grown slowly is because his critical writings have not been generally available. In fact, he was the leading British reviewer of contemporary poetry between 1900 and 1914: a period when poetry was in the melting-pot. He also reviewed editions of earlier poetry, which were proliferating at that date. His knowledge of English poetry was encyclopaedic as well as critically discriminating. This passage (from 1908) suggests the literary world that Thomas inhabited. It marks his close involvement with poetry, his belief in poetry, and his frustrations as an evangelist for new poetry:

> Our poets are seriously absorbed in the life, social, political, philosophic, and artistic of our day ... But we recognise that there are immense and, so far, insuperable difficulties in the way of [their] popularity and of the influence which is their due. Reprints of old, well tested, or well guaranteed poetry abound and catch the attention of the unobservant; and not only poetry but such prose as satisfies similar needs ... Foreign literatures and translations add still further defences which new poetry has to scale ... Then the multiplication of authors, and of writers of verse in particular, makes choice very difficult. An imbecile with ten pounds in his pocket can easily add one to the number of the volumes from which the lover of poetry has to choose. Finally, in a centrifugal age, in which principles and aims are numerous, vague, uncertain, confused, and in conflict, the lack of good criticism, or even of moderately good criticism that has any authority, defrauds many

事实上，1900—1914年（这期间诗歌处于相互融合状态）他曾是一名卓越的英国现代诗歌评论家。此外，他还评论过诸多当时盛行的早期英国诗集。除了其评论极具批判性与鉴别性之外，他的英语诗歌知识浩瀚犹如一部百科全书。以下这段评论为托马斯于1908年所作，暗示了其所处的文学世界，表明了其对诗歌的热爱，其诗歌信念，以及作为新诗布道者所呈现出来的挫折感：

> 我们的诗人认真地汲取当下生活、社会、政治、哲学和艺术的养分……然而，我们意识到他们在获取应有的声望与影响力的道路上历经巨大且截至目前难以逾越的诸多困难。经典的、深受好评的或品质精良的诗歌，重印数量丰硕，同时也引起了大众读者的关注；不只是诗歌，还有散文，皆满足类似的需求……外国文学和译作依旧增添了更为高深的防御之墙，而这需要新诗去不断攀登……此外，作者数量，尤其是诗人的数量倍增，令读者在选择上感到非常困惑。一名蠢货，口袋里装有10英镑，便能轻而易举地让诗歌爱好者必选的作品销量徒增1本。最后，在一个离心的时代，原则和目标不计其数、模糊不清、难以界定、混乱困惑，甚至相互冲突，并且缺乏好的批评，甚至缺乏略好的权威批评，所有这一切都蒙蔽

noble and beautiful voices of the ears which expect them.

Thomas was himself the kind of critic he desired. And he would later become a "noble and beautiful" poetic voice for the "centrifugal" modern age. Perhaps, without knowing it, he was already a poet-critic. Certainly, profound critical thinking underlies his poetry. He wrote prescient reviews of poets like W. B. Yeats and D. H. Lawrence, and especially of Robert Frost. Here Thomas's critical powers helped to awaken his poetic powers. The Anglo-American friendship between Thomas and Frost was one of the great literary friendships. It was the most important creative meeting between English-language poets since Wordsworth and Coleridge. In aesthetic terms, it also curiously resembles that earlier encounter. Like their Romantic precursors, Frost and Thomas believed that poetry should be animated by speech: by what Frost called "sentence-sounds". Thomas sums up Frost's poetic credo as "absolute fidelity to the postures which the voice assumes in the most expressive intimate speech".

Thomas and Frost (like Yeats) also believed that speech could revitalise the syntax and rhythm of so-called "traditional form". In this respect, they differed from "modernists" (like Ezra Pound and T. S. Eliot) who preferred more disjunctive forms. Thomas renewed traditional form by means of infinitely subtle rhythmic variations and his extraordinary range of stanza-shapes. Frost's example was crucial to the mysterious process by which Thomas changed from a prose-writer into a poet. But crucial, too, was his devotion to the whole corpus of English poetry: a devotion intensified by the war.

了预期想听到诸多高尚优美之语的听者。

托马斯本身就是自己梦寐以求的那种评论家。此后，他便在那个“离心”时代发出了“高尚优美”之诗音。或许，他并不知道，自己早已是一位诗评家了。当然，其诗作深藏着深刻的批判性思维。他对 W. B. 叶芝、D. H. 劳伦斯，尤其是罗伯特·佛罗斯特所作的诗评，极富先见之明。可见，托马斯对诗歌的批判性有助于唤醒他的诗歌创造性。托马斯和佛罗斯特之间的英美友谊是伟大文学友谊史上的一段佳话，是自华兹华斯和柯勒律治以降，英语诗人间最重要和富有创造力的一次相遇。从审美角度看，那也是与早期华翁和柯翁相遇有着异曲同工之妙。与浪漫主义先驱们一样，佛罗斯特和托马斯相信诗歌应洋溢着言语：即佛罗斯特所谓的“句—声”。托马斯将佛罗斯特的诗歌信条总结为“完全忠实于最富表现力的亲密言语所展示出来的口吻”。

托马斯和佛罗斯特（像叶芝一样）也认为，言语能让所谓的“传统形式”的句法和韵律节奏重新焕发生机。从这一层面看，他们与“现代主义”诗人，如埃兹拉·庞德、T. S. 艾略特等早已分道扬镳，因为后者喜爱更加转折反意的分离形式。托马斯则通过使用极其精巧的、富有韵律结构的变体，以及使用超凡脱俗的诗节形式，来更新传统诗歌形式。佛罗斯特以身示范，对托马斯从散文作家到诗人这一转变的过程，起到了举足轻重的作用。然而，同样重要的还有托马斯对整个英语诗歌事业的奉献精神——这种奉献精神被战争所强化。那

The Great War was an ambiguous Muse for Thomas. It led him to enlist in July 1915. It led him to be killed in April 1917. His dark poem "Gone, Gone Again" refers to the war as "turning young men to dung". Yet the war may have helped to call forth Thomas's poetry as an act of cultural defence or defiance. His close reading of the English poets underlies his own work. In "Lob", Thomas affirms the historical intercourse between language and landscape, which culminates in poetry:

This is tall Tom that bore
The logs in, and with Shakespeare in the hall
Once talked, when icicles hung by the wall ...

Thus, poetry was the ground of Thomas's patriotism.

Thomas as a Second Lieutenant in 1917

Edward Thomas's poems are a journey to war. For all his concern with Nature, his poems are symbolic rather than

场浩大的战役对于托马斯来说，犹如一位暧昧的缪斯。1915年7月，她带领他入伍参军，导致他1917年4月死于战场。他的黑暗之诗《流逝，再流逝》将战争看作"让青年变为粪丸"的毁灭力量，然而，战争或许有助于唤起读者将托马斯的诗歌看作是一种文化防御或反抗的行为方式。此外，其作品也潜藏着托马斯对其他英国诗人作品的品读。在《罗勃》一诗中，托马斯肯定了语言与风景紧密的历史关系，从下面的诗句中，可见一斑：

汤姆高个子，
搂抱柴火来，莎翁厅中遇，
开口便聊天，冰锥挂墙隅。……

故此，诗歌是托马斯抒发爱国主义情怀的阵地。

1917年陆军少尉托马斯

托马斯的诗歌，犹如一段通往战争的旅程。尽管极其关注自然，但他的诗歌与其说极具自然主义写实风格，

naturalistic. They encompass all the psychological and metaphysical questions whereby the Great War had made modernity still more "centrifugal". "Bob's Lane", another dark poem, was written in June 1916. In this parable Thomas reflects on the complex relations between name and thing, between poetry and history. A farmer, who loves trees, plants elms along a lane, which has lacked a name. By doing so, he unwittingly destroys the lane. The poem ends:

> Many years since, Bob Hayward died, and now
> None passes there because the mist and the rain
> Out of the elms have turned the lane to slough
> And gloom. The name alone survives, Bob's Lane.

The imagery of "slough/ And gloom" hints at the trenches. It symbolises the murky future into which Thomas's poetry faces. The "stormcock" (the missel-thrush) is Thomas as "war poet". Yet the name, which "survives", is a positive sign. It anticipates the survival of Thomas's poetry: a survival that this book wonderfully affirms.

Belfast

7 August, 2017

不如说更具象征主义意味，因为其诗作涉及了所有心理和玄学层面上的议题，借此揭露了“一战”早已让现代性更加“离心”这一特征。另一首幽暗之诗《鲍勃之道》，写于1916年6月。这首寓言诗反思了名与物、诗与史之间的复杂关系，讲述了一位农民喜欢树木，并沿着一条无名巷道种植榆树，而这样做无意中摧毁了这条巷道。正如诗歌结尾所言：

> 多年以后，鲍勃·海沃德离世，如今
> 无人经过那里，因为榆树外的火车
> 与迷雾已将小道变成阴郁之境
> 和泥沼，仅名字“鲍勃之道”幸存着。

这组意象“阴郁之境 / 和泥沼”暗示了战壕的情形，象征了托马斯诗歌所要面对的阴暗未来。“田鸫”(即槲鸫)指代“战争诗人”托马斯。这“幸存”下来的头衔却发出了一种积极的信号。它预示了托马斯诗歌的幸存：本书便很好地证明了这种幸存。

作于贝尔法斯特

2017年8月7日

Contents

目　录

The Year 1915

1915 年

The Year 1916

1916 年

The Year 1917

Afterword

1917 年

译后记

The Year 1914

1914 年

Up in the Wind

3 December, 1914

"I could wring the old thing's neck that put it here!
A public-house! It may be public for birds,
Squirrels, and such-like, ghosts of charcoal-burners
And highwaymen." The wild girl laughed. "But I
Hate it since I came back from Kennington.
I gave up a good place." Her Cockney accent
Made her and the house seem wilder by calling up —
Only to be subdued at once by wildness —
The idea of London, there in that forest parlour,
Low and small among the towering beeches
And the one bulging butt that's like a font.

Her eyes flashed up; she shook her hair away
From eyes and mouth, as if to shriek again;
Then sighed back to her scrubbing. While I drank
I might have mused of coaches and highwaymen,
Charcoal-burners and life that loves the wild.
For who now used these roads except myself,
A market waggon every other Wednesday,

风中飘荡

1914 年 12 月 3 日[1]

“我真想拧断那老家伙奄拉在这儿的脖子！
一家客栈！或许供鸟儿、
松鼠等鸟兽在此栖息，供炭炉幽灵、
拦路劫匪在此驻足。”野丫头笑道：“但我
讨厌它，因为我刚从肯宁顿回来，
放弃了那儿优越的环境。”她操着一口伦敦腔，
顿时让她和房子显得愈加乡野粗俗，不禁想起——
仅仅只是一下子被这荒野压抑罢了——
伦敦的林林总总。那林中客栈，
又矮又小，匿于高耸山毛榉林之中，
客栈凸出部分，犹如一尊洗礼盆。

她双眼怒闪；将头发从眼睛和嘴角处
甩开，好像要再次嚷嚷；
然后叹息，回身继续擦洗。醉意浓浓之时，
我便陷入了沉思，想象着马车、拦路劫匪、
烧炭工人，以及热爱荒野的一切生命。
如今使用这些道路的，除了我自己，
还有每隔周三的闹市马车、

❶ 全书每首诗歌标题后的时间皆为诗人托马斯创作诗歌的时间，除非另有特殊说明。——译者注

A solitary tramp, some very fresh one
Ignorant of these eleven houseless miles,
A motorist from a distance slowing down
To taste whatever luxury he can
In having North Downs clear behind, South clear before,
And being midway between two railway lines
Far out of sight or sound of them? There are
Some houses — down the by-lanes; and a few
Are visible — when their damsons are in bloom.
But the land is wild, and there's a spirit of wildness
Much older, crying when the stone-curlew yodels
His sea and mountain cry, high up in Spring.
He nests in fields where still the gorse is free as
When all was open and common. Common 'tis named
And calls itself, because the bracken and gorse
Still hold the hedge where plough and scythe have chased them.
Once on a time 'tis plain that "The White Horse"
Stood merely on the border of a waste
Where horse or cart picked its own course afresh.
On all sides then, as now, paths ran to the inn;
And now a farm-track takes you from a gate.

Two roads cross, and not a house in sight
Except "The White Horse" in this clump of beeches.

一位孤独的流浪汉、一些不知这方圆
十一英里[1]荒芜人烟的新来者，
还有远道而来的摩托车骑手，慢慢减速，
为了尽情享受奢美的瞬间：
身后北部丘原、前方南部景色清晰可见，
身处两条铁路之间的位置，
却不见其踪迹，不闻其声？有些
房子——沿着辅路而下；有些
清晰可见——正值西洋李树花容绽放。
然而，此地荒凉，带着一股荒野气息，
显得愈加古老，发出呐喊，呼应石鸻约德尔调的歌唱，
他[2]领略过的大海、高山也在呐喊，响彻整个春天。
在他驻扎过的地方，金雀花仍无拘无束地开着，
好像万物皆在绽放，甚是常见。之所以说常见，
如此形容，皆因蕨菜、金雀花
仍紧紧怀绕着树篱，虽曾被犁镰斩断。
曾经，显然这家“白马”客栈
就坐落在荒野的边缘，
马、车在此重新启程上路。
道路四通八达，一如既往，条条通往这家客栈；
如今，一条农场车道直通大门。

两道相交，不见一座房子，
除了山毛榉林中的“白马”客栈。

---

❶ 1 英里 =1609.3 米。

❷ 诗人托马斯在诗中经常用第三人称代词“他”或“她”来指代自然界中的动植物，将其拟人化，体现了诗人独特的动植物生态观。——译者注

It hides from either road, a field's breadth back,
And it's the trees you see, and not the house,
Both near and far, when the clump's the highest thing
And homely, too, upon a far horizon
To one that knows there is an inn within.

" 'Twould have been different" the wild girl shrieked, "suppose
That widow had married another blacksmith and
Kept on the business. This parlour was the smithy.
If she had done, there might never have been an inn;
And I, in that case, might never have been born.
Years ago, when this was all a wood
And the smith had charcoal-burners for company,
A man from a beech-country in the shires
Came with an engine and a little boy
(To feed the engine) to cut up timber here.
It all happened years ago. The smith
Had died, his widow had set up an alehouse —
I could wring the old thing's neck for thinking of it.
Well, I suppose they fell in love, the widow
And my great-uncle that sawed up the timber:
Leastways they married. The little boy stayed on.
He was my father." She thought she'd scrub again —
"I draw the ale and he grows fat" she muttered —
But only studied the hollows in the bricks
And chose among her thoughts in stirring silence.

站在每条道上，皆望不见它后面的那片旷野；
远近高低皆是树林，望不见那家客栈，
尤其每当毛榉林疯长至最高之时，
对于深知内有客栈的熟客来说，
从远处眺望，亦有宾至如归之感。

“一切将变得不一样”，那疯丫头嚷嚷着，“倘若
那位寡妇当初嫁给了另外一位铁匠，
并继操旧业。这家客栈原本是一间铁匠铺。
要是她当初真嫁了，今天就不会有这家客栈了；
倘若如此，这世上也就不会有我了。
多年前，这里曾是一片树林，
铁匠一家也有烧炭工人们作伴，
其中一位从郡里长满山毛榉的村庄而来，
带着一台引擎和一个小男孩儿
（为了供养引擎）在此砍伐树木。
那是多年前的事儿了。铁匠
已死，留下寡妇经营酒肆——
一想到这儿，我真想拧断那老家伙的脖子。
哎，我猜想寡妇和他当时相恋了，
而舅老爷当时是一名伐木工：
至少，他们结了婚。小男孩儿留下了。
他便是我后来的父亲。”她觉得得继续擦洗干活儿了——
“我酿过麦芽酒，他如今长膘了，”她自言自语——
琢磨着砖头上的坑坑洼洼，
在躁动的沉默中，角逐各种想法。

The clock ticked, and the big saucepan lid
Heaved as the cabbage bubbled, and the girl
Questioned the fire and spoke: "My father, he
Took to the land. A mile of it is worth
A guinea; for by that time all the trees
Except these few about the house were gone:
That's all that's left of the forest unless you count
The bottoms of the charcoal-burners' fires —
We plough one up at times. Did you ever see
Our signboard?" No. The post and empty frame
I knew. Without them I should not have guessed
The low grey house and its one stack under trees
Was a public-house and not a hermitage.
"But can that empty frame be any use?
Now I should like to see a good white horse
Swing there, a really beautiful white horse,
Galloping one side, being painted on the other."
"But would you like to hear it swing all night
And all day? All I ever had to thank
The wind for was for blowing the sign down.
Time after time it blew down and I could sleep.
At last they fixed it, and it took a thief
To move it, and we've never had another:
It's lying at the bottom of the pond.
But no one's moved the wood from off the hill

时钟滴答地走着，锅中白菜沸腾，
蒸汽顶起了大锅盖，姑娘
质问起炉火，说道：“我父亲，他
深爱这片土地。一英里值
一基尼[1]；尽管那时候所有的树，
除了房子周围的树之外，都被砍了：
那可是森林里仅剩的树啊，除非你数上
炭炉火堆里的那些残木——
我们时不时刨出一块儿来。你有没有见过
我们的标识牌？”没有。杆子和空架，
我倒是知道。没有他们，我绝对想不到
这座低矮的灰色房子，以及树下的那堆东西，
居然是一家客栈，而不是一个隐居之所。
“难道那空架没起任何作用吗？
如今我倒愿意瞧见这匹骏逸的白马
在那儿摇摆，一匹十分漂亮的白马，
一侧在飞奔疾驰，一侧被刷上了油漆。”
“然而你愿意听到它整日彻夜地
发出摇摆声吗？我曾感谢过风，
感谢它吹倒过那根标杆。
正因为每次的吹倒，我才能睡个安稳觉。
最后他们又把它修好，盗贼
却将它偷走，从此也就没再安上：
现在它正躺在池子底下呢。
但从来没人把后山的那片树林

[1] 即基尼币，出现在 1633 年，是英国第一代由机器生产的货币。——译者注

There at the back, although it makes a noise
When the wind blows, as if a train were running
The other side, a train that never stops
Or ends. And the linen crackles on the line
Like a wood fire rising." "But if you had the sign
You might draw company. What about Kennington?"
She bent down to her scrubbing with "Not me:
Not back to Kennington. Here I was born,
And I've a notion on these windy nights
Here I shall die. Perhaps I want to die here.
I reckon I shall stay. But I do wish
The road was nearer and the wind farther off,
Or once now and then quite still, though when I die
I'd have it blowing that I might go with it
Somewhere distant, where there are trees no more
And I could wake and not know where I was
Nor even wonder if they would roar again.
Look at those calves."

Between the open door
And the trees two calves were wading in the pond,
Grazing the water here and there and thinking,
Sipping and thinking, both happily, neither long.
The water wrinkled, but they sipped and thought,
As careless of the wind as it of us.
"Look at those calves. Hark at the trees again."

移走，尽管起风时，
噪声不断，好像火车在另一头
奔跑，永不停止，永无终点。
杆上的亚麻布发出阵阵爆裂声，
像一堆烈焰腾空的木火。”“倘若客栈挂起那标识，
一定会引来不少住客。聊聊肯宁顿吧？”
她边弯腰擦洗干活，边回答，“不了：
不回肯宁顿了，因为我生在这里，
这几夜狂风乱作，我萌生了一个想法：
我将死在这里。或许，我想死在这里。
我想我会留下来。不过，希望
路越来越近，风越来越远，
偶尔能平静些，尽管我死时，
希望风起，带我离去，
吹向远方，去到那没树的地方，
当我醒来，不知身在何方，
不在乎他们是否再次咆哮。
看看那些牛犊吧。”

介于敞开的门
和树林之间，其中有两只于池中跋涉，
水中四处觅草，略有所思，
啜饮思索，悠然自得，身材短小。
水起波纹，而他们啜饮思索，
不顾风吹，无视我们。
“看看那些牛犊！再听听这片树林！”

November

4 December, 1914

November's days are thirty:
November's earth is dirty,
Those thirty days, from first to last;
And the prettiest things on ground are the paths
With morning and evening hobnails dinted,
With foot and wing-tip overprinted
Or separately charactered,
Of little beast and little bird.
The fields are mashed by sheep, the roads
Make the worst going, the best the woods
Where dead leaves upward and downward scatter.
Few care for the mixture of earth and water,
Twig, leaf, flint, thorn,
Straw, feather, all that men scorn,
Pounded up and sodden by flood,
Condemned as mud.

But of all the months when earth is greener
Not one has clean skies that are cleaner.
Clean and clear and sweet and cold,

十一月

1914 年 12 月 4 日

十一月共三十天：
十一月大地脏乱不堪，
从始至终，三十天数；
地上至美之物为条条道路，
朝朝暮暮却为鞋钉所烙痕，
被足翼用力踩踏留痕，
痕迹疏密，错落有致，
犹如幼小鸟兽之迹。
麦田被羊蹂躏，道路
异常艰行，森林却肃穆，
尽管枯叶上下随处飘散。
极少有人介意水土混合物：
枝、叶、石、刺、
草、毛等人类所藐视的东西，
被洪水侵袭、浸湿，
演化成泥。

但在土地更葱郁的月份里，
十一月份最有晴空万里之势。
干净、晴朗、甜美、寒峭，

They shine above the earth so old,
While the after-tempest cloud
Sails over in silence though winds are loud,
Till the full moon in the east
Looks at the planet in the west
And earth is silent as it is black,
Yet not unhappy for its lack.
Up from the dirty earth men stare:
One imagines a refuge there
Above the mud, in the pure bright
Of the cloudless heavenly light:
Another loves earth and November more dearly
Because without them, he sees clearly,
The sky would be nothing more to his eye
Than he, in any case, is to the sky;
He loves even the mud whose dyes
Renounce all brightness to the skies.

在古老土地上照耀，
狂风暴雨后，天霄
安静，云游，任凭寒风咆哮，
直至圆月东方起，
眺望西边之际，
这土地方显静谧漆黑，
却不因稀缺而生悲。
人们从污泥中抬头凝视：
一人设想泥上伫立
一座避难所，光彩夺目，
在云淡天光中闪露；
另一人更爱十一月这片土地，
因为倘若无它，他心里
清楚：天对于他，他对于天，
皆一无是处，皆不以为然；
他爱泥土，因其颜色
拒绝天空的明亮色。

March

5 December, 1914

Now I know that Spring will come again,
Perhaps tomorrow: however late I've patience
After this night following on such a day.

While still my temples ached from the cold burning
Of hail and wind, and still the primroses
Torn by the hail were covered up in it,
The sun filled earth and heaven with a great light
And a tenderness, almost warmth, where the hail dripped,
As if the mighty sun wept tears of joy.
But 'twas too late for warmth. The sunset piled
Mountains on mountains of snow and ice in the west:
Somewhere among their folds the wind was lost,
And yet 'twas cold, and though I knew that Spring
Would come again, I knew it had not come,
That it was lost too in those mountains chill.

What did the thrushes know? Rain, snow, sleet, hail,
Had kept them quiet as the primroses.
They had but an hour to sing. On boughs they sang,

三月

1914 年 12 月 5 日

如今我察觉春天将再次来临，
或许明天：无论多晚，这一白昼之后，
过了今晚，我会耐心等待。

冰雹寒，风凛冽，太阳穴冷痛，
冰雹覆盖、包裹着报春花，
无奈最终压弯了报春花，
春阳向天地投下一缕光线
和柔嫩，极为温和，故冰雹滴落，
恰似骄阳挥洒欢乐之泪。
然温暖姗姗来迟。夕阳西落，
满山冰雪，山峦重叠：
风却消失在峰峦交叠处，
天寒地冻，虽然我深知春天
会再次来临，但它还未降临，
想必也消失在冰冷山间。

何为画眉所知？雨、雪、霰、雹
令画眉静如报春花。
画眉却早已欢唱一小时，或立于树梢，

On gates, on ground; they sang while they changed perches
And while they fought, if they remembered to fight:
So earnest were they to pack into that hour
Their unwilling hoard of song before the moon
Grew brighter than the clouds. Then 'twas no time
For singing merely. So they could keep off silence
And night, they cared not what they sang or screamed;
Whether 'twas hoarse or sweet or fierce or soft;
And to me all was sweet: they could do no wrong.
Something they knew — I also, while they sang
And after. Not till night had half its stars
And never a cloud, was I aware of silence
Stained with all that hour's songs, a silence
Saying that Spring returns, perhaps tomorrow.

或栖于门上，或停于地上；边变换栖息地，边放声歌唱。
斗歌时，如果他们记得“战斗”过：
趁着月亮比乌云更明亮前，他们迫切希望
在那一小时里勉为其难地唱完
自己私藏的曲目。而单单唱歌
已没时间。因此，他们拒绝安静
和夜晚，他们不在乎唱什么、喊什么，
不管声音粗糙或甜美，急促或柔慢；
对我而言，一切皆甜美：他们并未做错。
他们所知之事——我亦知，尤其歌唱之时
和之后。直至夜空一半繁星开始闪耀，
不见一片云彩，我方知这片宁静
糅杂着那一小时的歌唱，这片宁静
诉说着春天终会归来，或许就在明天。

Old Man

6 December, 1914

Old Man, or Lad's-Love, — in the name there's nothing
To one that knows not Lad's-Love, or Old Man,
The hoar-green feathery herb, almost a tree,
Growing with rosemary and lavender.
Even to one that knows it well, the names
Half decorate, half perplex, the thing it is:
At least, what that is clings not to the names
In spite of time. And yet I like the names.

The herb itself I like not, but for certain
I love it, as some day the child will love it
Who plucks a feather from the door-side bush
Whenever she goes in or out of the house.
Often she waits there, snipping the tips and shriveling
The shreds at last on to the path, perhaps
Thinking, perhaps of nothing, till she sniffs
Her fingers and runs off. The bush is still
But half as tall as she, though it is as old;
So well she clips it. Not a word she says;
And I can only wonder how much hereafter

老者

1914 年 12 月 6 日

“老者”或“伴侣之爱”，——名字毫无意义，
对于不熟悉这些俗称的人来说，
这株灰绿柔软如羽毛的艾草，恰如一棵树，
随迷迭香、薰衣草一同成长。
甚至对于深知此物的人来说，这些名字，
半典雅，半复杂，事实如此：
至少，物之存在，不困于名，
不念时光。而我，恋上了这些名字。

我不喜欢艾草本身，但毋庸置疑
我爱它，正如有朝一日稚童会爱上它：
每当她出入自家门口，
会从门前灌木丛摘下一片羽叶。
她常常待在那儿，掐断艾草尖端，
将它揉碎，最后撒落在小径上，若有
所思，又或许心无旁骛，接着嗅嗅
自己的手指，然后跑开。草丛至今仍然
只有她一半高，尽管年龄相仿；
她小心翼翼地将它剪下，默默无语；
而我只想知道此后她到底

She wlll remember, with that bitter scent,
Of garden rows, and ancient damson-trees
Topping a hedge, a bent path to a door,
A low thick bush beside the door, and me
Forbidding her to pick.

As for myself,
Where first I met the bitter scent is lost.
I, too, often shrivel the grey shreds,
Sniff them and think and sniff again and try
Once more to think what it is I am remembering,
Always in vain. I cannot like the scent,
Yet I would rather give up others more sweet,
With no meaning, than this bitter one.

I have mislaid the key. I sniff the spray
And think of nothing; I see and I hear nothing;
Yet seem, too, to be listening, lying in wait
For what I should, yet never can, remember:
No garden appears, no path, no hoar-green bush
Of Lad's-love, or Old Man, no child beside,
Neither father nor mother, nor any playmate;
Only an avenue, dark, nameless, without end.

会记住多少——那花园里一排排
艾草的苦涩香，老李树
长得比树篱高，蜿蜒小道通往门口，
门旁有一丛低矮浓密的灌木，而我
阻止过她采摘。

　　　　　　　　至于我自己，
记不清在哪里初闻过那苦涩香。
我也经常将灰艾草揉碎，
嗅着鼻子，思索着，然后再嗅着，
再次尝试回忆自己正在回忆之事，
却总是徒劳。我无法接受这味道，
不过，为了这苦涩香，倒愿意放弃
那些毫无意义的更香美之味。

我错悟其精要。嗅着弥散的香气，
我无思，无见，无闻；
然而，似乎也在聆听，静候
本应想到却始终无法记起之事：
“老者”或“伴侣之爱”花园、小道、灰绿灌木，
如今已无处可寻，稚童也难见踪迹，
父母、玩伴亦不在身旁；
唯剩一条大道，漆黑，难以名状，却一望无尽。

The Signpost

7 December, 1914

The dim sea glints chill. The white sun is shy,
And the skeleton weeds and the never-dry,
Rough, long grasses keep white with frost
At the hilltop by the finger-post;
The smoke of the traveller's-joy is puffed
Over hawthorn berry and hazel tuft.

I read the sign. Which way shall I go?
A voice says: You would not have doubted so
At twenty. Another voice gentle with scorn
Says: At twenty you wished you had never been born.

One hazel lost a leaf of gold
From a tuft at the tip, when the first voice told
The other he wished to know what 'twould be
To be sixty by this same post. "You shall see,"
He laughed — and I had to join his laughter —
"You shall see; but either before or after,
Whatever happens, it must befall,
A mouthful of earth to remedy all

路标

1914 年 12 月 7 日

大海昏暗，寒光闪烁，白日羞涩，
芦苇枯枝，山头漫草，从不干涩，
粗糙高长，布满白霜，
指示路标，立于近旁；
铁线莲，又名“游人欢愉”，喷吐烟气，
于山楂果、榛蔟之上旋辟。

我读着标识，心想何去何从？
一个声音说道：年方二十，不应有此困窘。
另一声音带着温柔又藐视的语气
说道：年方二十，你多希望自己尚未出世！

一片金叶从榛蔟顶端处
脱落之际，第一个声音告诉
另一个声音：“抵达此路标之际，
六十岁的人生何如？”“届时便知，”
他仰天长笑——我不禁言笑晏晏——
“届时便知；不管之后，不论之前，
发生何事，它终将临降，
一口泥土，若能治愈世间所有愿望

Regrets and wishes shall freely be given;
And if there be a flaw in that heaven
'Twill be freedom to wish, and your wish may be
To be here or anywhere talking to me,
No matter what the weather, on earth,
At any age between death and birth, —
To see what day or night can be,
The sun and the frost, the land and the sea,
Summer, Winter, Autumn, Spring, —
With a poor man of any sort, down to a king,
Standing upright out in the air
Wondering where he shall journey, O where?"

与后悔，理应自由享赐；
倘若天堂出现瑕疵，
那将是自由之盼，或许你希望
来此处或任何地方，与我交谈，
不顾风雨，不困世间
任何年龄，介于生死之间，——
欲知何为昼，何为夜，
太阳、冰霜、陆地、海河，
秋、冬、春、夏，——
穷人也好，国王也罢，
个个顶“天”立“地”，
思索何去何从，噢，何处旅寄？”

After Rain

14 December, 1914

The rain of a night and a day and a night
Stops at the light
Of this pale choked day. The peering sun
Sees what has been done.
The road under the trees has a border new
Of purple hue
Inside the border of bright thin grass:
For all that has
Been left by November of leaves is torn
From hazel and thorn
And the greater trees. Throughout the copse
No dead leaf drops
On grey grass, green moss, burnt-orange fern,
At the wind's return:
The leaflets out of the ash-tree shed
Are thinly spread
In the road, like little black fish, inlaid,
As if they played.
What hangs from the myriad branches down there
So hard and bare

雨后

1914 年 12 月 14 日

骤雨临至，昼夜寒洌，
次日方歇，
苍白窒息，旭日朝霞，
凝视穹下。
林中树下，道起新辙，
紫色光泽，
辙内青草，明亮细嫩：
十一月份，
万物唯剩：榛子荆棘，
落叶枯枝，
高树坠零。整片矮林，
草灰苔青，
蕨类焦黄，枯叶未坠。
寒风归兮：
桍树枝叶，细小脱落，
稀疏飘梭，
如小黑鱼，镶嵌路地。
宛若嬉戏。
树丛杂枝，坚硬光秃，
枝下垂露，

Is twelve yellow apples lovely to see
On one crab-tree,
And on each twig of every tree in the dell
Uncountable
Crystals both dark and bright of the rain
That begins again.

十二沙果，色黄夺目，
树上幽独。
谷中树林，枝条垂沐，
雨滴水珠，
不计其数，黑亮晶莹，
骤雨再临。

Interval

? December, 1914

Gone the wild day:
A wilder night
Coming makes way
For brief twilight.

Where the firm soaked road
Mounts and is lost
In the high beech-wood
It shines almost.

The beeches keep
A stormy rest,
Breathing deep
Of wind from the west.

The wood is black,
With a misty steam.
Above, the cloud pack
Breaks for one gleam.

间歇

1914 年 12 月某日

狂日去矣：
肆夜将临，
交替之际，
黄昏暂临。

硬道湿浸，
蜿蜒而上，
匿于榉林，
晶光闪闪。

林遭风雨，
静谧如息，
深深吸取：
西风徐疾。

林中幽肃，
烟雾缭荡。
天云密布，
缝中透光。

But the woodman's cot
By the ivied trees
Awakens not
To light or breeze.

It smokes aloft
Unwavering:
It hunches soft
Under storm's wing.

It has no care
For gleam or gloom:
It stays there
While I shall roam,

Die, and forget
The hill of trees,
The gleam, the wet,
This roaring peace.

樵夫之屋，
青藤环抱，
不见光束，
不闻风啸。

烟雾旋霞，
锲而不舍：
风暴翼下，
柔顺伏蛰。

漠不关心，
光明黑暗：
静待荫垠，
无视我恋、

我亡、我忘：
榉林、山峦、
阳光、雨滂，
咆哮、安恬。

The Other

? December, 1914

The forest ended. Glad I was
To feel the light, and hear the hum
Of bees, and smell the drying grass
And the sweet mint, because I had come
To an end of forest, and because
Here was both road and inn, the sum
Of what's not forest. But 'twas here
They asked me if I did not pass
Yesterday this way. "Not you? Queer."
"Who then? and slept here?" I felt fear.

I learnt his road and, ere they were
Sure I was I, left the dark wood
Behind, kestrel and woodpecker,
The inn in the sun, the happy mood
When first I tasted sunlight there.
I travelled fast, in hopes I should
Outrun that other. What to do
When caught, I planned not. I pursued
To prove the likeness, and, if true,

他者

1914 年 12 月某日

森林尽头，欢愉欣喜，
阳光和煦，蜜蜂嗡鸣，
草丛干枯，薄荷芳息，
阵阵扑鼻，开心庆幸，
已至尽头，来到福地，
道从此始，栈从此行，
此处难见，森林之态。
有人询问，是否昨日，
途径此道。“非也？奇怪。”
“何人夜宿？”倍感惊骇。

铭记此道，未等质询，
未被确认，远离黑林，
辞行鸳鸟，惜别茶隼，
走向客栈，快乐心境，
初尝阳曦，恐难再寻。
快速前行，期盼满心，
超越他者。倘若相撞，
如何是好？未曾预定。
欲证我他，何其相像，

To watch until myself I knew.

I tried the inns that evening
Of a long gabled high-street grey,
Of courts and outskirts, travelling
An eager but a weary way,
In vain. He was not there. Nothing
Told me that ever till that day
Had one like me entered those doors,
Save once. That time I dared: "You may
Recall" — but never-foamless shores
Make better friends than those dull boors.

Many and many a day like this
Aimed at the unseen moving goal
And nothing found but remedies
For all desire. These made not whole;
They sowed a new desire, to kiss
Desire's self beyond control,
Desire of desire. And yet
Life stayed on within my soul.
One night in sheltering from the wet
I quite forgot I could forget.

A customer, then the landlady
Stared at me. With a kind of smile

亲眼所见，方知真相。

夜幕降临，投宿客栈，
长墙靠山，坐落高街，
地处郊外，旅程切盼，
路途疲倦，徒劳而歇。
他不在此，尚未出现。
直到这天，我才了解，
他曾来过，登门而入，
仅此一次。壮胆去怯：
“可曾记起？”——河滨无沫，
较粗俗者，愈加友睦。

日复一日，光阴逝去，
追逐不懈，隐动目标，
毫无所获，唯获治愈，
欲望良方。药非所药；
旧欲正治，又来新欲，
欲望本身，难以治愈，
欲望之欲，难以控制。
灵魂深处，生命驻足。
夜晚骤雨，栈下躲避，
忘之所忘，忘之所忆。

客栈之内，顾客店主，
凝眸于我，面带微笑，

They hesitated awkwardly:
Their silence gave me time for guile.
Had anyone called there like me,
I asked. It was quite plain the wile
Succeeded. For they poured out all.
And that was naught. Less than a mile
Beyond the inn, I could recall
He was like me in general.

He had pleased them, but I less.
I was more eager than before
To find him out and to confess,
To bore him and to let him bore.
I could not wait: children might guess
I had a purpose, something more
That made an answer indiscreet.
One girl's caution made me sore,
Too indignant even to greet
That other had we chanced to meet.

I sought then in solitude.
The wind had fallen with the night; as still
The roads lay as the ploughland rude,
Dark and naked, on the hill.
Had there been ever any feud
'Twixt earth and sky, a mighty will

欲说还休，略显局促：
沉默之际，我便谋招。
像我之人，曾来贵处？
毋庸置疑，我计生效：
其便答复，全盘告知。
可惜无用。栈外转角，
一英里处，我便想起，
追寻之人，与我无异。

他擅取悦，我显逊色。
寻他之欲，甚于初始，
期盼遇见，向他忏责，
令其厌烦，使其生气。
迫不及待：稚童猜测，
我有图谋，绝非易事，
若求答案，难上加难。
女孩谨慎，令人憋气：
义愤填膺，不屑寒暄，
倘若我他，有缘相见。

苦苦追寻，寂寞孤独。
夜幕降临，风渐停息；
条条道路，如田荒芜。
幽暗裸露，穿梭山里。
倘若天地，出现仇怒，
发生纷争，强大意志，

Closed it: the crocketed dark trees,
A dark house, dark impossible
Cloud-towers, one star, one lamp, one peace
Held on an everlasting lease:

And all was earth's, or all was sky's;
No difference endured between
The two. A dog barked on a hidden rise;
A marshbird whistled high unseen;
The latest waking blackbird's cries
Perished upon the silence keen.
The last light filled a narrow firth
Among the clouds. I stood serene,
And with a solemn quiet mirth,
An old inhabitant of earth.

Once the name I gave to hours
Like this was melancholy, when
It was not happiness and powers
Coming like exiles home again,
And weaknesses quitting their bowers,
Smiled and enjoyed, far off from men,
Moments of everlastingness.
And fortunate my search was then
While what I sought, nevertheless,
That I was seeking, I did not guess.

使其终止：黑树卷叶，
黑暗之屋，无比黑漆；
云塔耸立，星灯祥和，
紧紧握住，永恒契约：

自然万物，天生地长，
天地之间，均无差异。
忽闻犬吠，隐隐渐强；
泽雀高鸣，无踪无迹；
乌鸫警觉，啼叫嘹亮，
戛然而止，万籁俱寂。
一束残光，投向浅湾，
云雾缭绕。安祥伫立，
宁静平和，肃穆庄严，
大地子民，古老欢颜。

悠悠时光，我曾名之，
尽显愁思，不乏忧郁，
无流亡者，再次归时，
幸福之感，权力之欲；
方显柔弱，弃离幽室，
欢颜悦心，远离人域，
享受刹那，时光永恒。
尽管当初，切盼相遇，
即使不知，所寻之人，
当时追寻，幸运之征。

That time was brief: once more at inn
And upon road I sought my man
Till once amid a tap-room's din
Loudly he asked for me, began
To speak, as if it had been a sin,
Of how I thought and dreamed and ran
After him thus, day after day:
He lived as one under a ban
For this: what had I got to say?
I said nothing. I slipped away.

And now I dare not follow after
Too close. I try to keep in sight,
Dreading his frown and worse his laughter.
I steal out of the wood to light;
I see the swift shoot from the rafter
By the inn door: ere I alight
I wait and hear the starlings wheeze
And nibble like ducks: I wait his flight.
He goes: I follow: no release
Until he ceases. Then I also shall cease.

时光短暂：客栈道路，
来回穿梭，寻找他者，
喧嚣酒肆，终究相遇：
唯见他者，朝我呼喝，
随即质问，寻他意图，
何故梦他，跟踪不舍，
日复一日，仿若犯罪：
他怨生活，处处受责：
如何答复？无言以对，
无话可说，悄悄离退。

太近追赶，如今不敢。
与他所距，视线之内，
怕其皱眉，更惧笑脸。
溜出森林，望见光蔚，
客栈梁椽，只见雨燕，
疾速飞出：未进栈内，
等候听闻，椋鸟喘息，
轻咬如鸭：待他飞起。
他走：我随：寸步不离，
直至他歇。我将停息。

Birds' Nests

? December, 1914

The summer nests uncovered by autumn wind,
Some torn, others dislodged, all dark,
Everyone sees them: low or high in tree,
Or hedge, or single bush, they hang like a mark.

Since there's no need of eyes to see them with
I cannot help a little shame
That I missed most, even at eye's level, till
The leaves blew off and made the seeing no game.

'Tis a light pang. I like to see the nests
Still in their places, now first known,
At home and by far roads. Boys knew them not,
Whatever jays and squirrels may have done.

And most I like the winter nests deep-hid
That leaves and berries fell into:
Once a dormouse dined there on hazel-nuts,
And grass and goose-grass seeds found soil and grew.

鸟巢

1914 年 12 月某日

秋风呼啸，夏巢掀揭，
撕毁腾挪，一片昏暗，
随处可见：树上树下，
篱上丛中，痕迹斑斑。

以眼望之，实属多余。
羞愧遗憾，涌上心间，
错失良机，视野所及，
树叶零落，无缘相见。

略感痛心。欲见鸟巢，
仍处原地，如今初露，
巢穴远路。男孩不知，
松鸡松鼠，筹运何物。

隐蔽冬巢，至爱之物，
叶莓坠落，沉入其盆：
偶见睡鼠，嚼食榛果，
扁草籽种，落地生根。

The Mountain Chapel

? December, 1914

Chapel and gravestones, old and few,
Are shrouded by a mountain fold
From sound and view
Of life. The loss of the brook's voice
Falls like a shadow. All they hear is
The eternal noise
Of wind whistling in grass more shrill
Than aught as human as a sword,
And saying still:
" 'Tis but a moment since man's birth,
And in another moment more
Man lies in earth
For ever; but I am the same
Now, and shall be, even as I was
Before he came;
Till there is nothing I shall be."
Yet there the sun shines after noon
So cheerfully
The place almost seems peopled, nor
Lacks cottage chimney, cottage hearth:

山中教堂

1914年12月某日

教堂墓碑，古老稀少，
蔽于青山重叠处，
不见生机，远离喧嚣。
河流之声，死寂沉沉，
幽灵一般。唯能闻见：
无休山风，
呼啸碧草，声刺万物，
尖锐甚于情义刀剑，
仍在吐露：
“人类诞生以来，此时，
以及其他时候更甚，
人类永躺于地里；
而此刻我便如此这般，
并且将会，甚至如前所为，
当他来临之前；
直到我化为乌有。”
而午后太阳闪耀，
如此欢悠，
似乎有人居于此地，
屋舍烟囱壁炉可见：

It is not more
In size than is a cottage, less
Than any other empty home
In homeliness.
It has a garden of wild flowers
And finest grass and gravestones warm
In sunshine hours
The year through. Men behind the glass
Stand once a week, singing, and drown
The whistling grass
Their ponies munch. And yet somewhere,
Near or far off, there's a man could
Be happy here,
Or one of the gods perhaps, were they
Not of inhuman stature dire,
As poets say
Who have not seen them clearly; if
At sound of any wind of the world
In grass-blades stiff
They would not startle and shudder cold
Under the sun. When gods were young
This wind was old.

教堂面积，
大小如村舍，
相较其他任何空荡家园，
少了些朴素简约。
教堂后有一座花园，
一年中，阳光普照的日子里，
野花盛开，绿草嫩鲜，
墓碑灼暖。人们
每周一次，站于窗玻之后，歌唱，淹没
青草的呼哨声、
马儿的咀嚼声。但是
不远不近，有人能
快乐地栖居于此地，
或是某位神仙，倘若
他们不怕这冷漠无情身形，
如诗人所说，
因看不清他们，假如
听到世间任何风声
在草片中僵卒，
他们便在阳光下不会惊倒，
不会颤抖。神仙年轻，
风儿已老。

The Manor Farm

24 December, 1914

The rock-like mud unfroze a little and rills
Ran and sparkled down each side of the road
Under the catkins wagging in the hedge.
But earth would have her sleep out, spite of the sun;
Nor did I value that thin gliding beam
More than a pretty February thing
Till I came down to the old Manor Farm,
And church and yew-tree opposite, in age
Its equals and in size. The church and yew
And farmhouse slept in a Sunday silentness.
The air raised not a straw. The steep farm roof,
With tiles duskily glowing, entertained
The midday sun; and up and down the roof
White pigeons nestled. There was no sound but one.
Three cart-horses were looking over a gate
Drowsily through their forelocks, swishing their tails
Against a fly, a solitary fly.

The Winter's cheek flushed as if he had drained
Spring, Summer, and Autumn at a draught

庄园农场

1914 年 12 月 24 日

硬如岩石的泥土松融了些，小溪
在道路两旁涓涓流淌，闪闪发亮，
柳絮纷飞，飘摆在树篱中。
而阳光下土地沉睡；
相较于二月芳菲，我也并未
更珍惜那束纤细流畅的晨光，
直到我造访这片古老庄园农场，
发现与教堂、紫衫相对而立，在年龄、
面积上相当。教堂、紫衫、
农房在周日的宁静中熟睡。
空气未飘起一根稻草。农场屋顶陡峭，
瓦片微微发亮，让正午阳光
笑逐颜开；屋顶上下筑满
白鸽巢穴。万籁俱静，唯剩一音。
三四车马透过马套望向大门，
昏昏欲睡，摇着尾巴，沙沙作响，
驱赶着苍蝇，一只孤独的苍蝇。

冬天的脸颊胀得通红，好像刚刚
一口气吞没了春、夏、秋三季，

And smiled quietly But 'twas not Winter —
Rather a season of bliss unchangeable
Awakened from farm and church where it had lain
Safe under tile and thatch for ages since
This England, Old already, was called Merry.

心中窃喜。然而那不是冬天——
更像是一个幸福的季节，永不褪色，
从农场、教堂中醒来：它已在
茅草、瓦顶下安详沉寂了很久
自从这古老的英格兰叫“福地”以来。

An Old Song I

25 December, 1914

I was not apprenticed nor ever dwelt in famous Lincolnshire;
I've served one master ill and well much more than seven year;
And never took up to poaching as you shall quickly find;
    But 'tis my delight of a shiny night in the season of the year.

I roamed where nobody had a right but keepers and squires, and there
I sought for nests, wild flowers, oak sticks, and moles, both far and near,
And had to run from farmers, and learnt the Lincolnshire song:
    "Oh, 'tis my delight of a shiny night in the season of the year."

I took those walks years after, talking with friend or dear,
Or solitary musing; but when the moon shone clear
I had no joy or sorrow that could not be expressed
    By " 'Tis my delight of a shiny night in the season of the year."

Since then I've thrown away a chance to fight a gamekeeper;
And I less often trespass, and what I see or hear
Is mostly from the road or path by day: yet still I sing:
    "Oh, 'tis my delight of a shiny night in the season of the year."

一首老歌（一）

1914 年 12 月 25 日

我未曾在著名的林肯郡住过，也未曾当过学徒，
曾超过七年精心服侍过一位师傅；
从来不非法狩猎，不久你便知分晓；
　　然我欣喜于一年中那季节里的璀璨夜幕。

我在只有守门者、乡绅的禁地漫步，
四处寻觅鸟巢、野花、橡树枝和鼹鼠，
必须逃离农场主，学习林肯郡之歌：
　　“噢，我欣喜于一年中那季节里的璀璨夜幕。”

多年后我故地重游，或与亲友倾诉，
或独自冥思；明月正当空光彩夺目，
我不喜不悲，此景此情也难以言状，
　　唯有“我欣喜于一年中那季节里的璀璨夜幕。”

从此，我便放弃机会与守门者角逐；
也很少再踏入禁地，所闻或所睹
大多源自“道听途说”：但我仍歌唱：
　　“噢，我欣喜于一年中那季节里的璀璨夜幕。”

For if I am contented, at home or anywhere,
Or if I sigh for I know not what, or my heart beats with some fear,
It is a strange kind of delight to sing or whistle just:
"Oh, 'tis my delight of a shiny night in the season of the year."

And with this melody on my lips and no one by to care,
Indoors, or out on shiny nights or dark in open air,
I am for a moment made a man that sings out of his heart:
"Oh, 'tis my delight of a shiny night in the season of the year."

倘若在家或任何地方，我开心满足，
或因见识浅薄叹息，因恐惧而心跳加速，
歌唱或吹口哨真是别有一番欣慰：
　　“噢，我欣喜于一年中那季节里的璀璨夜幕。”

唱着这美妙的旋律，心无旁骛，
室内或户外繁星璀璨或漆黑夜幕，
瞬间成为伶人，由衷而唱，从心而赋：
　　“噢，我欣喜于一年中那季节里的璀璨夜幕。”

An Old Song II

26 December, 1914

The sun set, the wind fell, the sea
Was like a mirror shaking:
The one small wave that clapped the land
A mile-long snake of foam was making
Where tide had smoothed and wind had dried
The vacant sand.

A light divided the swollen clouds
And lay most perfectly
Like a straight narrow footbridge bright
That crossed over the sea to me;
And no one else in the whole world
Saw that same sight.

I walked elate, my bridge always
Just one step from my feet:
A robin sang, a shade in shade:
And all I did was to repeat:
  "I'll go no more a-roving
  With you, fair maid."

一首老歌（二）

1914 年 12 月 26 日

日落，风势渐弱，大海
如一面镜子，摇晃：
一波小海浪拍击着陆地，
形成一英里蛇长似的沫浪，
潮水已平静，风已吹干
空旷的沙地。

光线劈裂了臃肿的云层，
非常完美地射出
一座又直又窄又明亮的跨桥，
越过大海，照在我身上；
全世界别无他人
见过如此美妙。

我步履心欢，跨桥总是
离我一步之遥：
知更鸟歌唱，凄冷旋律：
我所做的便是重复唱调：
　　“我不再与你漫步，
　　窈窕淑女。”

The sailors' song of merry loving
With dusk and sea-gull's mewing
Mixed sweet, the lewdness far outweighed
By the wild charm the chorus played:
"I'll go no more a-roving
With you, fair maid:
A-roving, a-roving, since roving's been my ruin,
I'll go no more a-roving with you, fair maid."

In Amsterdam there dwelt a maid —
Mark well what I do say —
In Amsterdam there dwelt a maid
And she was a mistress of her trade:
I'll go no more a-roving
With you, fair maid:
A-roving, a-roving, since roving's been my ruin,
I'll go no more a-roving with you, fair maid.

水手欢快的歌声
爱着黄昏，爱着海鸥声，
歌声混杂着甜蜜与淫荡
远被疯狂迷人的合唱声所扫荡：
“我不再与你漫步，
窈窕淑女：
漫步，漫步，因其已成梦魇，
我便不再与你漫步，窈窕淑女。”

阿姆斯特丹住着一位少女——
好好记住我的话语——
阿姆斯特丹住着一位少女
她是淑女中的翘楚：
我不再与你漫步，
窈窕淑女：
漫步，漫步，因其已成梦魇，
我便不再与你漫步，窈窕淑女。

The Combe

30 December, 1914

The Combe was ever dark, ancient and dark.
Its mouth is stopped with brambles, thorn, and briar;
And no one scrambles over the sliding chalk
By beech and yew and perishing juniper
Down the half precipices of its sides, with roots
And rabbit holes for steps. The sun of Winter,
The moon of Summer, and all the singing birds
Except the missel-thrush that loves juniper,
Are quite shut out. But far more ancient and dark
The Combe looks since they killed the badger there,
Dug him out and gave him to the hounds,
That most ancient Briton of English beasts.

峡谷

1914 年 12 月 30 日

峡谷历来幽暗、古老、黑暗。
谷口长满藤棘、荆棘、花刺；
无人攀过湿滑的白垩岩，
临近山毛榉、紫杉、枯杜松
垂落半崖壁间，树根蔓延，
野兔洞穴为阶。冬日阳光，
夏日月光，所有歌唱之鸟，
除了喜爱杜松的獬鸫外，
皆被拒之谷外。然而峡谷
愈显古老幽暗，因为他们
杀死獾熊，挖出交给猎犬，
英国兽中最古老的“土著”。

The Hollow Wood

31 December, 1914

Out in the sun the goldfinch flits
Along the thistle-tops, flits and twits
Above the hollow wood
Where birds swim like fish —
Fish that laugh and shriek —
To and fro, far below
In the pale hollow wood.

Lichen, ivy, and moss
Keep evergreen the trees
That stand half-flayed and dying,
And the dead trees on their knees
In dog's-mercury, and moss:
And the bright twit of the goldfinch drops
Down there as he flits on thistle-tops.

空林

1914 年 12 月 31 日

阳光下，金翅雀翔翱
顺着蓟尖，翔翱嬉闹
空林上方，
鸟儿遨游如鱼——
鱼儿嬉笑尖语——
游来游去，远在下方，
在黯淡的空林之中。

青苔、常青藤、苔藓
让树木永葆青绿，
虽然树皮半脱落枯死，
枯萎树木屈躺于
狗山靛和苔藓之间：
金翅雀翔翱在蓟尖上，
嬉闹正好坠入下方。

The Year 1915

1915 年

The New Year

1 January, 1915

He was the one man I met up in the woods
That stormy New Year's morning; and at first sight,
Fifty yards off, I could not tell how much
Of the strange tripod was a man. His body,
Bowed horizontal, was supported equally
By legs at one end, by a rake at the other:
Thus he rested, far less like a man than
His wheel-barrow in profile was like a pig.
But when I saw it was an old man bent,
At the same moment came into my mind
The games at which boys bend thus, *High-cockolorum*,
Or *Fly-the-garter*, and *Leap-frog*. At the sound
Of footsteps he began to straighten himself;
His head rolled under his cape like a tortoise's;
He took an unlit pipe out of his mouth
Politely ere I wished him "A Happy New Year",
And with his head cast upward sideways muttered —
So far as I could hear through the trees' roar —
"Happy New Year, and may it come fastish, too",
While I strode by and he turned to raking leaves.

元旦

1915 年 1 月 1 日

在风雨交加的元旦清晨，
他与我林中相遇；初见时，
五十码开外，无法说清他
有多像奇怪的三角架。身体
侧面看似鞠躬，一端双腿
平衡支撑，另一端搂耙支撑：
休息时，他极不像一个人，
他的独轮手推车轮廓倒像一头猪。
但我见他像驼背老人时，
那一瞬间，脑海中闪现过
男孩儿们玩耍的弯腰游戏：
“高跨其背”“飘袜带”和“跳蛙”[1]。
听到脚步声，他直起腰来：
披风下，头扭得像龟脑袋；
他嘴里刁着未点着的烟斗，
我恭敬地问候：“元旦快乐”，
他甩直头，侧着身子，咕哝——
透过树的咆哮，隐约听见——
“同祝元旦快乐，盼它快来”，
我大步向前，他去耙树叶。

---

[1] 此三种游戏为英国儿童游戏，皆要求参与玩耍人员至少有一人须躬身弯腰，以便剩余人员从其背上越过。——译者注

The Source

4 January, 1915

All day the air triumphs with its two voices
Of wind and rain:
As loud as if in anger it rejoices,
Drowning the sound of earth
That gulps and gulps in choked endeavour vain
To swallow the rain.

Half the night, too, only the wild air speaks
With wind and rain,
Till forth the dumb source of the river breaks
And drowns the rain and wind,
Bellows like a giant bathing in mighty mirth
The triumph of earth.

源头

1915 年 1 月 4 日

整日空气洋洋弥漫二音，
风咆雨哮：
咆哮声响犹如怒中欢欣，
淹没大地之声，
雨水哗啦，土地喘呛吞咬，
徒劳无效。

时值半夜闻听空气狂语，
风雨飕嚎，
直到静默水源突崩河隅，
吞没风雨之声，
咆哮犹如巨物沐浴高歌，
大地凯歌。

The Penny Whistle

5 January, 1915

The new moon hangs like an ivory bugle
In the naked frosty blue;
And the ghylls of the forest, already blackened
By Winter, are blackened anew.

The brooks that cut up and increase the forest,
As if they had never known
The sun, are roaring with black hollow voices
Betwixt rage and a moan.

But still the caravan-hut by the hollies
Like a kingfisher gleams between:
Round the mossed old hearths of the charcoal-burners
First primroses ask to be seen.

The charcoal-burners are black, but their linen
Blows white on the line;
And white the letter the girl is reading
Under that crescent fine;

六音哨笛

1915 年 1 月 5 日

新月垂挂，如一个象牙喇叭，
披着赤裸、霜冷的蓝色；
严冬里，林谷早已变黑，
又重新裹上一层黑色。

溪流切穿并滋养着树林，
仿佛他们从未知晓
阳光，溪流咆哮，带着黑暗空荡之音，
似呻吟，似怒号。

然而冬青树旁的大篷屋子，
像一只翠鸟，闪烁其间：
绕着爬满苔藓的旧烧炭炉边，
报春花邀请初次相见。

炭炉黑黝黝，而炉边的覆盖物
白乎乎，被吹成一线；
女孩儿读着一封白色的书信，
借着新月的皎洁光线；

And her brother who hides apart in a thicket,
Slowly and surely playing
On a whistle an old nursery melody,
Says far more than I am saying.

她的兄长藏在丛林中，
泰然自若地吹着哨笛，
演奏一曲古老的儿歌，
诉说着远胜我要讲的往事。

A Private

6, 7 January, 1915 and later

This ploughman dead in battle slept out of doors
Many a frozen night, and merrily
Answered staid drinkers, good bedmen, and all bores:
"At Mrs Greenland's Hawthorn Bush," said he,
"I slept." None knew which bush. Above the town,
Beyond "The Drover", a hundred spot the down
In Wiltshire. And where now at last he sleeps
More sound in France — that, too, he secret keeps.

列兵

1915 年 1 月 7 日前后

这位农夫战死，长眠户外，
历经无数冰冷夜晚，欣然
答复着沉静的酒鬼、好心的床匠，以及所有的烦赖情绪：
“在格林兰夫人的山楂树丛中，”他断言，
“我长眠。”没人知道哪个树丛。小镇上方，
“卓佛山”那头，威尔特郡丘原上
的百座坟头。而今他在法国长眠，
睡得更香——对此他也缄口不言。

Snow

7 January, 1915

In the gloom of whiteness,
In the great silence of snow,
A child was sighing
And bitterly saying: "Oh,
They have killed a white bird up there on her nest,
The down is fluttering from her breast."
And still it fell through that dusky brightness
On the child crying for the bird of the snow.

雪

1915 年 1 月 7 日

白茫茫，沮萧飒，
雪辽阔，静寂寥，
稚童咄咄，
喃喃诉：“呜呼哉，
白鸟毙，巢空荡，
胸绒毛，雪中颤。”
黄昏白，绒毛下，
落稚童，泣雪鸟。

Adlestrop

8 January, 1915

Yes. I remember Adlestrop —
The name, because one afternoon
Of heat the express-train drew up there
Unwontedly. It was late June.

The steam hissed. Someone cleared his throat.
No one left and no one came
On the bare platform. What I saw
Was Adlestrop — only the name

And willows, willow-herb, and grass,
And meadowsweet, and haycocks dry,
No whit less still and lonely fair
Than the high cloudlets in the sky.

And for that minute a blackbird sang
Close by, and round him, mistier,
Farther and farther, all the birds
Of Oxfordshire and Gloucestershire.

艾德斯卓普

1915 年 1 月 8 日

是的。我记得艾德斯卓普——
这名字，因为一个炎热的午后，
一列快速火车停靠那里，
出人意料。那是六月末。

汽笛嘶嘶。有人清嗓。
无人下车，无人上车，
站台空空荡荡。所能瞧见的
便是艾德斯卓普——名字罢了，

还有杨柳、柳兰、青草、
绣线菊、干草堆，
与天上高云一样，
一切皆静寂孤璀。

那一瞬间，听见一只画眉近处
歌唱，周围旋绕着一群
来自牛津郡和格洛斯特郡
的鸟儿，越飞越远，渐渐模糊。

Tears

8 January, 1915

It seems I have no tears left. They should have fallen —
Their ghosts, if tears have ghosts, did fall — that day
When twenty hounds streamed by me, not yet combed out
But still all equals in their rage of gladness
Upon the scent, made one, like a great dragon
In Blooming Meadow that bends towards the sun
And once bore hops: and on that other day
When I stepped out from the double-shadowed Tower
Into an April morning, stirring and sweet
And warm. Strange solitude was there and silence.
A mightier charm than any in the Tower
Possessed the courtyard. They were changing guard,
Soldiers in line, young English countrymen,
Fair-haired and ruddy, in white tunics. Drums
And fifes were playing "The British Grenadiers".
The men, the music piercing that solitude
And silence, told me truths I had not dreamed,
And have forgotten since their beauty passed.

泪水

1915 年 1 月 8 日

如今双眼似无泪。眼泪本应流落——
幽灵，倘若泪水中住着幽灵，确曾滴落——那日
正值二十只猎犬临我鱼贯而行，毛发不见梳理
却个个眼带欣喜的怒光，
嗅着气味，拧成一团，像一只巨龙
穿梭于“盛艳草甸”，躬身向着太阳，
曾一跃而起：就在那日
我走出双影塔，
进入撩人、甜美、温暖的四月
清晨。那里怪异的孤独和安静相伴。
相比塔内所有的一切，庭院充满着
更大的魅力。他们正在换岗，
士兵排成行，年轻的英格兰同胞们，
头发鲜亮，面容红润，身穿白外衣。大鼓
与横笛正在演奏《英国掷弹兵进行曲》。
士兵和那首划破孤独与沉寂
的进行曲向我吐露了真相，而我未曾梦见，
或早已忘却，自从美与我擦肩而过。

Over the Hills

9 January, 1915

Often and often it came back again
To mind, the day I passed the horizon ridge
To a new country, the path I had to find
By half-gaps that were stiles once in the hedge,
The pack of scarlet clouds running across
The harvest evening that seemed endless then
And after, and the inn where all were kind,
All were strangers. I did not know my loss
Till one day twelve months later suddenly
I leaned upon my spade and saw it all,
Though far beyond the sky-line. It became
Almost a habit through the year for me

翻山越岭[1]

1915 年 1 月 9 日

它常常浮现于脑海里：
那一日我越过那座山岭
来到新的国度，所寻之路
挨着曾是篱梯的半沟子，
一朵朵绯红的云彩横驰
收获的夜空，似无边无际，
客栈里人人友善却生疏。
我不知道自己有何损失，
直到一年后突然有一日，
依偎着铁锹，将它尽收眼底，
虽远远超过天际线。自此
一年里我已习惯于偎依，

---

[1] 此诗探讨记忆功能。诗人意识到回忆当初平静之态已无可能。溪流如人生的成年期，再往回爬上“瀑布”，回到原初似的湖里，已不可能实现。此处既可解读为诗人意识到自己抑郁的严重程度犹如焦躁不安的小溪流永远无法回到原初正常的平静状态，亦可从生态危机的视角解读为人类的发展如今已到了成熟期，生态危机四伏，若想回到当初的原始自然状态，已无法实现，而这一切只能变成有限的回忆。《老子》强调返回原初，托马斯也意识到这一重要性，通过诗歌表达了他对现实世界难以实现之事的惋惜。参看第 79 首诗，《梦》（“A Dream”）一诗认为，唯有梦才能带领诗人回到原初之境。欲知更多道学视角的阐释，详见拙作博士论文：XU J. Early Daoism, ecocriticism and the Anthropocene: the case of Edward Thomas[D]. Bangor: Prifysgol Bangor University, 2018.——译者注

To lean and see it and think to do the same
Again for two days and a night. Recall
Was vain: no more could the restless brook
Ever turn back and climb the waterfall
To the lake that rests and stirs not in its nook,
As in the hollow of the collar-bone
Under the mountain's head of rush and stone.

望着它，想着做同样的事，
虽又耗时两天一夜。回忆
即徒劳：焦躁不安的小溪
再也无法回溯，爬上瀑布，
回到湖中，湖水静谧如初，
仿佛坐落在锁骨的凹处，
位于湍流坚石山头下部。

The Lofty Sky

10 January, 1915

Today I want the sky,
The tops of the high hills,
Above the last man's house,
His hedges, and his cows,
Where, if I will, I look
Down even on sheep and rook,
And of all things that move
See buzzards only above: —
Past all trees, past furze
And thorn, where nought deters
The desire of the eye
For sky, nothing but sky.
I sicken of the woods
And all the multitudes
Of hedge-trees. They are no more
Than weeds upon this floor
Of the river of air
Leagues deep, leagues wide, where
I am like a fish that lives
In weeds and mud and gives

苍穹

1915 年 1 月 10 日

今日我想要这片天空，
高山之巅峰，
俯瞰最后一个人的房子、
奶牛与树篱，
在顶端处，若愿意，我向下
能瞧见羊群和白嘴鸦，
以及所有移动之物，
抬头望棕鵟：——
飞过树林，越过荆豆灌木
和荆棘，没有能阻挡
望向苍穹的欲眼，
因眼里唯有苍天。
我厌恶森林
及各种各样
的篱树。它们仅仅
只是水草，位于这一层面，
属于河流，属于空气，
生态群落又深又宽，
我像一只鱼儿栖息
在水草泥浆里，

What's above him no thought.
I might be a tench for aught
That I can do today
Down on the wealden clay.
Even the tench has days
When he floats up and plays
Among the lily leaves
And sees the sky, or grieves
Not if he nothing sees:
While I, I know that trees
Under that lofty sky
Are weeds, fields mud, and I
Would arise and go far
To where the lilies are.

不知头上何物。
我犹如一只鲤鱼，
今日能做之事，
唯在威尔德泥沼里。
甚至鲤鱼也有喜心之日：
他浮出跃起
嬉戏于百合花间，
仰望苍穹，不会感伤
若他什么都没看到：
而我心中知晓
苍穹之下，树
即水草、泥土；
我将起身，远徙
至百合花盛开之地。

The Cuckoo

15 January, 1915

That's the cuckoo, you say. I cannot hear it.
When last I heard it I cannot recall; but I know
Too well the year when first I failed to hear it —
It was drowned by my man groaning out to his sheep "Ho! Ho!"

Ten times with an angry voice he shouted
"Ho! Ho!" but not in anger, for that was his way.
He died that Summer, and that is how I remember
The cuckoo calling, the children listening, and me saying, "Nay."

And now, as you said, "There it is" I was hearing
Not the cuckoo at all, but my man's "Ho! Ho!" instead.
And I think that even if I could lose my deafness
The cuckoo's note would be drowned by the voice of my dead.

杜鹃

1915 年 1 月 15 日

你说，那是“咕咕”声。我却听不见。
上次何时听见，我已记不清；但我深知
第一次未听见其叫声的时间——
它淹没在丈夫朝着羊群的“吼！吼！”呻吟声里。

他带着怨声喊了十次“吼！吼！”，
并非真生气，而是他的习性。
那年夏天他死了，故此我便记得
杜鹃在啼叫，孩童在聆听，而我在哀鸣着“不”。

如今，正如你曾说“它在那儿”，我侧耳倾听
那完全不是“咕咕”声，而是我丈夫的“吼！吼！”声。
我心想着纵使我双耳不聋，
逝者的吼声也会淹没杜鹃的咕声。

Swedes

15 January, 1915

They have taken the gable from the roof of clay
On the long swede pile. They have let in the sun
To the white and gold and purple of curled fronds
Unsunned. It is a sight more tender-gorgeous
At the wood-corner where Winter moans and drips
Than when, in the Valley of the Tombs of Kings,
A boy crawls down into a Pharaoh's tomb
And, first of Christian men, beholds the mummy,
God and monkey, chariot and throne and vase,
Blue pottery, alabaster, and gold.

But dreamless long-dead Amen-hotep lies.
This is a dream of Winter, sweet as Spring.

大头菜

1915 年 1 月 15 日

他们将黏土顶山形墙用来
堆放大头菜。让阳光射进来，
照在未晒的白、金、紫卷菜
叶上。林中角落：冬日哭吟、滴泪，
真是一幅柔美华丽的景象，
不亚于另一番景象：皇陵
谷中，一个男孩儿爬进法老墓穴中，
首位基督徒，见到了木乃伊、
上帝、猴子、马车、王座和花瓶，
以及蓝彩瓷器、雪花石膏和黄金。

而无梦的阿门霍特普法老
却长眠于此。冬之梦，美如春。

The Unknown Bird

17 January, 1915

Three lovely notes he whistled, too soft to be heard
If others sang; but others never sang
In the great beech-wood all that May and June.
No one saw him: I alone could hear him
Though many listened. Was it but four years
Ago? or five? He never came again.

Oftenest when I heard him I was alone,
Nor could I ever make another hear.
La-la-la! he called, seeming far-off —
As if a cock crowed past the edge of the world,
As if the bird or I were in a dream.
Yet that he travelled through the trees and sometimes
Neared me, was plain, though somehow distant still
He sounded. All the proof is — I told men
What I had heard.

I never knew a voice,
Man, beast, or bird, better than this. I told
The naturalists; but neither had they heard

无名鸟

1915 年 1 月 17 日

他吹了三首妙曲，太过柔和以致没人听见，
假如他者也在唱；然而他者根本没唱，
那时正值五六月山毛榉林浓密时节。
没人见过他：唯有我一人能听见其歌唱，
尽管许多人也在听。那是四年前的事儿？
还是五年前？他再也没来了。

过去听见他时，我常常独自一人，
如今再也无法听到。
“啦—啦—啦！”他哼着，似乎远去——
犹如鸡鸣声传遍天涯海角，
仿佛鸟儿或我在睡梦中。
然而他的确穿越树林，有时候
靠近我，尽管他的声音听着似乎
还有点儿距离。所有证据便是——我告诉人们
我所听到的。

　　　　　　比起这个，我绝不会更了解
人、兽、禽的声音了。我告诉
博物学家；但是他们也从没听过

Anything like the notes that did so haunt me,
I had them clear by heart and have them still.
Four years, or five, have made no difference. Then
As now that La-la-la! was bodiless sweet:
Sad more than joyful it was, if I must say
That it was one or other, but if sad
'Twas sad only with joy too, too far off
For me to taste it. But I cannot tell
If truly never anything but fair
The days were when he sang, as now they seem.
This surely I know, that I who listened then,
Happy sometimes, sometimes suffering
A heavy body and a heavy heart,
Now straightway, if I think of it, become
Light as that bird wandering beyond my shore.

如此萦绕我心头的曲调，
我曾将它们铭记于心，至今仍记忆犹新。
四年或五年，毫无差别。往昔
如今，“啦—啦—啦！”皆成了无形无影的美：
曲调忧伤多于欢快，如果非要我
说出个子丑寅卯，但如说其悲伤，
那也是悲中带欢，对我来说，
太远而无法细品。但我无法告知
当他歌唱时是否一切
除了公平别无它物，就像现在一样。
我深知这点，当时在倾听的我，
时而开心，时而悲伤，
身体沉重，心情沉重。
如今每当我想起它时，便身心愉悦，
轻快地如那只鸟儿，飞离我的境地[1]。

[1] 此处鸟儿独特的声音，勾起了诗人的回忆，同时也具有带领诗人远离苦海的治愈功能。——译者注

The Mill-Pond

18 January, 1915

The sun blazed while the thunder yet
Added a boom:
A wagtail flickered bright over
The mill-pond's gloom:

Less than the cooing in the alder
Isles of the pool
Sounded the thunder through that plunge
Of waters cool.

Scared starlings on the aspen tip
Past the black mill
Outchattered the stream and the next roar
Far on the hill.

As my feet dangling teased the foam
That slid below
A girl came out. "Take care!" she said—
Ages ago.

磨坊池

1915 年 1 月 18 日

烈日灼耀，雷霆却
发出一声轰隆：
鹡鸰轻盈地振翅于
阴郁的磨坊池上空：

低于桤木中的咕哝声，
池中小岛屿
响起的雷声穿透冷水
跌落的音律。

山杨枝上受惊的欧椋鸟
飞过黑色磨坊，
惊叫声淹没了溪流的潺潺声和远山
再次发出的呼啸声。

当我摇晃双脚，戏弄水沫，
水下滑动之时，
一位女孩走出，对我说“小心！”——
仿若隔世。

She startled me, standing quite close
Dressed all in white:
Ages ago I was angry till
She passed from sight.

Then the storm burst, and as I crouched
To shelter, how
Beautiful and kind, too, she seemed,
As she does now!

她吓了我一跳，站得很近，
全身皆白：
多年前，我依旧生气
直到她消逝不在。

不久暴雨骤至，我蜷伏着
四处躲避，
她当时多么美丽善良，
如今也是！

Man and Dog

20 January, 1915

" 'Twill take some getting." "Sir, I think 'twill so."
The old man stared up at the mistletoe
That hung too high in the poplar's crest for plunder
Of any climber, though not for kissing under:
Then he went on against the north-east wind —
Straight but lame, leaning on a staff new-skinned,
Carrying a brolly, flag-basket, and old coat, —
Towards Alton, ten miles off. And he had not
Done less from Chilgrove where he pulled up docks.
'Twere best, if he had had "a money-box",
To have waited there till the sheep cleared a field
For what a half-week's flint-picking would yield.
His mind was running on the work he had done
Since he left Christchurch in the New Forest, one

人与狗

1915 年 1 月 20 日

“得花点儿时间慢慢适应。”“我想确实如此，先生。”
那位老人抬头凝望着槲寄生[1]，
见它高高地挂在白杨树的顶端，为了拼抢
压倒所有攀缘植物，尽管不是为了与下面接壤：
然后他迎着东北风继续行走向前——
身材笔挺却腿脚残疾，拄着一根新皮拐杖，
拿着一把伞，一个芦苇篮子和一件旧大衣，——
朝着十英里外的奥尔顿前行。他一直如此
装扮前行，自从在戚尔格拉夫码头搬运以来。
倘若他能有个“存钱罐”，最好在那儿等待，
直到山羊清理出一个空旷的地方，
足以存放供半周拾捡的燧石量。
自从七十年代某个春天他离开
新福里斯特基督教堂以来，

---

[1] 詹姆斯·乔治·弗雷泽（James George Frazer）在《金枝》（*The Golden Bough*）中对槲寄生进行了阐释。他将槲寄生与原始人类的灵魂寄存于体外的观念进行关联。众所周知，秋冬季节来临之际，万木萧萧下，万物暗淡如死寂一般，唯独槲寄生依然绿油油，生长于树枝之间。根据弗雷泽的解读，古人见状，便会自然而然地觉得树的灵魂走出体外，移到槲寄生上，进而认为只要掌握了槲寄生，便相当于掌握了它所寄生的那棵树的灵魂和精华。詹姆斯·弗雷泽．金枝 [M]. 徐育新，汪培基，张泽石，译．北京：大众文艺出版社，1998: 12。——译者注

Spring in the 'seventies, — navvying on dock and line
From Southampton to Newcastle-on-Tyne, —
In 'seventy-four a year of soldiering
With the Berkshires, — hoeing and harvesting
In half the shires where corn and couch will grow.
His sons, three sons, were fighting, but the hoe
And reap-hook he liked, or anything to do with trees.
He fell once from a poplar tall as these:
The Flying Man they called him in hospital.
"If I flew now, to another world I'd fall."
He laughed and whistled to the small brown bitch
With spots of blue that hunted in the ditch.
Her foxy Welsh grandfather must have paired
Beneath him. He kept sheep in Wales and scared
Strangers, I will warrant, with his pearl eye
And trick of shrinking off as he were shy,
Then following close in silence for — for what?
"No rabbit, never fear, she ever got,
Yet always hunts. Today she nearly had one:
She would and she wouldn't. 'Twas like that. The bad one!
She's not much use, but still she's company,
Though I'm not. She goes everywhere with me.
So Alton I must reach tonight somehow:
I'll get no shakedown with that bedfellow
From farmers. Many a man sleeps worse tonight
Than I shall." "In the trenches." "Yes, that's right.

便一门心思扑在这个职业上，——
当搬运工，在南安普顿到泰因河畔纽卡斯尔的航线与码头上，——
1874 年他当兵，
驻军在伯克郡，——在玉米和野草共生共邻
的半郡大小的地盘上锄草和收割。
他的三个儿子正在打仗，他却喜欢
铁钩和锄头，以及任何与树相关的东西。
有一次，他从一颗白杨树上摔下来，
在医院里人们给了他一个称呼——飞人。
"若我现在起飞，定会掉入另一世界中去。"
他放声大笑，朝着黄色小母狗吹起
口哨，狗身上蓝斑点点，正在阴沟里觅食。
她狡猾的威尔士祖父一定在他下面给她
配对好了。他在威尔士养着羊群，他
利用患有白内障的一只眼和害羞时的胆怯
伎俩，我敢断定，来恐吓所有的外来者，
然后静静地紧随着——目的何在？
"她不曾逮到过野兔，从不惊骇，
却总在搜寻。今天她差点逮到一只：
今后或许会，或许不会。就那样了。真是晦气！
她用处不大，却依旧陪伴左右，
虽然我不是她的伴侣。她随我四处奔走。
今晚我总能到达奥尔顿小镇：
我和她不会在农家打地铺过夜。
今晚很多人比我睡得更糟、更差。"
"在壕沟中。""是的，分毫不差。

But they'll be out of that — I hope they be —
This weather, marching after the enemy."
"And so I hope. Good luck." And there I nodded
"Good-night. You keep straight on." Stiffly he plodded;
And at his heels the crisp leaves scurried fast,
And the leaf-coloured robin watched. They passed,
The robin till next day, the man for good,
Together in the twilight of the wood.

但他们将会远离那儿——希望他们会——
在这种天气下，不断追杀敌队。”
“我也希望如此。祝好运。”我点头回应，
“晚安。您继续。”他迈着僵硬、沉重的步伐前行；
在他的脚跟处，酥脆的树叶疾走穿梭，
而那只叶色的知更鸟注视着。他们经过，
次日破晓前，那只知更鸟停留，和那位老人，永远地，一起
留在了那片树林的暮色里。

Beauty

21 January, 1915

What does it mean? Tired, angry, and ill at ease,
No man, woman, or child alive could please
Me now. And yet I almost dare to laugh
Because I sit and frame an epitaph —
"Here lies all that no one loved of him
And that loved no one." Then in a trice that whim
Has wearied. But, though I am like a river
At fall of evening when it seems that never
Has the sun lighted it or warmed it, while
Cross breezes cut the surface to a file,
This heart, some fraction of me, happily
Floats through the window even now to a tree
Down in the misting, dim-lit, quiet vale;
Not like a pewit that returns to wail
For something it has lost, but like a dove
That slants unswerving to its home and love.
There I find my rest, and through the dusk air
Flies what yet lives in me. Beauty is there.

美

1915 年 1 月 21 日

美是何意？疲惫、生气、心神不安，
男人、女人、孩子难以令我欢颜，
如今依然。但我敢于笑脸相迎，
因我坐着在构思一篇墓志铭——
“此地安息着世人厌他之忧愁
以及厌世之仇恨”。不久，那念头
瞬间令我生厌。但，我虽似一条
河流，夜幕降临之际，仍未得到
太阳的垂照和温暖，然而这时
横风切割着地表，犹如一把锉刀，
这个心脏，我的一部分，开心地
飘出窗外，如今甚至到了树梢，
飘落至迷雾笼罩、幽静的山谷；
不应像田凫那样因丢失某物
而重归哀嚎，理应像鸽子那般
百折不挠，斜着飞向爱和家园。
在那儿我找到安息地，透过薄暮
放飞体内的灵魂。美就在彼处。[1]

---

[1] 此诗反映了诗人忧郁的精神状态。对他而言，死是一种美。面对恶劣环境，诗人意识到唯有坦然地迎向鸽子所带领的栖息地，才能找到祥和、家园和爱。这种坦然面对死亡的意境与他的另一首诗《雨》（*Rain*）所展示出来的生死观有着异曲同工之妙。——译者注

The Gypsy

22 January, 1915

A fortnight before Christmas Gypsies were everywhere:
Vans were drawn up on wastes, women trailed to the fair.
"My gentleman," said one, "you've got a lucky face."
"And you've a luckier," I thought, "if such a grace
And impudence in rags are lucky." "Give a penny
For the poor baby's sake." "Indeed I have not any
Unless you can give change for a sovereign, my dear."
"Then just half a pipeful of tobacco can you spare?"
I gave it. With that much victory she laughed content.
I should have given more, but off and away she went
With her baby and her pink sham flowers to rejoin
The rest before I could translate to its proper coin
Gratitude for her grace. And I paid nothing then,
As I pay nothing now with the dipping of my pen
For her brother's music when he drummed the tambourine
And stamped his feet, which made the workmen passing grin,
While his mouth-organ changed to a rascally Bacchanal dance
"Over the hills and far away." This and his glance
Outlasted all the fair, farmer, and auctioneer,
Cheap-jack, balloon-man, drover with crooked stick, and steer,

吉卜赛人

1915 年 1 月 22 日

圣诞节前的两周里，吉普赛人到处都是：
大蓬货车停在废墟上，妇人们列队赶着集市。
有人夸赞，“先生，您长着一张要交好运的脸蛋”。
“您的看起来更走运”，我心想，“如果这褴褛衣衫、
外表下的通情达理和厚颜无耻是幸运的话”。“看在这可怜
孩子的份上，给我点儿钱吧。”“实际上，我真没钱，
亲爱的朋友，除非您能给一个君主找零钱啊。”
“那您总可以施舍半管的烟草吧？”
我给了。拿着胜利的果实，她笑了，心满意足。
我本可以多给她点，但她早已离去，
带着她的孩子和粉色花饰重新混入人群里，
我都没来得及将感激她的通情达理
换算成相应的钱数。我当时分文未付，
就像此刻我的笔头蘸墨间，我也未支付
她兄弟的音乐一样，当时他敲着小手鼓，跺着脚，
引起路过的工人们咧嘴而笑，
他吹完口琴便跳起无赖似的酒神节狂舞
“翻山越岭，遥远之地。”这一瞥，他的远顾
比市集上的一切都愈加耐人寻味：农民、拍卖商、
叫卖小贩、卖气球的、拄着拐杖的家畜商贩、拉客商，

Pig, turkey, goose, and duck, Christmas corpses to be.
Not even the kneeling ox had eyes like the Romany.
That night he peopled for me the hollow wooded land,
More dark and wild than the stormiest heavens, that I searched and scanned
Like a ghost new-arrived. The gradations of the dark
Were like an underworld of death, but for the spark
In the Gypsy boy's black eyes as he played and stamped his tune,
"Over the hills and far away," and a crescent moon.

以及猪、火鸡、鹅、鸭等即将成为圣诞节的祭品。
甚至跪着的牛的双眼也不像这位吉普赛人的神情。
那晚他替我在我曾经追寻并见过的林中空地[1]上栖息过夜，
比最狂暴的天堂更加黑暗、更加狂野，
犹如一位新来的幽灵。那黑暗的层级，
就像死亡的地狱，除了那位吉普赛男孩儿的
黑色双眼所透露出的星光：他踩着节奏，唱着曲乐，
“翻山越岭，遥远之地”，当空垂挂着一轮新月。

---

❶ 林中空地变成了一个与大地、大自然最为亲近的隐喻，诗人虽向往却不像吉普赛人那样洒脱地睡于林地，可见诗人未能真正摆脱世俗的束缚，未能超脱一切。——译者注

Ambition

23 January, 1915

Unless it was that day I never knew
Ambition. After a night of frost, before
The March sun brightened and the South-west blew,
Jackdaws began to shout and float and soar
Already, and one was racing straight and high
Alone, shouting like a black warrior
Challenges and menaces to the wide sky.
With loud long laughter then a woodpecker
Ridiculed the sadness of the owl's last cry.
And through the valley where all the folk astir
Made only plumes of pearly smoke to tower
Over dark trees and white meadows happier
Than was Elysium in that happy hour,
A train that roared along raised after it
And carried with it a motionless white bower
Of purest cloud, from end to end close-knit,
So fair it touched the roar with silence. Time
Was powerless while that lasted. I could sit
And think I had made the loveliness of prime,
Breathed its life into it and were its lord,

志向

1915 年 1 月 23 日

若不是那日，我一直不知
何为雄心壮志。霜夜之后，
三月阳未明，西南风未至，
寒鸦方啼鸣，翱空展翅游，
径直飞起，独自翱空，
犹如一位黑暗勇士发出
挑战和恐吓，奔向那长空。
不久，啄木鸟大笑并长呼，
嘲讽猫头鹰最后的悲咏。
整个山谷中，万物皆骚动，
将一缕缕珍珠般的白烟
悬于黑林、白色草地的上空，
比一小时的极乐世界更欢愉，
火车咆哮驶来，加速追跑，
载着一个静止的纯净云团，
如白色树荫，头尾相缭绕，
它完美地以静谧抚咆哮。
时光柔弱，然而烟雾长绕。
我坐下思索，已将此美好，
赋予了生命，仿若创世者，

And no mind lived save this 'twixt clouds and rime.
Omnipotent I was, nor even deplored
That I did nothing. But the end fell like a bell:
The bower was scattered; far off the train roared.
But if this was ambition I cannot tell.
What 'twas ambition for I know not well.

除了云霜，再无其他思考。
我虽然全能，却从未谴责
自己无为。然而结局如铃而至：
树荫消散逝去，火车长鸣远去。
然此若为志向，我难以释解。
志向何用之有？我不甚了解。

House and Man

3, 4 February, 1915[1]

One hour: as dim he and his house now look
As a reflection in a rippling brook,
While I remember him; but first, his house.
Empty it sounded. It was dark with forest boughs
That brushed the walls and made the mossy tiles
Part of the squirrels' track. In all those miles
Of forest silence and forest murmur, only
One house — "Lonely!" he said, "I wish it were lonely" —
Which the trees looked upon from every side,
And that was his.

He waved good-bye to hide
A sigh that he converted to a laugh.
He seemed to hang rather than stand there, half

---

[1] In early February when Thomas composed this poem and two poems that followed it (i.e., "House and Man" "Parting" and "First Known When Lost"), Frost was departing with Thomas's son Mervyn for the USA. For more details about Frost's departure and saying goodbyes to Thomas in Hampshire, England on 6th February, 1915, please see HOLLIS M. Now all roads lead to France: the last years of Edward Thomas[M]. London: Faber and Faber, 2011: 206–11.

房与人

1915 年 2 月 3、4 日[1]

一小时：他和房子如今昏暗不清，
犹如溪中泛着涟漪的倒影，
当我想起他时；首先，说说他的房子。
它空荡荡、黑咕隆咚，因为树林繁枝
刷着屋墙，将长满青苔的瓦片
变成松鼠的通道。森林时而阒然、
时而低语，方圆几英里内独独
就这一所房子——“孤独！”，他说，“真希望它孤独”——
周围树木环绕俯瞰着，那便是
他的屋舍。

他挥手告别致意，
忍着叹息，转而喜笑开颜。
他看似吊在那儿，不像站着，一半

---

[1] 二月初，正值托马斯创作此诗和后两首（即“房与人”“离别”“失去时方知”）期间，佛罗斯特带着托马斯之子默文离开英国前往美国。欲知更多有关佛罗斯特 1915 年 2 月 6 日在英格兰汉普郡与托马斯辞行情形的细节，参见 HOLLIS M. Now all roads lead to France: the last years of Edward Thomas[M]. London: Faber and Faber, 2011: 206–11.——译者注

Ghost-like, half like a beggar's rag, clean wrung
And useless on the briar where it has hung
Long years a-washing by sun and wind and rain.

But why I call back man and house again
Is that now on a beech-tree's tip I see
As then I saw — I at the gate, and he
In the house darkness, — a magpie veering about,
A magpie like a weathercock in doubt.

像幽灵，一半像乞丐的破布，被拧得
干净却一无是处，在野蔷薇上，它被晾着，
经年累月，遭日晒、风吹、雨洗。

而我之所以再次想起人与房子，
是因为在山毛榉树梢，我如今所略
正如曾经所见——我在门口，他却
在房子的幽暗处，——一只喜鹊，盘旋围绕，
这只喜鹊犹如一个困惑的风向标。

Parting

11 February, 1915

The Past is a strange land, most strange.
Wind blows not there, nor does rain fall:
If they do, they cannot hurt at all.
Men of all kinds as equals range

The soundless fields and streets of it.
Pleasure and pain there have no sting,
The perished self not suffering
That lacks all blood and nerve and wit,

And is in shadow-land a shade.
Remembered joy and misery
Bring joy to the joyous equally;
Both sadden the sad. So memory made

Parting today a double pain:
First because it was parting; next
Because the ill it ended vexed
And mocked me from the Past again,

离别

1915 年 2 月 11 日

昔日陌地，甚是陌生。
不闻风吹，不见雨落：
若有风雨，不痛不嗦。
天地之间，众生平等。

原野街道，万籁俱寂，
喜乐痛楚，皆无刺感，
消亡自我，无痛无难：
身体无血，神无气智，

陌生之地，又浅又阴。
回忆苦难，追忆欢乐，
喜者亦喜，乐者亦乐；
悲者亦悲。追忆之情，

今日离别，雪上加霜：
先是离别，而后生疾，
继而疾去，往事追忆，
扰乱心思，嘲笑心伤，

Not as what had been remedied
Had I gone on, — not that, oh no!
But as itself no longer woe;
Sighs, angry word and look and deed

Being faded: rather a kind of bliss,
For there spiritualized it lay
In the perpetual yesterday
That naught can stir or strain like this.

忧愁痛苦，已被治愈？
我已前行？绝非如此！
自身而言，不再悲思；
叹息愁容，艰行怒语，

逐渐褪去：愿是喜福，
净化精神，存于永恒，
昨日之境，情难以生，
不囿于惑，永无痛楚。

First Known When Lost

11 February, 1915

I never had noticed it until
'Twas gone, — the narrow copse
Where now the woodman lops
The last of the willows with his bill.

It was not more than a hedge overgrown.
One meadow's breadth away
I passed it day by day.
Now the soil is bare as a bone,

And black betwixt two meadows green,
Though fresh-cut faggot ends
Of hazel made some amends
With a gleam as if flowers they had been.

Strange it could have hidden so near!
And now I see as I look
That the small winding brook,
A tributary's tributary, rises there.

失去时方知

1915 年 2 月 11 日

我从未留意过它，直到
它消逝，——狭小的灌木林
如今，最后的那片柳林，
被樵夫用镰刀给伐倒。

当时，仅仅是树篱蔓芜。
一片草地大小的宽度，
我曾每日经过它的路。
如今，土地贫瘠如骸骨，

两片绿地间露出一片黑，
虽然刚剪的榛树末端
做了些修饰，微光闪闪，
好像它们曾开满鲜花。

奇怪它能隐藏得如此近！
如今，我已领悟，当望见
那条小溪，曲折蜿蜒，
支流的支流，起源于此地。

May 23

15 February, 1915

There never was a finer day,
And never will be while May is May, —
The third, and not the last of its kind;
But though fair and clear the two behind
Seemed pursued by tempests overpast;
And the morrow with fear that it could not last
Was spoiled. Today ere the stones were warm
Five minutes of thunderstorm
Dashed it with rain, as if to secure,
By one tear, its beauty the luck to endure.

At midday then along the lane
Old Jack Noman appeared again,
Jaunty and old, crooked and tall,
And stopped and grinned at me over the wall,
With a cowslip bunch in his button-hole
And one in his cap. Who could say if his roll
Came from flints in the road, the weather, or ale?
He was welcome as the nightingale.
Not an hour of the sun had been wasted on Jack.
"I've got my Indian complexion back"

五月二十三日

1915 年 2 月 15 日

过去不曾且未来亦不会有哪一日
像现在如此美好，当五月是，——
五月三日，而非五月最后一日；
然而尽管它美丽与清澈，二者已逝，
似被狂风暴雨追逐，甩在后面；
担心它不能持久，明天，
早已幻灭。今天，石头温暖前，
电闪雷鸣，大雨滂沱，飞速猛窜，
持续五分钟，仿佛要撕开一缝罅去
守护它的美丽，让幸运永驻。

之后晌午时分，沿着小路漫步，
老杰克·诺曼再次现露，
精神抖擞却已年迈，身体弯曲却还高挑，
驻足，朝一墙之隔的我咧齿而笑，
他胸前的扣眼和头上的帽檐
各别着一束报春花。谁知道他摇晃
是因为路中燧石、天气还是喝了麦芽酒？
他像夜莺一样深受欢迎，不遭人羞。
阳光照在他身上，毫无浪费可言。
“我又重获了印度人的肤色”，他坦言。

Said he. He was tanned like a harvester,
Like his short clay pipe, like the leaf and bur
That clung to his coat from last night's bed,
Like the ploughland crumbling red.
Fairer flowers were none on the earth
Than his cowslips wet with the dew of their birth,
Or fresher leaves than the cress in his basket.
"Where did they come from, Jack?" "Don't ask it,
And you'll be told no lies." "Very well:
Then I can't buy." "I don't want to sell.
Take them and these flowers, too, free.
Perhaps you have something to give me?
Wait till next time. The better the day . . .
The Lord couldn't make a better, I say;
If he could, he never has done."
So off went Jack with his roll-walk-run,
Leaving his cresses from Oakshott rill
And his cowslips from Wheatham hill.

'Twas the first day that the midges bit;
But though they bit me, I was glad of it:
Of the dust in my face, too, I was glad.
Spring could do nothing to make me sad.
Bluebells hid all the ruts in the copse,
The elm seeds lay in the road like hops,
That fine day, May the twenty-third,
The day Jack Noman disappeared.

他被晒得像一位收割的农者，
像他那把陶瓷短烟嘴，像昨夜
睡觉时黏在外衣上的树叶和芒刺，
像一片田地被犁碎，通红满地。
他的报春花带着出生时的露珠，
成了世间无与伦比的花簇，
他篮中的水芹叶是世间最鲜嫩的叶。
“杰克，这些哪儿弄来的？”“别问了，
反正不会骗你。”“既然如此，
我便不能买。”“我没打算卖给你。
这些都拿走，还有花，免费送你。
或许你要回赠我什么东西？
等下次吧。等天更好的时候了……
我想，上帝不会赏赐更好的天气了；
如果会，他早就赏赐了。”
说完，杰克摇晃着身子，又走又跑地离开了，
却留下了奥克肖特小溪的水芹，
还有那些维特哈姆山的报春花英。

第一天蠓虫便四处叮咬；
我对它却满心欢喜，虽然被咬，
且满脸粉尘，却仍无比欢欣。
或许春天不会令我伤心。
蓝铃花遮住了灌木林中所有的车辙，
铺在路中的榆树籽似跳跃着，
那天便是美丽的五月二十三日，
而那天杰克·诺曼消失得渺无踪迹。

The Barn

22 February, 1915

They should never have built a barn there, at all —
Drip, drip, drip! — under that elm tree,
Though then it was young. Now it is old
But good, not like the barn and me.

Tomorrow they cut it down. They will leave
The barn, as I shall be left, maybe.
What holds it up? 'Twould not pay to pull down.
Well, this place has no other antiquity.

No abbey or castle looks so old
As this that Job Knight built in '54,
Built to keep corn for rats and men.
Now there's fowls in the roof, pigs on the floor.

What thatch survives is dung for the grass,
The best grass on the farm. A pity the roof
Will not bear a mower to mow it. But
Only fowls have foothold enough.

谷仓

1915 年 2 月 22 日

他们本不该在那儿建谷仓，绝对不行——
滴答，滴答，滴答！——在那颗榆树下面，
尽管它当时还年轻。如今虽已老，
却依旧完好，不像我和那座谷仓。

明日他们将把它伐倒，会留下
谷仓，我也将被留下，或许。
它何以支撑？不值得将它砍倒。
哎，此处再无其他古迹建筑。

无一座寺庙或城堡像约伯·奈特
1854 年所建的谷仓那样古色古香，
用来贮存玉米，供鼠耗和人食用。
如今飞禽落在仓顶，猪躺在地板上。

幸存的茅草屋顶已成为草的养粪，
那可是农场上最肥沃的草地。可惜
屋顶恐难承受修葺员的修葺。不过，
足以支撑飞禽的落脚之力。

Starlings used to sit there with bubbling throats
Making a spiky beard as they chattered
And whistled and kissed, with heads in air,
Till they thought of something else that mattered.

But now they cannot find a place,
Among all those holes, for a nest any more.
It's the turn of lesser things, I suppose.
Once I fancied 'twas starlings they built it for.

欧椋鸟曾经常驻足，鼓动着喉咙，
竖起尖尖的颊毛，时而喳喳叽叽，
时而吹哨，时而亲吻，时而仰着头，
直到想起其他一些要紧之事。

如今他们在那些洞穴中，
无法找到一隅之地来筑巢。
我心想，这便是物种变少的转折点。
我曾幻想谷仓是为欧椋鸟而造。

Home (Not the End)

23 February, 1915

Not the end: but there's nothing more.
Sweet Summer and Winter rude
I have loved, and friendship and love,
The crowd and solitude:

But I know them: I weary not;
But all that they mean I know.
I would go back again home
Now. Yet how should I go?

This is my grief. That land,
My home, I have never seen;
No traveller tells of it,
However far he has been.

And could I discover it,
I fear my happiness there,
Or my pain, might be dreams of return
Here, to these things that were.

家园（非尽头）

1915 年 2 月 23 日

非尽头：然也仅此而已。
夏日甜美，冬日粗鲁
我都曾爱过，友情、爱情，
人群与孤独：

但我知道他们：我不厌烦；
但我明白其所蕴含之意。
如今我将再次回家。
然而我该如何走起？

悲从中来。那片土地，
我的家园，未曾看见；
未闻游者提起，
无论他多遥远。

如若能找到它，
我怕在那儿的幸福
或痛苦，会变成一个个梦想，
重新变回这些熟悉的事物。

Remembering ills, though slight
Yet irremediable,
Brings a worse, an impurer pang
Than remembering what was well.

No: I cannot go back,
And would not if I could.
Until blindness come, I must wait
And blink at what is not good.

回忆各种疾病，尽管轻微，
却难以治愈，
相比回忆安康
则带来更痛、更浑的闷郁。

不：我不能回去，
如果可以，也不回去。
我必须等，眨眼望着不幸，
直至双眼失明。

The Owl

24 February, 1915

Downhill I came, hungry, and yet not starved;
Cold, yet had heat within me that was proof
Against the North wind; tired, yet so that rest
Had seemed the sweetest thing under a roof.

Then at the inn I had food, fire, and rest,
Knowing how hungry, cold, and tired was I.
All of the night was quite barred out except
An owl's cry, a most melancholy cry

Shaken out long and clear upon the hill,
No merry note, nor cause of merriment,
But one telling me plain what I escaped
And others could not, that night, as in I went.

And salted was my food, and my repose,
Salted and sobered, too, by the bird's voice
Speaking for all who lay under the stars,
Soldiers and poor, unable to rejoice.

猫头鹰

1915 年 2 月 24 日

下山饿意正起，却未饥不择食；
外面寒冷凛冽，体内尚存热气，
足以抵抗北风；筋疲力尽之时，
方觉檐下歇息，实乃极美之事。

而后栈内就餐，烘火暖身安歇，
方知肚饥身寒，精疲力竭不堪。
夜下屋内温馨，阻挡屋外一切，
不敌枭鸟哭泣，异常凄楚悲婉，

响彻万里，地动山摇，
曲调沉闷，毫无欣喜，
进店之时，我才知晓：
我已离苦境，他人却未离。

食物咸苦，歇息咸苦，
清醒咸苦，鸟声嘹亮，
诉说星空之下，躺着穷人士卒，
难以欢欣暖歇，无限凄苦悲凉。

The Child on the Cliffs

11 March, 1915

Mother, the root of this little yellow flower
Among the stones has the taste of quinine.
Things are strange today on the cliff. The sun shines so bright,
And the grasshopper works at his sewing-machine
So hard. Here's one on my hand, mother, look;
I lie so still. There's one on your book.

But I have something to tell more strange. So leave
Your book to the grasshopper, mother dear, —
Like a green knight in a dazzling market-place, —
And listen now. Can you hear what I hear
Far out? Now and then the foam there curls
And stretches a white arm out like a girl's.

Fishes and gulls ring no bells. There cannot be
A chapel or church between here and Devon,
With fishes or gulls ringing its bell, — hark! —
Somewhere under the sea or up in heaven.
"It's the bell, my son, out in the bay
On the buoy. It does sound sweet today."

悬崖上的稚童

1915 年 3 月 11 日

母亲，这朵小黄花的根部
长在乱石间，有着奎宁的气息。
今日崖上一切倍感奇异。阳光如此灿烂，
一只蚱蜢在他的缝纫机上如此努力地
工作。现在，我手中就有一只，母亲，看；
我静静地躺着。一只蚱蜢落在您的书上。

但我还有更诡异之事要讲。因此把
您的书留给那只蚱蜢，亲爱的母亲，——
在眼花缭乱的集市中，如一名绿色骑士，——
现在请听。您能否和我一样听见那声音
响彻远方？那泡沫时不时地卷起
又舒展着像少女的一只白臂。

鱼鸥没有鸣起响钟。不可能有
任何教堂，在此地与德文海滩之间，
同时鱼鸥鸣起响钟，——听！——
在海底或天堂某个地方。
“那是响钟，我的孩子，在海湾之外，
浮标之上。今天它听起来甚是美哉。”

Sweeter I never heard, mother, no, not in all Wales.
I should like to be lying under that foam,
Dead, but able to hear the sound of the bell,
And certain that you would often come
And rest, listening happily.
I should be happy if that could be.

1915 年

更美之声，我从未听闻，母亲，不，并非整个威尔士皆能听到。
我宁愿躺在那泡沫下方，
虽死，却还能听见那钟声，
同时相信您也会经常
前来歇息，开心地听着此妙音。
倘若如此，我将感到幸福欢欣。

The Bridge

12 March, 1915

I have come a long way today:
On a strange bridge alone,
Remembering friends, old friends,
I rest, without smile or moan,
As they remember me without smile or moan.

All are behind, the kind
And the unkind too, no more
Tonight than a dream. The stream
Runs softly yet drowns the Past,
The dark-lit stream has drowned the Future and the Past.

No traveller has rest more blest
Than this moment brief between
Two lives, when the Night's first lights
And shades hide what has never been,
Things goodlier, lovelier, dearer, than will be or have been.

桥

1915 年 3 月 12 日

今日我走了很长的路：
独自来到一座陌生的桥，
想起了朋友，老朋友，
我歇了歇，不笑，不怨，
正如他们记起我的模样：不笑，不怨。

一切皆抛诸脑后，善也好，
恶也罢，今晚只剩
一个梦想。这条小溪
缓缓流淌，淹没过往，
昏暗的溪流早已淹没了将来与过往。

游人无不感到此刻歇息
介于俩生命之间，最受庇佑，
虽然短暂：夜晚初放光芒，
撒下阴影，遮蔽从未存在之物，
遮蔽那些比将来或过往更美、更有活力、更珍贵之物。

Good-Night

16 March, 1915

The skylarks are far behind that sang over the down;
I can hear no more those suburb nightingales;
Thrushes and blackbirds sing in the gardens of the town
In vain: the noise of man, beast, and machine prevails.

But the call of children in the unfamiliar streets
That echo with a familiar twilight echoing,
Sweet as the voice of nightingale or lark, completes
A magic of strange welcome, so that I seem a king

Among man, beast, machine, bird, child, and the ghost
That in the echo lives and with the echo dies.
The friendless town is friendly; homeless, I am not lost;
Though I know none of these doors, and meet but strangers' eyes.

Never again, perhaps, after tomorrow, shall
I see these homely streets, these church windows alight,
Not a man or woman or child among them all:
But it is All Friends' Night, a traveller's good-night.

良宵

1915 年 3 月 16 日

云雀远处旋飞，在原野上放声歌唱；
我再也听不见那些市郊的夜莺；
画眉、乌鸫栖息小镇花园中歌唱
徒然：人类、野兽、机器皆轰鸣。

而稚童的叫声响彻陌生的道路，
与那熟悉的朝霞共鸣，相得益彰，
甜美如夜莺或百灵鸟之音，谱出
一首奇妙的欢迎曲，故此，我好像

在人类、野兽、机器、鸟儿、稚童、幽灵中称王，
在共鸣回音中，与之共存亡。
冷漠之城显得友善；无家可归，我却没有迷失方向；
尽管我不知这些人家，并且遇到的皆是陌生的眼光。

或许，明天之后，我将再也看不见
这些如家的街道，一扇扇教堂窗户亮着，
没有一个男人或女人或稚童待在里面：
而这正是友人之夜，游子之良夜。

But These Things Also

18 March, 1915

But these things also are Spring's —
On banks by the roadside the grass
Long-dead that is greyer now
Than all the Winter it was;

The shell of a little snail bleached
In the grass; chip of flint, and mite
Of chalk; and the small birds' dung
In splashes of purest white:

All the white things a man mistakes
For earliest violets
Who seeks through Winter's ruins
Something to pay Winter's debts,

While the North blows, and starling flocks
By chattering on and on
Keep their spirits up in the mist,
And Spring's here, Winter's not gone.

然此物亦属

1915 年 3 月 18 日

然此物亦属春天——
路边堤岸上的杂草
早已枯死，如今显得
比冬天时更加苍老；

一枚小蜗壳在草丛中
被漂白；燧石片片，
白垩零星；鸟屎坨坨，
甚是洁白，四处飞溅：

所有白物，人们误识，
以为最早的紫罗兰，
似在冬日的废迹中
寻宝，以补冬日之债款，

正值北风吹，一群欧椋鸟
叽叽喳喳、喋喋不休，
在迷雾中精神振奋，
春天已至，冬天未去。

The New House

19 March, 1915

Now first, as I shut the door,
I was alone
In the new house; and the wind
Began to moan.

Old at once was the house,
And I was old;
My ears were teased with the dread
Of what was foretold,

Nights of storm, days of mist, without end;
Sad days when the sun
Shone in vain: old griefs, and griefs
Not yet begun.

All was foretold me; naught
Could I foresee;
But I learnt how the wind would sound
After these things should be.

新房

1915 年 3 月 19 日

房门紧闭时，初感
孤身伶仃
在新房之中，那风
开始呻吟。

房子瞬间变老，
我也变老；
两耳被揶揄，恐惧
那预言谶兆，

每夜风暴，每日薄雾，无休无止；
忧伤时节，日照徒然：
旧愁、旧怨
尚未开始。

一切已被预兆；
非我能预筹；
但我学会辨别风声，
在历经诸事之后。

The Barn and the Down

22, 23 March, 1915

It stood in the sunset sky
Like the straight-backed down,
Many a time — the barn
At the edge of town,

So huge and dark that it seemed
It was the hill
Till the gable's precipice proved
It impossible.

Then the great down in the west
Grew into sight,
A barn stored full to the ridge
With black of night;

And the barn fell to a barn
Or even less

谷仓与丘原

1915 年 3 月 22—23 日

夕阳中它屹立着
像一片平坦的丘原，
经常如此——谷仓
坐落于小镇边缘，

看起来又大又黑，
犹如一座小山，
直到山形墙的峭壁
证明其非然。

西边广阔的丘原
渐入眼帘，
一仓储量满至边缘，
夜幕垂帘。

全仓[1]降至一仓
或更少一点儿，

---

[1] barn 一词除了表示“谷仓”之意，在威尔士传统中亦有“观点，视角，判断”之意。——译者注

Before critical eyes and its own
Late mightiness.

But far down and near barn and I
Since then have smiled,
Having seen my new cautiousness
By itself beguiled

To disdain what seemed the barn
Till a few steps changed
It past all doubt to the down;
So the barn was avenged.

在犀利的双眼和它自身
迟来的威力面前。

而远处之下，谷仓附近，我
从那时起便笑容满面，
觉察到自己新添的谨慎
已被自身所诱骗，

以致藐视类似谷仓之物，
直至挪动几步：
它把所有疑惑留给了丘原；
故此，谷仓之仇已被复。

Sowing

23 March, 1915

It was a perfect day
For sowing; just
As sweet and dry was the ground
As tobacco-dust.

I tasted deep the hour
Between the far
Owl's chuckling first soft cry
And the first star.

A long stretched hour it was;
Nothing undone
Remained; the early seeds
All safely sown.

And now, hark at the rain,
Windless and light,
Half a kiss, half a tear,
Saying good-night.

播种

1915 年 3 月 23 日

那日正是播种
最好时机；
土地祥美、干燥，
如烟草一灰。

我沉浸于时光中：
远处鸥鸮
初次轻声笑唤，
初星寥寥。

那时光，若千年；
万物已造，
一切依旧；早期种子
皆已种好。

如今聆听雨声，
无风、轻淡，
仿若吻，仿若泪，
道声晚安。

March the Third

23 March, 1915

Here again (she said) is March the third
And twelve hours singing for the bird
'Twixt dawn and dusk, from half-past six
To half-past six, never unheard.

'Tis Sunday, and the church-bells end
When the birds do. I think they blend
Now better than they will when passed
Is this unnamed, unmarked godsend.

Or do all mark, and none dares say,
How it may shift and long delay,
Somewhere before the first of Spring,
But never fails, this singing day?

And when it falls on Sunday, bells
Are a wild natural voice that dwells
On hillsides; but the birds' songs have
The holiness gone from the bells.

三月三

1915 年 3 月 23 日

一晃（她说）又是三月三，
整日整夜为鸟儿歌唱，
朝起暮降，从六点半
到六点半，歌声不断。

今儿周日，教堂的钟声
随鸟曲而终。二者合声
胜过平日路过时所闻，
此乃无名、无迹天赐之声。

或许人们留意，却不敢言，
在欢歌时节，初春来前，
它怎会变更路线，长期
滞留某地，却从不食言？

倘若它周日来临，钟声
如自然狂野之音，存生
山坡之上；但鸟儿歌声
拥有钟声遗失的神圣。

This day unpromised is more dear
Than all the named days of the year
When seasonable sweets come in,
Because we know how lucky we are.

这一天，尚未兑现，相比
所有已知岁日，更加珍贵，
因为幸运早已垂青自己，
当美好季节来临之际。

Two Pewits

24 March, 1915, revised 4 May, 1915

Under the after-sunset sky
Two pewits sport and cry,
More white than is the moon on high
Riding the dark surge silently;
More black than earth. Their cry
Is the one sound under the sky.
They alone move, now low, now high,
And merrily they cry
To the mischievous Spring sky,
Plunging earthward, tossing high,
Over the ghost who wonders why
So merrily they cry and fly,
Nor choose 'twixt earth and sky,
While the moon's quarter silently
Rides, and earth rests as silently.

两只凤头麦鸡

1915 年 3 月 24 日，改于 1915 年 5 月 4 日

夕阳西下，夜幕临现，
凤头麦鸡，穿梭呼喊，
白胜皓月，当空璀璨，
驰骋夜空，祥和静谧；
暗胜黑土。其声呼喊，
苍穹之下，久久不散。
踽踽旋飞，时高时低，
激情欢悦，高声呼喊，
淘气响彻春意蓝天，
朝东猛冲，飞摇直窜，
悬于幽灵，迷惑之感：
何故欢呼、何故翱旋，
非抉择于天地之间，
正当明月悄然升起，
土地悄然入息之时。

Will You Come

25 March, 1915

Will you come?
Will you come?
Will you ride
So late
At my side?
O, will you come?

Will you come?
Will you come
If the night
Has a moon,
Full and bright?
O, will you come?

Would you come?
Would you come
If the noon
Gave light,
Not the moon?
Beautiful, would you come?

你会来吗

1915 年 3 月 25 日

你会来吗？
你会来吗？
你会姗姗
来迟
到我身边？
啊，你会来吗？

你会来吗？
你会来吗，
如果夜晚
明月当空，
又亮又圆？
啊，你会来吗？

你能来吗？
你能来吗，
倘若是正午
发亮，
而非月亮？
美丽的你，能来吗？

Would you have come?
Would you have come
Without scorning,
Had it been
Still morning?
Beloved, would you have come?

If you come,
Haste and come.
Owls have cried;
It grows dark
To ride.
Beloved, beautiful, come.

你已经来了吗？
你已经来了吗，
若免受指摘，
若晨光
依旧在？
亲爱的，你已经来了吗？

你若来，
速速来。
猫头鹰已哭泣；
夜幕临近，
行路难矣。
亲爱的，美丽的你，来吧！

The Path

26 March, 1915

Running along a bank, a parapet
That saves from the precipitous wood below
The level road, there is a path. It serves
Children for looking down the long smooth steep,
Between the legs of beech and yew, to where
A fallen tree checks the sight: while men and women
Content themselves with the road and what they see
Over the bank, and what the children tell.
The path, winding like silver, trickles on,
Bordered and even invaded by thinnest moss
That tries to cover roots and crumbling chalk
With gold, olive, and emerald, but in vain.
The children wear it. They have flattened the bank
On top, and silvered it between the moss
With the current of their feet, year after year.
But the road is houseless, and leads not to school.
To see a child is rare there, and the eye
Has but the road, the wood that overhangs
And underyawns it, and the path that looks
As if it led on to some legendary
Or fancied place where men have wished to go
And stay; till, sudden, it ends where the wood ends.

小道

1915 年 3 月 26 日

沿着河岸，一堵矮墙
将下面陡峭的林地与平路
隔开，辟出一条小道。它帮助
孩子们俯瞰那又长又顺的陡坡，
介于山毛榉和紫衫树干之间，直到
一棵倒地的树挡住了视线：而人们
对此道和岸上所见，
以及孩童们所诉倍感欣慰。
此道蜿蜒如银色细流，
为极细苔藓所分界、侵蚀，
苔藓竭尽全力将树根、碎白垩
裹成金黄、橄榄绿和祖母绿，却是徒劳。
孩子们磨损了小道，踏平了河岸
顶部，随着脚下的流水，年复一年
将介于苔藓间的河岸磨得银亮。
然而此路“无家可归”，也不通至学校。
在那儿很难撞见孩童，所见之物
唯有此路，为密林所笼罩，
形成一方幽洞，它似
通往某个神话般的世界
或迷人的地方，人们早已向往
去栖居；直到，突然，它终结于森林尽头。

The Wasp Trap

27 March, 1915

This moonlight makes
The lovely lovelier
Than ever before lakes
And meadows were.

And yet they are not,
Though this their hour is, more
Lovely than things that were not
Lovely before.

Nothing on earth,
And in the heavens no star,
For pure brightness is worth
More than that jar,

For wasps meant, now
A star — long may it swing
From the dead apple-bough,
So glistening.

黄蜂陷阱

1915 年 3 月 27 日

这月光使
甜美之物更美
而湖泊、草地
较之不美。

然而他们不——
虽光彩依然——更加
甜美，相比此前不
美之物华。

世间皆寥茫，
天辰不见星，
清明价非凡，
雄胜罐与瓶，

黄蜂如今似
朗星——久久振翅，
飞离苹果枯枝，
闪耀无比。

A Tale

28 March, 1915

There once the walls
Of the ruined cottage stood.
The periwinkle crawls
With flowers in its hair into the wood.

In flowerless hours
Never will the bank fail,
With everlasting flowers
On fragments of blue plates, to tell the tale.

传说

1915 年 3 月 28 日

曾经那小屋坍塌，
围墙却巍然屹立。
玉黍螺随处蔓爬，
蔓上花须伸进树林里。

花落凋零之际，
堤岸绝不会忘记，
对着蓝碟碎器
上印着的常盛花，讲述这个故事。

Wind and Mist

1 April, 1915

They met inside the gateway that gives the view,
A hollow land as vast as heaven. "It is
A pleasant day, sir." "A very pleasant day."
"And what a view here. If you like angled fields
Of grass and grain bounded by oak and thorn,
Here is a league. Had we with Germany
To play upon this board it could not be
More dear than April has made it with a smile.
The fields beyond that league close in together
And merge, even as our days into the past,
Into one wood that has a shining pane
Of water. Then the hills of the horizon —
That is how I should make hills had I to show
One who would never see them what hills were like."
"Yes. Sixty miles of South Downs at one glance.
Sometimes a man feels proud of them, as if
He had just created them with one mighty thought."
"That house, though modern, could not be better planned
For its position. I never liked a new
House better. Could you tell me who lives in it?"

风与雾

1915 年 4 月 1 日

他们相聚门内，门外好视野，
一片空凹地，广阔如天。“先生，
今天天气真好。”“是的，非常好。”
“这里美不胜收。如果你喜欢
橡棘环绕视野宽广的麦草地，
这儿便是集萃园。倘若与德国
一起角逐此地，这便是风水
宝地：四月面带微笑，将它精心打扮了一番。
园外一片片原野，相互挨着，
相互交融，仿佛将我们带入往昔时光，
进入一片林地，闪耀着光彩夺目的水窗。
还有地平线上的群山——
那是我所希望建造的群山，
倘若我陪同一位从未见过山的人来参观。”
“是。一眼望尽六十英里南丘。
有时候人们以此为傲，仿佛
刚用强大意念将他们造出。”
“那房子，虽现代，因地理位置
已是最好设计。我从不认为
新房更好。知道谁住里面吗？”

"No one." "Ah — and I was peopling all
Those windows on the south with happy eyes,
The terrace under them with happy feet;
Girls —" "Sir, I know. I know. I have seen that house
Through mist look lovely as a castle in Spain,
And airier. I have thought: ''Twere happy there
To live.' And I have laughed at that
Because I lived there then." "Extraordinary."
"Yes, with my furniture and family
Still in it, I, knowing every nook of it
And loving none, and in fact hating it."
"Dear me! How could that be? But pardon me."
"No offence. Doubtless the house was not to blame,
But the eye watching from those windows saw,
Many a day, day after day, mist — mist,
Like chaos surging back — and felt itself
Alone in all the world, marooned alone.
We lived in clouds, on a cliff's edge almost
(You see), and if clouds went, the visible earth
Lay too far off beneath and like a cloud.
I did not know it was the earth I loved
Until I tried to live there in the clouds
And the earth turned to cloud." "You had a garden
Of flint and clay, too." "True; that was real enough.
The flint was the one crop that never failed.
The clay first broke my heart, and then my back;

“没人。”“啊——我想着里面有人住：
所有南面窗露着幸福的双眼，
窗下平台站满了幸福的双脚；
皆是女孩儿——”“先生，我知道，见过
雾中那房，美如西班牙城堡，
但更飘逸。我曾想：‘住在那里
多么幸福。’我对此还嘲笑过，
因我曾在那里住过。”“太棒了。”
“是的，我的家具和家人仍在
里面，每一个角落我都熟悉
但一无所恋，实际上还厌恶。”
“天呐！怎么可能？原谅我的惊讶。”
“无妨。无疑不该谴责那房子，
但那些窗后的眼睛向外望着
迷雾好几日，日复一日——迷雾
像混沌翻涌归来——感觉自身
孤独于世，独自形成一座‘孤岛’。
我们住在云中，似悬崖峭壁之上
（你看），如果云消散，可见底下
土地远远地躺着，仿若云彩。
我不知道那是我爱的土地，
直到我尝试居住在云中后，
发现地变成了云。”“你还有一花园
的燧石和粘土。”“是，的确如此。
燧石如一粒谷物，如我所愿。
粘土先是伤我心，后伤我背；

And the back heals not. There were other things
Real, too. In that room at the gable a child
Was born while the wind chilled a summer dawn:
Never looked grey mind on a greyer one
Than when the child's cry broke above the groans."
"I hope they were both spared." "They were. Oh yes.
But flint and clay and childbirth were too real
For this cloud castle. I had forgot the wind.
Pray do not let me get on to the wind.
You would not understand about the wind.
It is my subject, and compared with me
Those who have always lived on the firm ground
Are quite unreal in this matter of the wind.
There were whole days and nights when the wind and I
Between us shared the world, and the wind ruled
And I obeyed it and forgot the mist.
My past and the past of the world were in the wind.
Now you will say that though you understand
And feel for me, and so on, you yourself
Would find it different. You are all like that
If once you stand here free from wind and mist:
I might as well be talking to wind and mist.
You would believe the house-agent's young man
Who gives no heed to anything I say.
Good morning. But one word. I want to admit
That I would try the house once more, if I could;
As I should like to try being young again."

至今伤未愈。还有其他真事儿。
在那山墙房间里，一个孩子
诞生，而风正寒透夏日清晨：
孩子哭声划破阵阵呻吟时，
脑海从未如此灰暗迟钝过。”
“愿他们都能幸免。”“哦，他们能。
对云堡来说，燧石、粘土、孩子
出生，皆是真事儿。寒风我已忘。
求你不要让我继续提到风。
你无法理解这寒风的寓意。
它是我的主题，和我相比较，
一直住在坚实土地上的人
无法真真切切体悟这寒风。
记得曾经日日夜夜，风与我
共享着我们之间的世界，风
主宰一切，我顺从，并忘了雾。
我和世界的过去皆在风中。
如今你或许会说，虽然理解，
也会设身处地等诸如此类的话，你自己
会有不同的体验。一样的感受，
除非你站这儿不受风吹雾绕：
我不妨算是在和风雾聊天。
你或许会信那年轻的房产经纪人，
而他对我的所述置若罔闻。
早安。但是有一点。我想承认
倘若可以，我会再住一次这房子；
因我想试着重回青春年少。”

A Gentleman

2 April, 1915

"He has robbed two clubs. The judge at Salisbury
Can't give him more than he undoubtedly
Deserves. The scoundrel! Look at his photograph!
A lady-killer! Hanging's too good by half
For such as he." So said the stranger, one
With crimes yet undiscovered or undone.
But at the inn the Gypsy dame began:
"Now he was what I call a gentleman.
He went along with Carrie, and when she
Had a baby he paid up so readily
His half a crown. Just like him. A crown'd have been
More like him. For I never knew him mean.
Oh! But he was such a nice gentleman. Oh!
Last time we met he said if me and Joe
Was anywhere near we must be sure and call.
He put his arms around our Amos all
As if he were his own son. I pray God
Save him from justice! Nicer man never trod."

绅士

1915 年 4 月 2 日

“他打劫了俩酒吧。索尔兹伯里法官按律
判他应有之罪，无疑他咎由自取。
恶棍流氓！看看他的照片！
少妇杀手！绞刑算是太慈善，
只抵其一半罪过。”一位罪恶滔天
却逍遥法外的陌生人发言。
然而，酒吧里一位吉普赛女士开始
讲述：“他曾是我口中称赞的一位绅士。
他曾与凯莉交往，并且当她
怀有孩子时，他很爽快地给了她
半克朗。真像他。一克朗可能
更像他。因为我从不觉得他抠门。
噢，可他曾是如此善良的绅士。噢！
上次我们见面时，他说如果我和乔
在附近的话，我们务必要拜访。
他把双臂搭在我们的阿摩司[1]上
好像他是自己的儿子。我祈祷上帝
让他免受审判！更善之人，不应被蹂躏。”

---

[1] 《圣经》旧约中公元前 8 世纪的希伯来先知。——译者注

Lob

3, 4 April, 1915

At hawthorn-time in Wiltshire travelling
In search of something chance would never bring,
An old man's face, by life and weather cut
And coloured, — rough, brown, sweet as any nut, —
A land face, sea-blue-eyed, — hung in my mind
When I had left him many a mile behind.
All he said was: "Nobody can't stop 'ee. It's
A footpath, right enough. You see those bits
Of mounds — that's where they opened up the barrows
Sixty years since, while I was scaring sparrows.
They thought as there was something to find there,
But couldn't find it, by digging, anywhere."

To turn back then and seek him, where was the use?
There were three Manningfords,— Abbots, Bohun, and Bruce:
And whether Alton, not Manningford, it was,
My memory could not decide, because
There was both Alton Barnes and Alton Priors.
All had their churches, graveyards, farms, and byres,
Lurking to one side up the paths and lanes,

罗勃

1915 年 4 月 3—4 日

山楂灿烂时，游威尔特郡，
寻奇闻轶事，非机缘可寻，
老人脸沧桑，饱经风与霜，——
黄脸粗且糙，恰似坚果香，——
双眼蓝如海，脸庞大如地，——
依晰我脑中，虽隔数英里。
其语绕耳边：“无人不阻你。
直走小径道。道旁土丘立，
堆积成山岗——开凿为盗墓，
已有六十载，麻雀为我逐。
墓中藏珍宝？盗贼常疑惑，
四处凿且挖，终究无所获。”

转身想寻他，何用之有焉？
曼宁三家族——阿博斯、波罕、
布鲁斯：奥顿，非曼宁难析，
奥顿·巴恩斯，奥顿·普莱斯，
二者易混淆，非记忆所斟：
教堂与墓地，农场与牛棚，
皆暗立路旁，匿于小巷处，

Seldom well seen except by aeroplanes;
And when bells rang, or pigs squealed, or cocks crowed,
Then only heard. Ages ago the road
Approached. The people stood and looked and turned,
Nor asked it to come nearer, nor yet learned
To move out there and dwell in all men's dust.
And yet withal they shot the weathercock, just
Because 'twas he crowed out of tune, they said:
So now the copper weathercock is dead.
If they had reaped their dandelions and sold
Them fairly, they could have afforded gold.

Many years passed, and I went back again
Among those villages, and looked for men
Who might have known my ancient. He himself
Had long been dead or laid upon the shelf,
I thought. One man I asked about him roared
At my description: " 'Tis old Bottlesford
He means, Bill." But another said: "Of course,
It was Jack Button up at the White Horse.
He's dead, sir, these three years." This lasted till
A girl proposed Walker of Walker's Hill,
"Old Adam Walker. Adam's Point you'll see
Marked on the maps."

"That was her roguery,"

不为人所见，唯乘机可睹；
铃声响起时，猪嗷伴鸡鸣，
只会闻其声，恐难见其形。
路通已久远。行人站望离。
不求路更近，不栖红尘世：
无意往外迁，不愿离此地。
村中奇事多：射死风信鸡，
村民怪因由：鸣时常跑调；
铜色风信鸡，如今死翘翘。
民若施初计：收割蒲公英，
出售价合理，现能买黄金。

几度春秋往，我再次归来，
行走村落间，寻根问祖脉，
每逢知情人。祖先何处寻？
作古已多年，架上族谱询。
上前问一人，惊呼我所述：
“波特斯福德，老鬼我清楚，
小名叫比尔。”他人却透露：
或杰克·巴顿，白马客栈住。
去世已三年。”路人复如此，
唯有一少女，谈及游山士，
“游士老亚当。亚当游世点，
图上皆可寻。”

“她一派胡言。”

The next man said. He was a squire's son
Who loved wild bird and beast, and dog and gun
For killing them. He had loved them from his birth,
One with another, as he loved the earth.
"The man may be like Button, or Walker, or
Like Bottlesford, that you want, but far more
He sounds like one I saw when I was a child.
I could almost swear to him. The man was wild
And wandered. His home was where he was free.
Everybody has met one such man as he.
Does he keep clear old paths that no one uses
But once a life-time when he loves or muses?
He is English as this gate, these flowers, this mire.
And when at eight years old Lob-lie-by-the-fire
Came in my books, this was the man I saw.
He has been in England as long as dove and daw,
Calling the wild cherry tree the merry tree,
The rose campion Bridget-in-her-bravery;
And in a tender mood he, as I guess,
Christened one flower Love-in-idleness,
And while he walked from Exeter to Leeds
One April called all cuckoo-flowers Milkmaids.
From him old herbal Gerard learnt, as a boy,
To name wild clematis the Traveller's-joy.
Our blackbirds sang no English till his ear
Told him they called his Jan Toy 'Pretty dear'.

有人驳斥道。其为乡绅子，
痴恋野鸟兽，爱狗喜枪支，
嗜枪为屠戮。出生便痴迷，
一物又一物，不亚恋土地。
“此人似巴顿，或像游世匠，
波特斯福德，正如尔所想。
然其音容貌，如从小所见。
发誓无谎言。他狂野疯癫，
爱四处漂泊：自由便是家。
无人不知晓，人人见过他。
他一生深情，常冥思凝望，
可曾清古道，若无人过往？
国籍英格兰，如同门花潭。
时值我八岁，罗勃火堆旁，
书中有描述，初识其容色。
久住英格兰，居史如鸦鸽，
野樱桃树者，谓之‘欢乐树’，
毛剪秋罗者，‘布里奇勇女’；
正如我所猜，他性情温雅，
为花儿赐名，名曰‘爱懒花’；
埃克塞特起，至利兹之旅，
四月杜鹃花，谓之‘挤奶女’。
药王杰勒德，从小习于他，
野铁线莲者，曰‘游者欢嘉’。
乌鸫齐欢唱，用语非英语，
倾耳知芳名，‘挚爱’珍·托好。

(She was Jan Toy the Lucky, who, having lost
A shilling, and found a penny loaf, rejoiced.)
For reasons of his own to him the wren
Is Jenny Pooter. Before all other men
'Twas he first called the Hog's Back the Hog's Back.
That Mother Dunch's Buttocks should not lack
Their name was his care. He too could explain
Totteridge and Totterdown and Juggler's Lane:
He knows, if anyone. Why Tumbling Bay,
Inland in Kent, is called so, he might say."
"But little he says compared with what he does.
If ever a sage troubles him he will buzz
Like a beehive to conclude the tedious fray:
And the sage, who knows all languages, runs away.
Yet Lob has thirteen hundred names for a fool,
And though he never could spare time for school
To unteach what the fox so well expressed,
On biting the cock's head off, — Quietness is best, —
He can talk quite as well as anyone
After his thinking is forgot and done.
He first of all told someone else's wife,
For a farthing she'd skin a flint and spoil a knife
Worth sixpence skinning it. She heard him speak:
'She had a face as long as a wet week'
Said he, telling the tale in after years.
With blue smock and with gold rings in his ears,

（珍乃幸运女，曾丢一先令，
却得一麵包，鼓舞且欢欣。）
鹧鸪名为何？甄妮·普特尔！
因由他自知，别人不知耳。
猪背谓‘猪背’，他乃第一人。
‘母亲邓奇臂’，至今无名分，
其心忧如焚。托特里奇镇、
托顿驹格巷，他如数家珍：
他无所不知。肯特郡内域，
缘何‘翻滚湾’？他喃喃自语。”
“然言行不一，他行多言少。
若遇圣人扰，回应似蜂巢，
嗡嗡止枯燥，呜呜终争吵：
圣人懂万言，无言却逃跑。
罗勃知愚人，赐名一千三，
不曾入学堂，却了如指掌，
狐狸断鸡头，圣人证其信，
他却证其伪，——沉默便是金，——
得意而忘言，得意且忘思，
他能言会道，与常人无异。
话匣一打开，先论他人妻，
为赚一法新，她剥打火石，
费六便士刀。闻见他讥评：
‘她脸色阴沉，长如一周阴’。
述说此轶事，一年复一年。
身穿蓝宽袍，双耳戴金环，

Sometimes he is a pedlar, not too poor
To keep his wit. This is tall Tom that bore
The logs in, and with Shakespeare in the hall
Once talked, when icicles hung by the wall.
As Herne the Hunter he has known hard times.
On sleepless nights he made up weather rhymes
Which others spoilt. And, Hob being then his name,
He kept the hog that thought the butcher came
To bring his breakfast. 'You thought wrong', said Hob.
When there were kings in Kent this very Lob,
Whose sheep grew fat and he himself grew merry,
Wedded the king's daughter of Canterbury;
For he alone, unlike squire, lord, and king,
Watched a night by her without slumbering;
He kept both waking. When he was but a lad
He won a rich man's heiress, deaf, dumb, and sad,
By rousing her to laugh at him. He carried
His donkey on his back. So they were married.
And while he was a little cobbler's boy
He tricked the giant coming to destroy
Shrewsbury by flood. 'And how far is it yet?'
The giant asked in passing. 'I forget;
But see these shoes I've worn out on the road
and we're not there yet.' He emptied out his load
Of shoes for mending. The giant let fall from his spade

一副小贩相，精明且伶俐，
毫无穷酸样。汤姆高个子，
搂抱柴火来，莎翁厅中遇，
开口便聊天，冰锥挂墙隅。
如猎人赫恩，历经坎与坷。
无数不眠夜，谱写气象歌，
旁人无不爱。他曾叫霍布，
养过一头猪，猪见一屠夫，
错感送餐来。霍布讥荒唐。
列王治肯特，罗勃领群羊，
膘肥胖肉圆，欣喜犹独尊，
坎特伯雷王，嫁女他成婚；
无乡绅之福，无君王之冕，
独自守护她，彻夜不睡眠；
二者皆清醒。昔日少年郎，
富家继承女，聋哑易伤感，
何计令欢颜？罗勃驮大驴，
此计甚是妙，终娶富家女。
昔日少年郎，淘气鞋匠孩，
施计骗巨怪，巨怪发洪灾，
欲毁舒伯利[1]。‘离城还多远？’
巨怪趁机问。‘具体我已忘；
瞧瞧一路上，穿破多少鞋，
便知未到达。’他清出破鞋，
修好继续穿。巨怪帮铲土，

[1] 指英格兰西部城镇舒兹伯利。——译者注

The earth for damming Severn, and thus made
The Wrekin hill; and little Ercall hill
Rose where the giant scraped his boots. While still
So young, our Jack was chief of Gotham's sages.
But long before he could have been wise, ages
Earlier than this, while he grew thick and strong
And ate his bacon, or, at times, sang a song
And merely smelt it, as Jack the giant-killer
He made a name. He too ground up the miller,
The Yorkshireman who ground men's bones for flour."

"Do you believe Jack dead before his hour?
Or that his name is Walker, or Bottlesford,
Or Button, a mere clown, or squire, or lord?
The man you saw, — Lob-lie-by-the-fire, Jack Cade,
Jack Smith, Jack Moon, poor Jack of every trade,
Young Jack, or old Jack, or Jack What-d'ye-call,
Jack-in-the-hedge, or Robin-run-by-the-wall,
Robin Hood, Ragged Robin, lazy Bob,
One of the lords of No Man's Land, good Lob, —
Although he was seen dying at Waterloo,
Hastings, Agincourt, and Sedgemoor too, —
Lives yet. He never will admit he is dead
Till millers cease to grind men's bones for bread,
Not till our weathercock crows once again
And I remove my house out of the lane

筑堤塞汶河，倾土复倾土，
堆成瑞金山；巨怪擦靴革，
土落变山岗，名曰‘迩克勒’。
杰克年轻郎，统领圣哥谭。
追溯更久远，天资聪慧显，
遥想其当年，厚实一壮夫，
培根为其食，时常哼小曲，
嗅闻培根香，杰克名自诩：
‘巨怪捕杀手’。约克磨坊主，
人骨磨成粉，反遭杰克磨。”

“信不信由你：杰克已短折；
小名‘游世侠’、波特斯福德，
别名叫巴顿，地位高或低。
——瞧火旁罗勃，看弃儿杰克，
杰克苦与累，行行穷杰克，
杰克老与少，人人似杰克，
这墙垣罗宾，那篱笆杰克，
罗宾施与乞，懒人之鲍勃，
主无主之地，英雄之罗勃，——
战死滑铁卢，或阿金库尔，
或黑斯廷斯，或塞奇莫尔，——
他虽死犹存。世人皆仰慕：
面包作坊主，停止磨人骨；
教堂风信鸡，复鸣声声尖；
我宅迁出巷，挪至马路间。”

On to the road." With this he disappeared
In hazel and thorn tangled with old-man's-beard.
But one glimpse of his back, as there he stood,
Choosing his way, proved him of old Jack's blood,
Young Jack perhaps, and now a Wiltshireman
As he has oft been since his days began.

如此方安息，松萝缠榛棘，
罗勃藏其间，从此无踪迹。
一瞥其项背，仿若择其道，
根根血脉明，杰克老与少，
今威尔特郡，自诞生以来，
无论贵与贱，皆承罗勃脉。

Digging (Today I Think)

4 April, 1915

Today I think
Only with scents, — scents dead leaves yield,
And bracken, and wild carrot's seed,
And the square mustard field;

Odours that rise
When the spade wounds the root of tree,
Rose, currant, raspberry, or goutweed,
Rhubarb or celery;

The smoke's smell, too,
Flowing from where a bonfire burns
The dead, the waste, the dangerous,
And all to sweetness turns.

It is enough
To smell, to crumble the dark earth,
While the robin sings over again
Sad songs of Autumn mirth.

挖掘（今日思绪）

1915 年 4 月 4 日

今日思绪
围绕味道——枯叶散发的味道、
蕨菜的味道、野萝卜籽的味道，
还有广阔的芥末地的味道；

气味儿升起，
当铁锹铲伤树的根基，
斩断玫瑰、醋栗、山梅、羊角芹、
大黄和芹菜之时；

烟味儿也足，
从焚烧尸体、废物、凶物
的篝火中飘出，
一切化为芬馥。

黑色泥土，
闻着、搓着，足矣，
知更鸟反复吟唱
秋颂的忧伤曲子。

Lovers

5 April, 1915

The two men in the road were taken aback.
The lovers came out shading their eyes from the sun,
And never was white so white, or black so black,
As her cheeks and hair. "There are more things than one
A man might turn into a wood for, Jack,"
Said George; Jack whispered: "He has not got a gun.
It's a bit too much of a good thing, I say.
They are going the other road, look. And see her run." —
She ran. — "What a thing it is, this picking may!"

恋人

1915年4月5日

路上两位行人看得目瞪口呆。
一对恋人出现，为防日晒，用手遮着眼睛，
黑色从未如此的黑，白色从未如此的白，
正如她的头发和脸颊。“杰克，人们进入树林
或许有诸多的由来”，
乔治说道；杰克悄声回应：“他没带‘枪’。
有点儿好事多磨啊，我想。
看，他们改道儿了。看，她跑着呢。”——
她跑了。——“真是妙极了，这山楂花摘得！”

In Memoriam (Easter, 1915)

6 April, 1915

The flowers left thick at nightfall in the wood
This Eastertide call into mind the men,
Now far from home, who, with their sweethearts, should
Have gathered them and will do never again.

悼念（复活节，1915）

1915 年 4 月 6 日

林中夜幕临，采采百花吟，
复活正当季，思存壮士音，
离家千万里，爱恋暖人心，
本应相逢庆，君将恐难寻。

Head and Bottle

14 April, 1915

The downs will lose the sun, white alyssum
Lose the bees' hum;
But head and bottle tilted back in the cart
Will never part
Till I am cold as midnight and all my hours
Are beeless flowers.
He neither sees, nor hears, nor smells, nor thinks,
But only drinks,
Quiet in the yard where tree trunks do not lie
More quietly.

头与瓶

1915 年 4 月 14 日

丘原将失去阳光，白庭荠
无蜂嬉戏；
而头与瓶在车厢里往后斜，
永不分别，
午夜寒气袭人，平生全部光阴
如花无蜂临。
他不见、不闻、不嗅，亦不念，
只顾饮咽，
静谧弥漫庭院，树桩睡息，
无声无息。

Home (Often I had Gone)

17 April, 1915

Often I had gone this way before:
But now it seemed I never could be
And never had been anywhere else;
'Twas home; one nationality
We had, I and the birds that sang,
One memory.

They welcomed me. I had come back
That eve somehow from somewhere far:
The April mist, the chill, the calm,
Meant the same thing familiar
And pleasant to us, and strange too,
Yet with no bar.

The thrush on the oaktop in the lane
Sang his last song, or last but one;
And as he ended, on the elm
Another had but just begun
His last; they knew no more than I
The day was done.

家园（过去我常常走）

1915 年 4 月 17 日

过去我常常走这条路：
但如今似乎我绝不能去
也从未曾去过其他地方；
那曾是家园；同一民族，
共同拥有。我与鸟儿同唱，
同一记忆。

它们欢迎我。那夜我已
归来，似乎从远方某地：
四月的迷雾，寒冷又静谧，
使我们感到同样的熟悉，
同样的美好，也倍感陌生，
却隔阂无遗。

画眉栖息道上橡树枝头
唱着最后一曲，或倒数第二首，
正当它唱完，在榆树枝头
另一只画眉则刚开始吟奏
终曲；它们与我一样不知
白昼已逝。

Then past his dark white cottage front
A labourer went along, his tread
Slow, half with weariness, half with ease;
And, through the silence, from his shed
The sound of sawing rounded all
That silence said.

走过他的黑白屋前，
劳工继续前行，他的脚步
放缓，半带疲惫，半带轻畅；
划破宁静，从他的小屋
传来锯木声，笼罩一切
宁静陈述。

Health

18 April, 1915

Four miles at a leap, over the dark hollow land,
To the frosted steep of the down and its junipers black,
Travels my eye with equal ease and delight:
And scarce could my body leap four yards.

This is the best and the worst of it —
Never to know,
Yet to imagine gloriously, pure health.

Today, had I suddenly health,
I could not satisfy the desire of my heart
Unless health abated it,
So beautiful is the air in its softness and clearness, while Spring
Promises all and fails in nothing as yet;
And what blue and what white is I never knew
Before I saw this sky blessing the land.

For had I health I could not ride or run or fly
So far or so rapidly over the land
As I desire: I should reach Wiltshire tired;

健康

1915 年 4 月 18 日

一跃四英里，越过那片黑凹地，
来到丘原寒霜覆盖的陡坡，瞧见黑杜松，
眼睛轻松愉悦地旅行着：
身体却难以跃出四码远。

这是最好和最坏的体验——
从未知道，
竟是奢望——身心健康。

今日，如若我突然康健，
我不会满足内心的欲望，
除非健康削弱了它，
空气如此柔美、清新，而春天
允诺万物，未曾让人失望；
我从不知何为蓝、何为白，
直到瞧见这片庇佑大地的苍穹。

倘若康健，我不会骑得、跑得、飞得
这么远或这么快地越过那片土地，
如己所愿：我定会疲惫地到达威尔特郡；

I should have changed my mind before I could be in Wales.
I could not love; I could not command love.
Beauty would still be far off
However many hills I climbed over;
Peace would still be farther.
Maybe I should not count it anything
To leap these four miles with the eye;
And either I should not be filled almost to bursting with desire,
Or with my power desire would still keep pace.

Yet I am not satisfied
Even with knowing I never could be satisfied.
With health and all the power that lies
In maiden beauty, poet and warrior,
In Caesar, Shakespeare, Alcibiades,
Mazeppa, Leonardo, Michelangelo,
In any maiden whose smile is lovelier
Than sunlight upon dew,
I could not be as the wagtail running up and down
The warm tiles of the roof slope, twittering
Happily and sweetly as if the sun itself
Extracted the song
As the hand makes sparks from the fur of a cat:

I could not be as the sun.
Nor should I be content to be

本应在自己来到威尔士时改变主意。
我不能爱；也不能掌控爱。
美依旧在千里之外，
尽管我越过无数的山岭；
祥和依旧更加遥远。
或许我不该计较这一切
用眼睛来眺望这四英里；
要么不该激情满满去爆发欲望，
要么欲望仍应与我的能力保持一致。

然而我甚至不满足
于知道自己从不会被满足。
倘若健康和所有力量源自
少女的美貌、诗人、勇士、
凯撒、莎士比亚、亚西比德、
马泽帕、莱奥纳多、米开朗基罗，
以及源自比露珠上的阳光
更加灿烂的少女微笑，
我不会像鹡鸰一样上下穿梭，
在斜顶的暖瓦上，叽叽喳喳，
幸福美满，好像太阳自己
选粹了此曲，
仿佛一只手从猫皮上擦出火花来：

我不会像太阳一样。
也不应该满足于

As little as the bird or as mighty as the sun.
For the bird knows not of the sun,
And the sun regards not the bird.
But I am almost proud to love both bird and sun,
Though scarce this Spring could my body leap four yards.

羸弱如鸟，刚强如日。
因为鸟儿不懂太阳，
而太阳不关心鸟儿。
我却自豪地爱上了鸟儿和太阳，
虽然这个春天我的身体难以跃出四码远。

The Huxter

20 April, 1915

He has a hump like an ape on his back;
He has of money a plentiful lack;
And but for a gay coat of double his girth
There is not a plainer thing on the earth
        This fine May morning.

But the huxter has a bottle of beer;
He drives a cart and his wife sits near
Who does not heed his lack or his hump;
And they laugh as down the lane they bump
        This fine May morning.

小商贩

1915 年 4 月 20 日

他驼着背犹如猿猴；
身无分文，捉襟见肘；
倘若没有艳服裹束，
世上无更平坦之物，
　　五月清晨，阳光明媚。

商贩却有一瓶啤酒；
拉着车，妻子挨坐瞅，
不嫌他贫穷与驼背；
颠簸下行，喜笑眼眉，
　　五月清晨，阳光明媚。

She Dotes

21 April, 1915

She dotes on what the wild birds say
Or hint or mock at, night and day, —
Thrush, blackbird, all that sing in May,
        And songless plover,
Hawk, heron, owl, and woodpecker.
They never say a word to her
        About her lover.

She laughs at them for childishness,
She cries at them for carelessness
Who see her going loverless
        Yet sing and chatter
Just as when he was not a ghost,
Nor ever ask her what she has lost
        Or what is the matter.

Yet she has fancied blackbirds hide
A secret, and that thrushes chide
Because she thinks death can divide
        Her from her lover;
And she has slept, trying to translate
The word the cuckoo cries to his mate
        Over and over.

她痴爱

1915 年 4 月 21 日

她痴爱野鸟的声色、
示意、嘲讽，日日夜夜，——
画眉、乌鸫、所有五月的歌者，
　　　以及无歌的千鸟、
雄鹰、鹭、猫头鹰、啄木鸟。
他们从不与她谈唠，
　　　关于她的比翼鸟。

她嘲笑他们的幼稚，
哭诉他们的粗心大意，
眼望着她失去伴侣，
　　　却在歌唱、絮语，
仿佛他还未仙逝，
也不曾问她何所失，
　　　或何事忧虑。

但她幻想乌鸫隐藏
秘密，画眉发出责难，
因为她觉得死神会让
　　　自己与爱人别离；
她已入睡，尝试翻译
杜鹃对同伴喊出的词，
　　　一次又一次。

Song

22 April, 1915

She is beautiful
With happiness invincible:
If cruel she be,
It is the hawk's proud innocent cruelty.

At poet's tears,
Sweeter than any smiles but hers,
She laughs; I sigh;
And yet I could not live if she should die.

And when in June
Once more the cuckoo spoils his tune,
She laughs at sighs;
And yet she says she loves me till she dies.

歌

1915 年 4 月 22 日

伊美若天仙，
幸福难遮掩；
伊狠若骄鹰，
凶残亦天真。

若见诗人泪，
伊笑最甜美，
吾叹心不悔，
伊死吾相随。

六月正当时，
杜鹃再哭啼，
伊叹息而笑，
起誓共偕老。

A Cat

24 April, 1915

She had a name among the children;
But no one loved though someone owned
Her, locked her out of doors at bedtime
And had her kittens duly drowned.

In Spring, nevertheless, this cat
Ate blackbirds, thrushes, nightingales,
And birds of bright voice and plume and flight,
As well as scraps from neighbours' pails.

I loathed and hated her for this;
One speckle on a thrush's breast
Was worth a million such; and yet
She lived long, till God gave her rest.

猫

1915 年 4 月 24 日

猫名稚童顽；
人养无人喜，
常驱门外眠。
崽生即溺死。

春来鸟飞至，
羽洁声脆清，
猫恶邻馊食，
遂食鹂鸫莺。

吾义愤填膺；
鸫胸斑如金，
猫命长且硬，
除非死“神”临。

Melancholy

25 April, 1915

The rain and wind, the rain and wind, raved endlessly.
On me the Summer storm, and fever, and melancholy
Wrought magic, so that if I feared the solitude
Far more I feared all company: too sharp, too rude,
Had been the wisest or the dearest human voice.
What I desired I knew not, but whate'er my choice
Vain it must be, I knew. Yet naught did my despair
But sweeten the strange sweetness, while through the wild air
All day long I heard a distant cuckoo calling
And, soft as dulcimers, sounds of near water falling,
And, softer, and remote as if in history,
Rumours of what had touched my friends, my foes, or me.

愁思

1915 年 4 月 25 日

夏日风雨，疯狂咆哮，无休无止。
强风暴雨，躁动狂热，忧郁愁思，
如幻如魔，恍然大悟——吾若惧独，
更惧喧嚣：人类至明，至亲至熟，
然其声色，时常刺耳，不时粗俗。
不知己所欲，不为己所取，
所取皆徒劳。绝望非吾为，
奇美自然成，奇美变甜美；
空气狂野，远处杜鹃，整日啼唱，
柔美如笙，近处流水，落声潺潺，
愈加柔缓，历史谣言，随之流远：
所传之事，曾伤敌友，令吾心寒。

Tonight

30 April, 1915

Harry, you know at night
The larks in Castle Alley
Sing from the attic's height
As if the electric light
Were the true sun above a summer valley:
Whistle, don't knock, tonight.

I shall come early, Kate:
And we in Castle Alley
Will sit close out of sight
Alone, and ask no light
Of lamp or sun above a summer valley:
Tonight I can stay late.

今夜

1915 年 4 月 30 日

哈里，你知夜里
阿里城堡内云雀
阁楼高处欢啼
仿佛电光熠熠
宛若一轮夏日徘徊于谷岳：
哨响，今夜别起！

凯特，我会早来：
阿里城堡中，你我
近坐却不相见
独处，不问光源
来自灯台还是夏谷之阳波：
今夜我将晚待。

April

2 May, 1915

The sweetest thing, I thought
At one time, between earth and heaven
Was the first smile
When mist has been forgiven
And the sun has stolen out,
Peered, and resolved to shine at seven
On dabbled lengthening grasses,
Thick primroses and early leaves uneven,
When earth's breath, warm and humid, far surpasses
The richest oven's, and loudly rings "cuckoo"
And sharply the nightingale's "tsoo, troo, troo, troo":
To say "God bless it" was all that I could do.

But now I know one sweeter
By far since the day Emily
Turned weeping back
To me, still happy me,
To ask forgiveness, —
Yet smiled with half a certainty
To be forgiven, — for what

四月

1915年5月2日

最美好之物，我曾
认为，介于天地之间，
便是初笑。
每当迷雾被宽谅，
太阳便偷偷溜出、
窥视，决定七点闪现
照耀在湿漉漉的长草、
浓密的报春花和参差不齐的嫩叶之上，
每当土地的气息，又暖又潮，远超
最浓烈的炉息和高声响起的"布谷"，
及刺耳的夜莺声"啾啾啾啾"，
而我所能做的便是"愿上帝保佑"。

但如今我悟到更美之物
自那天艾米莉
向我哭泣，
我依旧满心欢喜，
乞求原谅，——
却面带微笑半信半疑
能否被宽恕，——因为

She had never done; I knew not what it might be,
Nor could she tell me, having now forgot,
By rapture carried with me past all care
As to an isle in April lovelier
Than April's self. "God bless you" I said to her.

她从未如此做过；结果如何，不得而知，
她亦不会告知我，如今早已忘记，
因为狂喜载着我越过所有忧虑
仿佛来到四月里的一座岛屿
比四月本身更美。“上帝佑你”是我对她的祝福。

The Glory

? early May, 1915

The glory of the beauty of the morning, —
The cuckoo crying over the untouched dew;
The blackbird that has found it, and the dove
That tempts me on to something sweeter than love;
White clouds ranged even and fair as new-mown hay;
The heat, the stir, the sublime vacancy
Of sky and meadow and forest and my own heart: —
The glory invites me, yet it leaves me scorning
All I can ever do, all I can be,
Beside the lovely of motion, shape, and hue,
The happiness I fancy fit to dwell
In beauty's presence. Shall I now this day
Begin to seek as far as heaven, as hell,
Wisdom or strength to match this beauty, start
And tread the pale dust pitted with small dark drops,
In hope to find whatever it is I seek,
Hearkening to short-lived happy-seeming things
That we know naught of, in the hazel copse?
Or must I be content with discontent
As larks and swallows are perhaps with wings?

荣耀

1915 年 5 月初某日

清晨之美，荣耀绽放，
露珠未移，杜鹃哭泣；
乌鸫知美，信鸽善美，
诱我寻美：爱不胜美；
云如干草，整洁清新；
天空草地，森林我心，
炽热涌动，空荡壮美：
荣耀盛邀，自感汗颜，
成事已能，疚愧我心；
动态形色，优雅秀丽，
幸福快乐，我心所求，
美中栖居。是否如今，
上天入地，开始寻求
智慧力量，以配此美？
脚踏白尘，身披幽露，
独入榛林，寻之所求，
万物无常，其福我依，
纵使你我，不知何述？
虽有不满，能否知足，
犹如燕雀，知足其翼？

And shall I ask at the day's end once more
What beauty is, and what I can have meant
By happiness? And shall I let all go,
Glad, weary, or both? Or shall I perhaps know
That I was happy oft and oft before,
Awhile forgetting how I am fast pent,
How dreary-swift, with naught to travel to,
Is Time? I cannot bite the day to the core.

夜幕降临，美为何物，
幸福何意，能否再询？
或喜或悲，随风而逝，
顺其自然？回忆往昔，
我心欢喜，倍感幸福，
暂忘今愁，不困忧愠，
光阴郁逝，不念去向，
是否知晓？大美不言！

July

7 May, 1915

Naught moves but clouds, and in the glassy lake
Their doubles and the shadow of my boat.
The boat itself stirs only when I break
This drowse of heat and solitude afloat
To prove if what I see be bird or mote,
Or learn if yet the shore woods be awake.

Long hours since dawn grew, — spread, — and passed on high
And deep below, — I have watched the cool reeds hung
Over images more cool in imaged sky:
Nothing there was worth thinking of so long;
All that the ring-doves say, far leaves among,
Brims my mind with content thus still to lie.

七月

1915 年 5 月 7 日

云朵缓步，湖面如镜，
艘艓泛影，相辉悦目。
艘艓微动，荡桨划醒——
炎热沉闷，孤寂恍惚——
为辨所见之物，鸟或尘土，
欲知岸上之林，是否苏醒。

晨曦隐现，朝霞舒展，天晴波碧，
久久伫立，凝望芦苇，青葱微凉，
影中浮动，天云相映，愈显凉意：
陶醉之境，物我相忘；
林鸽柔语，树远叶密，
置身其境，心满神爽。

The Chalk-Pit

8 May, 1915

"Is this the road that climbs above and bends
Round what was once a chalk-pit: now it is
By accident an amphitheatre.
Some ash trees standing ankle-deep in briar
And bramble act the parts, and neither speak
Nor stir." "But see: they have fallen, every one,
And briar and bramble have grown over them."
"That is the place. As usual no one is here.
Hardly can I imagine the drop of the axe,
And the smack that is like an echo, sounding here."
"I do not understand." "Why, what I mean is
That I have seen the place two or three times
At most, and that its emptiness and silence
And stillness haunt me, as if just before
It was not empty, silent, still, but full
Of life of some kind, perhaps tragical.
Has anything unusual happened here?"
"Not that I know of. It is called the Dell.
They have not dug chalk here for a century.
That was the ash trees' age. But I will ask."

白垩矿场

1915 年 5 月 8 日

“确定这条路向上蜿蜒盘绕
至曾为白垩矿场的地方：如今
却意外成了一座露天圆形剧场？！
蔷薇荆棘丛中，几棵足踝高的白蜡树，
成了那儿的主角，一语不发，
一动不动。”“请看：他们一棵棵已倒下，
而那蔷薇荆棘丛早已盖过它们了。”
“这地方就那样了。通常无人造访。
我难以想象斧头的垂落声
和回音般的击打声曾在此响起”。
“我不明白。”“为什么，我的意思是
我曾经来过这儿最多两三次，
每次放眼望去，它空荡荡、静悄悄、
死气沉沉，常常萦绕在我心头，就好像
它以前并非空荡荡，并非静悄悄，
而是生机盎然，或许是悲剧般的喧嚣。
此地可曾有过不同寻常之事？”
“不曾听闻，只知道它叫‘林谷’。
一个世纪前这个白垩矿就已被弃。
曾是白蜡树时代。不过我会找人问问。”

"No. Do not. I prefer to make a tale,
Or better leave it like the end of a play,
Actors and audience and lights all gone;
For so it looks now. In my memory
Again and again I see it, strangely dark,
And vacant of a life but just withdrawn.
We have not seen the woodman with the axe.
Some ghost has left it now as we two came."
"And yet you doubted if this were the road?"
"Well, sometimes I have thought of it and failed
To place it. No. And I am not quite sure,
Even now, this is it. For another place,
Real or painted, may have combined with it.
Or I myself a long way back in time..."
"Why, as to that, I used to meet a man —
I had forgotten, — searching for birds' nests
Along the road and in the chalk-pit too.
The wren's hole was an eye that looked at him
For recognition. Every nest he knew.
He got a stiff neck, by looking this side or that,
Spring after spring, he told me, with his laugh, —
A sort of laugh. He was a visitor,
A man of forty, — smoked and strolled about.
At orts and crosses Pleasure and Pain had played
On his brown features; — I think both had lost; —
Mild and yet wild too. You may know the kind.

“不，不用了。我喜欢自己发挥想象，
或最好不管它，像剧终一样，
演员、观众、灯光皆已离场；
如今它便是如此。在我记忆中，
它不断闪现，显得诡异幽黑，
毫无生气，似刚刚谢幕。
我们未曾见过拿着斧头的樵夫。
我们到来之际，某个幽灵刚好退场。”
“但是你起初怀疑过这条路？”
“哎呀，有时我确实想起过，
后来却忘了。不，甚至现在还不敢
肯定就是它。因为另一个地方
不管真实或是虚构，或许早已跟它混淆。
或者时光流逝，我自己早已混淆不清……”
“同样问题，为何我曾常常遇见一人——
现已忘记，——在寻找鸟巢，
沿着马路找，也在白垩矿中寻。
鹪鹩巢穴犹如一只眼，盯着他
直到辨认出。他清楚每个巢穴。
他春复一春地左顾右看，
最后导致脖子僵硬，他笑着告诉我，——
是那种大笑。他是一名游客，
四十岁出头的男人，吸烟，四处游荡。
皮肤呈褐色，因曾草行露宿，饱经风霜，
历经沧桑；——我想幸福与苦难皆已消逝；——
性情温和却也狂野。这类人或许你并不陌生。

And once or twice a woman shared his walks,
A girl of twenty with a brown boy's face,
And hair brown as a thrush or as a nut,
Thick eyebrows, glinting eyes —" "You have said enough.
A pair, — free thought, free love, — I know the breed:
I shall not mix my fancies up with them."
"You please yourself. I should prefer the truth
Or nothing. Here, in fact, is nothing at all
Except a silent place that once rang loud,
And trees and us — imperfect friends, we men
And trees since time began; and nevertheless
Between us still we breed a mystery."

曾经一两次，有位女郎陪他一起浪迹天涯，
一位二十岁的少女，长着一张棕色男生脸，
褐色头发，活脱脱像一只画眉或一粒坚果，
双眉浓密，双眼炯炯有神——”“够了，你说得够详细了。
一对情侣嘛，——思想开放，自由恋爱——我知道这玩意儿：我还不至于胡说八道吧。”
“你就自我陶醉吧。我喜欢讲真话，
否则干脆不说。说实话，此地一无是处，
除了曾经的喧哗，如今只剩下沉寂、
树木与你我——有史以来，我们人类
与树木是一对不完美的朋友；尽管如此，
彼此之间却依然相隔一份神秘。”

Fifty Faggots

13 May, 1915

There they stand, on their ends, the fifty faggots
That once were underwood of hazel and ash
In Jenny Pinks's Copse. Now, by the hedge
Close packed, they make a thicket fancy alone
Can creep through with the mouse and wren. Next Spring
A blackbird or a robin will nest there,
Accustomed to them, thinking they will remain
Whatever is for ever to a bird:
This Spring it is too late; the swift has come.
'Twas a hot day for carrying them up:
Better they will never warm me, though they must
Light several Winters' fires. Before they are done
The war will have ended, many other things
Have ended, maybe, that I can no more
Foresee or more control than robin and wren.

五十捆柴

1915 年 5 月 13 日

五十捆柴在那儿立着，整齐划一，
他们曾是榛树和椤树下的灌木丛，
位于珍妮·平克斯林[1]中。如今，挨着树篱
堆得密密麻麻，灌木丛只剩下了幻想，
耗子和鹪鹩匍匐穿行其间。明年春天，
乌鸫或知更鸟将会在那儿筑巢，
习惯那柴堆，希望他们会留存
直到永远，无论对于鸟儿所谓何物：
今年春天姗姗来迟；雨燕却早已到来。
抱起柴堆那天正值天气炎热：
我不要被它们温暖，虽然它们必须
燃起几场冬天的篝火。在它们燃尽之前，
或许战争已结束，其他诸多事情
也已终结，然而我与知更鸟和鹪鹩
一样无法预知或控制这一切。

---

[1] 据朗利教授所言，此为英格兰南部斯迪坡村（Steep）一个地名，位于汉格山脊（Ridge Hanger）山顶。详见 LONGLEY E. Edward Thomas: the annotated collected poems [M]. Glasgow: Bell & Bain Limited, 2008: 240. ——译者注

Sedge-Warblers

23 May, 1915

This beauty made me dream there was a time
Long past and irrecoverable, a clime
Where any brook so radiant racing clear
Through buttercup and kingcup bright as brass
But gentle, nourishing the meadow grass
That leans and scurries in the wind, would bear
Another beauty, divine and feminine,
Child to the sun, a nymph whose soul unstained
Could love all day, and never hate or tire,
A lover of mortal or immortal kin.

And yet, rid of this dream, ere I had drained
Its poison, quieted was my desire
So that I only looked into the water,
Clearer than any goddess or man's daughter,
And hearkened while it combed the dark green hair
And shook the millions of the blossoms white
Of water-crowfoot, and curdled to one sheet
The flowers fallen from the chestnuts in the park
Far off. And sedge-warblers, clinging so light

莎草

1915 年 5 月 23 日

此美驱我梦，依稀旧时光，
往昔难挽回，寻梦至远方：
溪流耀光芒，清澈又湍急，
夹岸毛茛丛，亮泽如黄铜，
金凤花香柔，绿茵享滋泓，
簇簇顺风倾，棵棵随风疾，
另美清流载，神圣且柔雌，
如阳日之稚，似仙女灵善，
暖爱终日浓，不坠恶与倦，
仙凡一家亲，生死自然移。

欲消此梦境，抽竭此毒前，
问我何所求，先平我所欲，
如此心方静，流泓望眼去，
清澈又洁净，不逊仙人女，
附耳且聆听，青丝水梳妆，
玉柏溪中白，万花水摇摆，
远处公园现，园中百栗林，
栗花飘零落，沾水汇成图。
柳条岸边垂，莎草轻依怀，

To willow twigs, sang longer than the lark,
Quick, shrill, or grating, a song to match the heat
Of the strong sun, nor less the water's cool,
Gushing through narrows, swirling in the pool.
Their song that lacks all words, all melody,
All sweetness almost, was dearer then to me
Than sweetest voice that sings in tune sweet words.
This was the best of May — the small brown birds
Wisely reiterating endlessly
What no man learnt yet, in or out of school.

合奏吟长歌，久胜百灵曲，
乐声急尖刺，却合烈日心，
乐音沁心凉，清冷似流溪，
喷涌出狭道，旋涡起塘池。
此乐尽瑕疵：缺词少旋律，
甜美亦难寻；至美千百曲，
词声极动听，心犹醉此音。
最美五月季，鷓鸪复啼鸣，
聪明又伶俐，絮絮无尽语，
鸿儒难解译，白丁不知意。

I Built Myself a House of Glass

25 June, 1915

I built myself a house of glass:
It took my years to make it:
And I was proud. But now, alas,
Would God someone would break it.

But it looks too magnificent.
No neighbour casts a stone
From where he dwells, in tenement
Or palace of glass, alone.

亲手建了一座玻璃房

1915 年 6 月 25 日

我亲手建了一座玻璃房：
耗时多年才建好：
曾经自豪，如今悲伤，
上帝，有人会将它推倒？！

但它看起来真辉煌。
没有邻居会投石，
从其住所，或出租房，
或玻璃宫殿偷袭。

Words

26 – 28 June, 1915

Out of us all
That make rhymes,
Will you choose
Sometimes —
As the winds use
A crack in a wall
Or a drain,
Their joy or their pain
To whistle through —
Choose me,
You English words?

I know you:
You are light as dreams,
Tough as oak,
Precious as gold,
As poppies and corn,
Or an old cloak:
Sweet as our birds
To the ear,

话语

1915 年 6 月 26—28 日

从我们所有
作诗之人当中，
您是否有时会
选择——
当阵阵凉风吹过
墙上的缝隙
或阴沟，
他们的欢乐或悲伤
呼啸而过——
您英语话语
会选择我吗？

我懂您：
您轻如梦，
坚如橡树，
贵如黄金、
罂粟花和玉米，
或旧斗篷：
甜如鸟声
悦耳动听，

As the burnet rose
In the heat
Of Midsummer:
Strange as the races
Of dead and unborn:
Strange and sweet
Equally,
And familiar,
To the eye,
As the dearest faces
That a man knows,
And as lost homes are:
But though older far
Than oldest yew, —
As our hills are, old, —
Worn new
Again and again:
Young as our streams
After rain:
And as dear
As the earth which you prove
That we love.

Make me content
With some sweetness
From Wales

如地榆玫瑰
在盛夏
的热浪中：
陌生如死者，
如未生之人：
陌生却同样
甜美，
亲切熟悉，
映入眼帘，
如人们见过
最亲切的脸庞，
如失去的家园：
虽远老于
最古老的紫衫，——
正如山峦，古老，——
吐故纳新
一次又一次：
年轻如雨后
溪流：
亲切如
土地，如您所证
为我们所爱。

让我心满意足：
甜美芳香
来自威尔士，

Whose nightingales
Have no wings, —
From Wiltshire and Kent
And Herefordshire,
And the villages there, —
From the names, and the things
No less.

Let me sometimes dance
With you,
Or climb
Or stand perchance
In ecstasy,
Fixed and free
In a rhyme,
As poets do.

她的夜莺
没有羽翼，——
来自威尔特郡[1]、肯特郡
和赫里福郡[2]
以及那儿的村庄，——
这些名字、事物，
同样芬芳。

让我偶尔与您
共舞，
或攀爬，
或站立，可能
会欣喜若狂，
在韵律上，
循规蹈矩或随心所欲，
正如诗人一样。

❶ 英国英格兰南部的一郡。——译者注
❷ 英国英格兰旧郡名。——译者注

The Word

5 July, 1915

There are so many things I have forgot,
That once were much to me, or that were not,
All lost, as is a childless woman's child
And its child's children, in the undefiled
Abyss of what can never be again.
I have forgot, too, names of the mighty men
That fought and lost or won in the old wars,
Of kings and fiends and gods, and most of the stars.
Some things I have forgot that I forget.
But lesser things there are, remembered yet,
Than all the others. One name that I have not —
Though 'tis an empty thingless name — forgot
Never can die because Spring after Spring
Some thrushes learn to say it as they sing.
There is always one at midday saying it clear
And tart — the name, only the name I hear.
While perhaps I am thinking of the elder scent
That is like food, or while I am content
With the wild rose scent that is like memory,
This name suddenly is cried out to me
From somewhere in the bushes by a bird
Over and over again, a pure thrush word.

言道

1915 年 7 月 5 日

往事如烟云，消散已成忘，
其意曾于我，浓重或轻淡，
如无子妇孺，孺子之孺子，
坠洁净深渊，迷失至消逝，
一去不复返，恐难再相见。
威武万能者，曾骁勇奋战，
不管得与失，却忘其英名。
神魔君王星，终归忘其名。
往事如烟云，终忘其轮廓。
万事万物全，忆少且忘多，
该忘终须忘。一名仍铭记，
虽空洞无物，却从未消逝，
盖春来复始，画眉尽歌言，
学会鸣其名。晌午画眉旋，
必鸣此虚名，清脆又酸辛，
耳濡且目染，此名闻于心。
思绪方渐起，脑海忆古香，
古香似食香；野玫沁芳香，
称心如我意，熟悉若思忆，
灌木深幽处，芳名蓦然袭，
竟是画眉嗟，无休且无止，
画眉自然语，纯洁无瑕疵。

Under the Woods

5 July, 1915

When these old woods were young
The thrushes' ancestors
As sweetly sung
In the old years.

There was no garden here,
Apples nor mistletoe;
No children dear
Ran to and fro.

New then was this thatched cot,
But the keeper was old,
And he had not
Much lead or gold.

Most silent beech and yew:
As he went round about
The woods to view
Seldom he shot.

树林之下

1915 年 7 月 5 日

古老的树林年轻时，
画眉的祖先
在旧时光里
甜蜜地歌唱。

此处没有园子、
苹果或槲寄生；
无可爱的童稚
来回奔跑。

那时，这是间崭新的草屋，
而守护者是位老人家，
他手头并无
多少铅或金子。

山毛榉、紫衫树很静谧：
当他环绕四处
巡视这树林时，
很少杀戮。

But now that he is gone
Out of most memories,
Still lingers on,
A stoat of his,

But one, shrivelled and green,
And with no scent at all,
And barely seen
On this shed wall.

可如今他已逝去，
淡出多数人的记忆，
而他的一只白鼬
仍逗留歇息，

它皮皱、色绿，
无半点儿臭气，
但在此屋墙上却屡屡
不见其踪迹。

Haymaking

6–8 July, 1915

After night's thunder far away had rolled
The fiery day had a kernel sweet of cold,
And in the perfect blue the clouds uncurled,
Like the first gods before they made the world
And misery, swimming the stormless sea
In beauty and in divine gaiety.
The smooth white empty road was lightly strewn
With leaves — the holly's Autumn falls in June —
And fir cones standing stiff up in the heat.
The mill-foot water tumbled white and lit
With tossing crystals, happier than any crowd
Of children pouring out of school aloud.
And in the little thickets where a sleeper
For ever might lie lost, the nettle-creeper
And garden warbler sang unceasingly;
While over them shrill shrieked in his fierce glee
The swift with wings and tail as sharp and narrow
As if the bow had flown off with the arrow.
Only the scent of woodbine and hay new-mown
Travelled the road. In the field sloping down,

刍事

1915 年 7 月 6—8 日

夜晚的雷声早已滚滚远逝，
躁热的一天迎来了一丝芬芳沁心的凉意，
净蓝的天空，云展云舒，
犹如创世诸神，在创世与
造苦难之前，遨游风平浪静的海洋，
美轮美奂，神圣欢畅。
路面平坦白净，落叶稀疏
点缀——六月常见冬青树之秋辉——
高温下，冷杉果粒粒僵硬直立。
磨坊水洁白地翻滚着，被抛起
的水晶点亮，比放学回家
熙熙攘攘的孩子，更加幸福安佳。
在睡眠者躺着便可能永远消失
的小灌木丛中，荨麻蜂雀，以及
园莺奏响了无休无止的歌声；
头顶上的雨燕急促地发出欢快的尖叫声，
它的羽翼和尾部窄小而锋利，
仿若一把弯弓连同弦箭飞起。
唯有忍冬和刚割下的干草气息
飘满整条道路。一块儿公园似的空地，

Park-like, to where its willows showed the brook,
Haymakers rested. The tosser lay forsook
Out in the sun; and the long waggon stood
Without its team, it seemed it never would
Move from the shadow of that single yew.
The team, as still, until their task was due,
Beside the labourers enjoyed the shade
That three squat oaks mid-field together made
Upon a circle of grass and weed uncut,
And on the hollow, once a chalk-pit, but
Now brimmed with nut and elder-flower so clean.
The men leaned on their rakes, about to begin,
But still. And all were silent. All was old,
This morning time, with a great age untold,
Older than Clare and Cobbett, Morland and Crome,
Than, at the field's far edge, the farmer's home,

斜下延展直到看见小河潺潺、杨柳依依，
割草人在那儿休息。一台抛草机
弃于阳光之下；而一台运货长车没有
马队显得孤单孑立，好像从来没有
走出过那棵孤单紫衫树的荫庇。
那支马队在工作结束前照旧
在农夫身旁享受那片阴蔽，
那是空地中央三颗矮胖的橡树一起
在未割的草地上投下的一圈绿荫；
空地低洼地带，曾是白垩坑，如今
却装满了坚果和凋零的花朵，非常洁净。
人们依偎在铲耙上，准备辛勤
劳作，却一动不动。万籁俱寂。万物古老，
今晨时光，若一个未知的伟大时代，
比克莱尔❶、科贝特❷、莫兰❸、克罗姆❹更加古老，
比远处田地尽头的农夫房子还要古老，

---

❶ 指约翰·克莱尔（John Clare，1793—1864），英国 19 世纪浪漫主义乡村诗人，一生居住在英格兰北安普敦郡（Northamptonshire）彼得伯勒（Peterborough）附近的海尔伯斯通村（Helpston），其诗歌着重描写田园牧歌般的自然风景。——译者注

❷ 指威廉·科贝特（William Cobbett，1763—1835），英国 19 世纪散文作家、政治家和记者，其主要成就在于曾推动英国政治制度民主化进程。诗人托马斯曾在科贝特作品《乡村记事》(*Rural Rides*，1912 年版)引言中对这位散文作家、政治活动家给予崇高的敬意和评价。——译者注

❸ 指乔治·莫兰(George Morland，1763—1804)，英国 18 世纪画家，生前虽穷困潦倒、酗酒，却热衷于画画，其画作颇有特色，以画风景和动物见长。——译者注

❹ 指约翰·克罗姆（John Crome，1768—1821），英国风景画家，通常被称为“老克罗姆”，以便区别于其儿子；是英国浪漫主义时期诺维奇画派（Norwich School）的创始人。——译者注

A white house crouched at the foot of a great tree.
Under the heavens that know not what years be
The men, the beasts, the trees, the implements
Uttered even what they will in times far hence —
All of us gone out of the reach of change —
Immortal in a picture of an old grange.

一座蹲伏在一颗参天大树根旁的白房。
苍穹不知今朝是何年，
苍穹之下，人、兽、树、器共同
道出了今后他们将何去何从——
我们所有人超脱于沧海桑田——
永垂不朽于这古老田庄之画景。

A Dream

7, 8 July, 1915

Over known fields with an old friend in dream
I walked, but came sudden to a strange stream.
Its dark waters were bursting out most bright
From a great mountain's heart into the light.
They ran a short course under the sun, then back
Into a pit they plunged, once more as black
As at their birth: and I stood thinking there
How white, had the day shone on them, they were,
Heaving and coiling. So by the roar and hiss
And by the mighty motion of the abyss
I was bemused, that I forgot my friend
And neither saw nor sought him till the end,
When I awoke from waters unto men
Saying: "I shall be here some day again."

梦

1915年7月7—8日

梦中与故友走过故地，
突然来到陌生河溪。
溪水乌黑，湍流晶莹，
从大山深处流向光明。
阳光下奔流而复回，
流入洼地后一泻流坠，
黑如源水。我伫立冥思：
如白昼照耀，河流白皙，
起伏蜿蜒。它咆哮唏嘘，
深渊中，威猛旋流壮举
令我惊奇而忘了朋友，
到最终也未寻到见着，
我从溪中醒来，回到人世，
发誓："我将会再来此地。"❶

---

❶ 诗人所梦见的河流境地是如此庄严肃穆，河流源头，河曲直流在白日无法照耀下显得乌黑清澈，犹如道家的玄"道"一般。在现实中，诗人意识到正如他在《翻山越岭》（"Over the Hills"）一诗中所意识到的一样，即人如河流一样，从源头流出之后，便会历经曲折，焦躁不安，道德败坏，而唯有梦才能带他来到他所向往的清静简朴之地："我将会再来此地"。——译者注

The Brook

10 July, 1915

Seated once by a brook, watching a child
Chiefly that paddled, I was thus beguiled.
Mellow the blackbird sang and sharp the thrush
Not far off in the oak and hazel brush,
Unseen. There was a scent like honeycomb
From mugwort dull. And down upon the dome
Of the stone the cart-horse kicks against so oft
A butterfly alighted. From aloft
He took the heat of the sun, and from below.
On the hot stone he perched contented so,
As if never a cart would pass again
That way; as if I were the last of men
And he the first of insects to have earth
And sun together and to know their worth.
I was divided between him and the gleam,
The motion, and the voices, of the stream,
The waters running frizzled over gravel,
That never vanish and for ever travel.
A grey flycatcher silent on a fence
And I sat as if we had been there since

小溪

1915 年 7 月 10 日

曾坐溪流旁，望稚童戏水，
陶醉似痴迷。乌鸫歌声美，
画眉啼音曲，刺耳尖如吵，
近处橡榛丛，灌木叶枝茂，
隐约不可见。阴暗艾蒿处，
香气如蜂巢。石头圆顶秃，
马车蹄踏过，蝴蝶常停息。
烈日悬于天，炎石躺于地。
头顶骄阳烈，脚踩炎灼石，
他驻足栖息，怡然甚惬意，
仿佛此道路，马车不再来；
仿若万物间，我已末人哉，
他为原初虫，拥有此大地，
享受此阳光，深知其价值。
潺潺溪流水，涓涓似滴答，
微光晶闪闪，分离我与他，
清泉石上流，吱吱响声曲，
砾石不消逝，遇波不随去。
篱上立灰鹟，安祥且清恬；
坐歇养心静，仿若已千年，

The horseman and the horse lying beneath
The fir-tree-covered barrow on the heath,
The horseman and the horse with silver shoes,
Galloped the downs last. All that I could lose
I lost. And then the child's voice raised the dead.
"No one's been here before" was what she said
And what I felt, yet never should have found
A word for, while I gathered sight and sound.

自从车夫马，静躺车辕下，
冷杉萋萋密，覆延满车架，
车夫与车马，闪闪银铁蹄，
飞驰阔原野。弃我所能弃。
不久稚童声，唤醒死者矣。
她坦言相告，“无人到此地”。
我感亦如是，无法言于表，
唯有望此景，聆听此声调。

Aspens

11 July, 1915

All day and night, save winter, every weather,
Above the inn, the smithy, and the shop,
The aspens at the cross-roads talk together
Of rain, until their last leaves fall from the top.

Out of the blacksmith's cavern comes the ringing
Of hammer, shoe, and anvil; out of the inn
The clink, the hum, the roar, the random singing —
The sounds that for these fifty years have been.

The whisper of the aspens is not drowned,
And over lightless pane and footless road,
Empty as sky, with every other sound
Not ceasing, calls their ghosts from their abode,

A silent smithy, a silent inn, nor fails
In the bare moonlight or the thick-furred gloom,
In tempest or the night of nightingales,
To turn the cross-roads to a ghostly room.

山杨

1915年7月11日

日日夜夜，除了冬季，各种天气，
盘旋于客栈、铁匠铺、商店之上，
山杨树排列交叉于路两旁，相互谈及
雨季，直到树梢最后的树叶凋散。

铁匠铺时时传出铁锤之声、
鞋砧之声；客栈不时飘来
叮当声、嗡嗡声、咆哮声和随意吟唱声——
声音交织混杂，已有五十载。

山杨树窃窃私语，未被淹盖，
飘过无灯之窗，无迹之路，
空荡如天，夹杂着其他声籁
无休无止，引诱幽灵逃出房屋，

逃出沉寂的铁铺、安静的客栈，
在稀疏的月华或毛密般的忧郁里，
在狂风暴雨或夜莺之夜，其私语让
交叉路变成了一座幽灵府邸。

And it would be the same were no house near.
Over all sorts of weather, men, and times,
Aspens must shake their leaves and men may hear
But need not listen, more than to my rhymes.

Whatever wind blows, while they and I have leaves
We cannot other than an aspen be
That ceaselessly, unreasonably grieves,
Or so men think who like a different tree.

情形亦如此，若周围屋舍不现。
经历各种天气、人和时序，
山杨树叶必会摇坠，人们或许听见
但无须倾听，不仅仅我的韵律。

任凭风吹，他们和我皆有树叶，
然而我们不可能不像山杨树
那样永无休止地过度悲咽，
否则人们会想谁会爱上一种怪树。

The Mill-Water

12 July, 1915

Only the sound remains
Of the old mill;
Gone is the wheel;
On the prone roof and walls the nettle reigns.

Water that toils no more
Dangles white locks
And, falling, mocks
The music of the mill-wheel's busy roar.

Pretty to see, by day
Its sound is naught
Compared with thought
And talk and noise of labour and of play.

Night makes the difference.
In calm moonlight,
Gloom infinite,
The sound comes surging in upon the sense:

磨坊水

1915 年 7 月 12 日

古老磨坊
唯剩其声；
磨轮塌崩；
屋顶墙壁倾斜，荨麻苍苍。

水不辛勤，
垂晃白锁，
涓涓流落，
戏弄磨轮繁忙咆哮之音。

白天一睹，
磨坊之音，
相比辛勤、
玩逸之思之语之音，却显短绌。

夜景奇异。
月光静旅，
无穷忧郁，
声音涌现，和韵此情此意：

Solitude, company, —
When it is night, —
Grief or delight
By it must haunted or concluded be.

Often the silentness
Has but this one
Companion;
Wherever one creeps in the other is:

Sometimes a thought is drowned
By it, sometimes
Out of it climbs;
All thoughts begin or end upon this sound,

Only the idle foam
Of water falling
Changelessly calling,
Where once men had a work-place and a home.

陪伴、孤独，——
夜幕降临，——
悲痛、欢欣
缭绕其音，或终结其曲。

通常寂然，
唯有这位
友伴相陪；
寂静匍匐潜入，磨坊依然：

时而思绪
被其吞噬，
时而爬离；
千思万绪沉浮于此音此曲，

水流降落，
泡沫清闲，
单调召唤
人类曾经劳作和栖居之所。

For These

13, 14 July, 1915

An acre of land between the shore and the hills,
Upon a ledge that shows my kingdoms three,
The lovely visible earth and sky and sea,
Where what the curlew needs not, the farmer tills:

A house that shall love me as I love it,
Well-hedged, and honoured by a few ash-trees
That linnets, greenfinches, and goldfinches
Shall often visit and make love in and flit:

A garden I need never go beyond,
Broken but neat, whose sunflowers every one
Are fit to be the sign of the Rising Sun:
A spring, a brook's bend, or at least a pond:

For these I ask not, but, neither too late
Nor yet too early, for what men call content,
And also that something may be sent
To be contented with, I ask of fate.

心之所盼

1915 年 7 月 13—14 日[1]

山滨之间，土地显现，
地壳之上，坐落三界，
天蓝地丰，海清水澈，
农夫耕耘，麻鹬不恋：

房子爱我，我爱房子，
篱笆坚固，白蜡守护，
红绿金雀，时常光顾，
停留示爱，飞掠树篱：

屋后花园，整洁崩颓，
我心追随，园中葵花，
朵朵向阳，生机勃发：
清泉河曲，一弯池水：

不恋不贪，不晚不早，
异于众人，不求欲满，
不困于欲，随心所盼，
自朴知足，命运所抱。

---

[1] 1915 年 7 月 14 日托马斯决定从军。——译者注

Digging (What Matter Makes My Spade)

21 July, 1915

What matter makes my spade for tears or mirth,
Letting down two clay pipes into the earth?
The one I smoked, the other a soldier
Of Blenheim, Ramillies, and Malplaquet
Perhaps. The dead man's immortality
Lies represented lightly with my own,
A yard or two nearer the living air
Than bones of ancients who, amazed to see
Almighty God erect the mastodon,
Once laughed, or wept, in this same light of day.

挖掘（何事令我铁锹）

1915 年 7 月 21 日

何事令我铁锹或哭或笑，
若将两烟管埋入泥土中？
一管我抽，一管士兵抽，
他来自布伦海姆、拉米伊
或马尔普拉凯。死者永生，
而我的命显得轻如鸿毛，
相距一两码便活在人间，
先人尸骨却惊喜地发现
全能上帝竖起大乳齿象，
在同一光线下，或笑，或哭。

Two Houses

22 July, 1915

Between a sunny bank and the sun
The farmhouse smiles
On the riverside plat:
No other one
So pleasant to look at
And remember, for many miles,
So velvet-hushed and cool under the warm tiles.

Not far from the road it lies, yet caught
Far out of reach
Of the road's dust
And the dusty thought
Of passers-by, though each
Stops, and turns, and must
Look down at it like a wasp at the muslined peach.

But another house stood there long before:
And as if above graves
Still the turf heaves
Above its stones:

两间农舍

1915 年 7 月 22 日

在阳光海岸与太阳之间
一间农舍喜笑开颜，
坐落于河滨之上：
无其他物产，
看起来如此美祥，
绵延数英里，令人流连忘返，
暖瓦之下，如丝绒般肃静凉爽。

它位于不远的路边，看着
远离路上
纷扰的尘灰，
以及路人尘染着
的思绪，虽然有人
驻足，转身离去时，也必定会
俯瞰它，犹如一只黄蜂叮在印花般的桃上。

而另一间农舍早先便在那儿立着：
似在墓地上方，
草皮在石头上
依旧喘嗽：

Dark hangs the sycamore,
Shadowing kennel and bones
And the black dog that shakes his chain and moans.

And when he barks, over the river
Flashing fast,
Dark echoes reply,
And the hollow past
Half yields the dead that never
More than half hidden lie:
And out they creep and back again for ever.

1915 年

悬铃树黑漆漆地夯拉着，
遮蔽了犬舍和骨头，
还有那只摇着铁链在呻吟的黑狗。

当犬吠声越过江河
闪烁疾驰之时，
黑暗回响答问，
那空洞的往昔
一半造就了死者，
而一半死者默默无闻：
他们来回匍匐，永不停歇。

Cock-Crow

23 July, 1915

Out of the wood of thoughts that grows by night
To be cut down by the sharp axe of light, —
Out of the night, two cocks together crow,
Cleaving the darkness with a silver blow:
And bright before my eyes twin trumpeters stand,
Heralds of splendour, one at either hand,
Each facing each as in a coat of arms:
The milkers lace their boots up at the farms.

鸡鸣

1915 年 7 月 23 日

夜幕降临，思绪如林，
光闪如斧，斩断思林，——
两鸡出林，夜下啼叫，
利如银光，劈裂黑罩：
号兵突现，光荣使者，
眼前闪耀，左右站立，
面面相望，身着徽章：
农场奶员，系靴整装。

October

15, 16 October, 1915

The green elm with the one great bough of gold
Lets leaves into the grass slip, one by one, —
The short hill grass, the mushrooms small milk-white,
Harebell and scabious and tormentil,
That blackberry and gorse, in dew and sun,
Bow down to; and the wind travels too light
To shake the fallen birch leaves from the fern;
The gossamers wander at their own will.
At heavier steps than birds' the squirrels scold.

The rich scene has grown fresh again and new
As Spring and to the touch is not more cool
Than it is warm to the gaze; and now I might
As happy be as earth is beautiful,
Were I some other or with earth could turn
In alternation of violet and rose,
Harebell and snowdrop, at their season due,
And gorse that has no time not to be gay.

十月

1915 年 10 月 15—16 日[1]

绿榆长着一根硕大金枝
让树叶片片坠入草丛中，——
山草矮短，蘑菇乳白娇小，
风铃草、委陵菜和轮峰菊、
黑莓、荆豆，沐浴在露阳中，
弯腰鞠躬，风履过于轻飘
难以摇坠蕨上桦树落叶；
蛛丝自由自在漂浮游旅。
步履比鸟更沉，松鼠呵斥。

万千景象不断重新焕发，
仿若春天，触感无比清丽，
视觉无比温馨；如今我会
幸福快乐如美丽的大地，
若我与地为伴，或与他者
能适时更替紫罗兰、玫瑰、
风铃草和雪花莲的花季，
还有无时不欢的金雀花。

---

❶ 1915 年 10 月，托马斯被送往埃塞克斯郡（Essex）劳顿（Loughton）附近的山毛榉高地军营（camp at High Beech），担任一名地图识读教官。——译者注

But if this be not happiness, — who knows?
Some day I shall think this a happy day,
And this mood by the name of melancholy
Shall no more blackened and obscured be.

但若此非幸福，——谁知道呢？
或许日后我会以此为乐，
此种心境以愁思之名义
将永不会变暗或被遮蔽。

There's Nothing like the Sun

18, 19 November, 1915

There's nothing like the sun as the year dies,
Kind as it can be, this world being made so,
To stones and men and beasts and birds and flies,
To all things that it touches except snow,
Whether on mountains side or street of town.
The south wall warms me: November has begun,
Yet never shone the sun as fair as now
While the sweet last-left damsons from the bough
With spangles of the morning's storm drop down
Because the starling shakes it, whistling what
Once swallows sang. But I have not forgot
That there is nothing, too, like March's sun,
Like April's, or July's, or June's, or May's,
Or January's, or February's, great days:
And August, September, October, and December
Have equal days, all different from November.
No day of any month but I have said —
Or, if I could live long enough, should say —
"There's nothing like the sun that shines today."
There's nothing like the sun till we are dead.

唯剩阳煦

1915年11月18—19日[1]

当岁月消逝时，唯有阳日，
和煦仁慈，今世造物如是：
石、人、兽、鸟、蝇皆感其祥慈，
除了雪，万物皆沐其曦，
无论山之侧或城镇街道。
南墙暖人心：十一月已至，
然而今曦美妙胜于往曦，
清晨暴雨银珠闪耀之际，
最后的甜李从枝头坠落，
因欧椋鸟摇晃，鸣哨昔日
雨燕之歌。但我从未忘记
万物亦逊色于三月之阳煦，
不如四、五、六、七月之荣光，
不及一、二月之美好时光：
八月、九月、十月和十二月
天数相同，皆异于十一月。
但没有哪月哪日，我曾说——
或，我若活得足够长，该说——
“万物唯有阳日今日熠烁。”
唯剩阳煦伴我们至殂殁。

---

[1] 1915年11月18日，托马斯迁往埃塞克斯郡（Essex）罗姆福德市（Romford）季迪亚公园（Gidea Park）黑尔厅军营（Hare Hall Camp），担任一名读图教官。——译者注

The Thrush

? November, 1915

When Winter's ahead,
What can you read in November
That you read in April
When Winter's dead?

I hear the thrush, and I see
Him alone at the end of the lane
Near the bare poplar's tip,
Singing continuously.

Is it more that you know
Than that, even as in April,
So in November,
Winter is gone that must go?

Or is all your lore
Not to call November November,
And April April,
And Winter Winter — no more?

画眉

1915 年 11 月某日

当冬日即临时，
十一月你能读出何意
正如四月所读到的一般
当冬日消逝时？

我听见画眉叫，瞧见
他独自在小巷尽头
临近光秃的白杨树尖，
歌唱，连续不断。

尽管在四月，正如在
十一月，冬日已逝
且必须消逝，你
是否了解更多，除此之外？

抑或你的全部知识：
不叫十一月为十一月，
四月为四月，
冬日为冬日——仅此而已？

But I know the months all,
And their sweet names, April,
May and June and October,
As you call and call

I must remember
What died in April
And consider what will be born
Of a fair November;

And April I love for what
It was born of, and November
For what it will die in,
What they are and what they are not,

While you love what is kind,
What you can sing in
And love and forget in
All that's ahead and behind.

然而所有月份我皆知晓，
包括其芳名，四月、
五月、六月、十月，
正如你叫之又叫；

我必须记住
四月中已逝之物，
思索美妙的十一月
将诞生何物；

我喜爱四月因其
所诞生之物，还有十一月
因其所要消逝之物，
物类有别，必有其意，

你却亲仁爱之事，
爱所歌唱之物，
爱之所爱，爱之所忘，
不困于来往之事。

Liberty

26 November, 1915

The last light has gone out of the world, except
This moonlight lying on the grass like frost
Beyond the brink of the tall elm's shadow.
It is as if everything else had slept
Many an age, unforgotten and lost
The men that were, the things done, long ago,
All I have thought; and but the moon and I
Live yet and here stand idle over the grave
Where all is buried. Both have liberty
To dream what we could do if we were free
To do some thing we had desired long,
The moon and I. There's none less free than who
Does nothing and has nothing else to do,
Being free only for what is not to his mind,
And nothing is to his mind. If every hour
Like this one passing that I have spent among
The wiser others when I have forgot
To wonder whether I was free or not,
Were piled before me, and not lost behind,
And I could take and carry them away

自由

1915 年 11 月 26 日

最后一缕光线从世界消退，
除了月光，如霜般躺在草上，
越过挺拔榆树的阴影边缘。
而其他万物好像皆已沉睡，
仿若隔世，迷失，不被遗忘
人类、物类皆如此，由来已久，
皆我所料；然而月亮与我
仍“活”着，站在此处，闲望那
埋葬一切之墓。我们有自由
去梦力所能及之事，若自由
去做我们期盼已久之事，
仅月亮与我之间。自由顶多是
游手好闲，无所事事，
自由仅意味着何事不自由，
或一切皆不自由。倘若每小时
能像我所度过的这个小时
在与更聪慧的他者共度时光中，我早已忘忧，
不去思考自己是否自由，
尽管它们摆在我面前，不消失于身后，
我会带着、驮着它们离去，

I should be rich; or if I had the power
To wipe out every one and not again
Regret, I should be rich to be so poor.
And yet I still am half in love with pain,
With what is imperfect, with both tears and mirth,
With things that have an end, with life and earth,
And this moon that leaves me dark within the door.

那么我将变得富有；我若有权力
去消灭一切，并不再陷入
懊悔，那么我的富有终将归于贫穷。
然而我仍然半爱着痛苦、
瑕疵之事，还有泪水与欢喜、
终逝之物、生命和土地，以及
这置我于漆黑门内的月光。

This is No Case of Petty Right or Wrong

26 December, 1915

This is no case of petty right or wrong
That politicians or philosophers
Can judge. I hate not Germans, nor grow hot
With love of Englishmen, to please newspapers.
Beside my hate for one fat patriot
My hatred of the Kaiser is love true: —
A kind of god he is, banging a gong.
But I have not to choose between the two,
Or between justice and injustice. Dinned
With war and argument I read no more
Than in the storm smoking along the wind
Athwart the wood. Two witches' cauldrons roar.
From one the weather shall rise clear and gay;
Out of the other an England beautiful
And like her mother that died yesterday.
Little I know or care if, being dull,
I shall miss something that historians
Can rake out of the ashes when perchance
The phoenix broods serene above their ken.
But with the best and meanest Englishmen

此事无关对与错

1915 年 12 月 26 日

对错难辨，黑白难分，
哲人难辩，政客难判。
英人不爱，德人不厌，
报纸新闻，吾不迎合。
爱国狂子，德皇凯泽，
恨之爱之，真假难获：——
其虽似上帝，却鸣锣战争。
爱国叛国，不作言说，
正义邪恶，无须抉取。
战争辩论，喋喋不休，狂风暴雨，
不妨读书，抽烟吐气，随风入林。
两位女巫，胸前热锅，翻滚咆吟。
一锅气候，欢快清洁。
一锅景象，美丽英伦，
宛若母亲，昨日殉节。
吾识浅薄，无趣迟钝，
漠不关切：是否错过，灰烬之中，
史学发现，恰巧此刻，凤凰旋空，
安详沉思，史家虽明，难见其形。
英国人士，不管善恶，不论忠佞，

I am one in crying, God save England, lest
We lose what never slaves and cattle blessed.
The ages made her that made us from the dust:
She is all we know and live by, and we trust
She is good and must endure, loving her so:
And as we love ourselves we hate her foe.

吾愿携手，共同祈祷，主佑英伦，
以免生灵奴牛，傴傴受辱福损。
岁月筑英伦，尘土造吾辈：
英伦之所悉，吾辈之所偎，
坚信其安好，定会永长存，爱其终不悔：
爱己方兴，恶敌便随。

The Year 1916

1916 年

Rain

7 January, 1916

Rain, midnight rain, nothing but the wild rain
On this bleak hut, and solitude, and me
Remembering again that I shall die
And neither hear the rain nor give it thanks
For washing me cleaner than I have been
Since I was born into this solitude.
Blessed are the dead that the rain rains upon:
But here I pray that none whom once I loved
Is dying tonight or lying still awake
Solitary, listening to the rain,
Either in pain or thus in sympathy
Helpless among the living and the dead,
Like a cold water among broken reeds,
Myriads of broken reeds all still and stiff,
Like me who have no love which this wild rain
Has not dissolved except the love of death,
If love it be towards what is perfect and
Cannot, the tempest tells me, disappoint.

雨

1916 年 1 月 7 日

雨，午夜之雨，唯有此暴雨
光临这凄冷之屋，留下孤独。
使我又想起我将告别于人世，
既听不见雨声，也不为之感激。
因为雨一次又一次把我洗净，
自从我降落至此孤独世界来。
被雨淋着的死者受上帝垂爱：
但我祈祷希望曾经爱过的人
不要死于今晚，或难以入睡、
孤独寂寞，聆听着这雨滴声，
或痛苦，或怜悯，或无助，
从生者、死者中难得慰藉，
犹如枯残芦苇中一滩冷水，
无数残苇僵直，毫无生气，
就像此刻的我，心中所有的爱
被暴雨浇融，唯剩对死亡的爱。
倘若此爱能达到完美之彼岸，
暴雨告诉我，它不会令人失望。

The Clouds That Are So Light

15 January, 1916

As the clouds that are so light,
Beautiful, swift, and bright,
Cast shadows on field and park
Of the earth that is so dark,

And even so now, light one!
Beautiful, swift and bright one!
You let fall on a heart that was dark,
Unillumined, a deeper mark.

But clouds would have, without earth
To shadow, far less worth:
Away from your shadow on me
Your beauty less would be,

And if it still be treasured
An age hence, it shall be measured
By this small dark spot
Without which it were not.

云霞如此轻淡

1916 年 1 月 15 日

云霞如此轻淡、
美丽、敏捷、明亮，
投影至大地田园
和公园，无比黑暗，

甚至如今，轻淡、
美丽、敏捷、明亮！
您让更深的印记
坠落漆黑、不明的心底。

然而，云霞因无地
投影，价值将更低：
远离您投给我的阴影，
您的美将变得差劲，

倘若美仍被珍视
一世之久，其圭尺
应由此细小黑点置论，
无它，美将荡然无存。[1]

[1] 此诗明显反映了诗人道家似的“阴阳”观。云彩明亮美丽与其黑暗阴影紧密相连，既相互对立，又相互依存，离开了后者，前者将变得一无是处，美丽也将荡然无存。——译者注

Roads

22 January, 1916

I love roads:
The goddesses that dwell
Far along invisible
Are my favourite gods.

Roads go on
While we forget, and are
Forgotten like a star
That shoots and is gone.

On this earth 'tis sure
We men have not made
Anything that doth fade
So soon, so long endure:

The hill road wet with rain
In the sun would not gleam
Like a winding stream
If we trod it not again.

路

1916 年 1 月 22 日

我喜欢路：
仙女们在其中
遥居，无影无踪，
是我至爱的天主。

路继续前行
我们却忘记，并
被遗忘，像一颗星
发射后，永无踪影。

地球上，肯定的是
我们人类还未造出
稍纵即逝的事物、
持之以恒的东西：

大雨浸湿的山路
在阳光下不像
蜿蜒的河流闪亮，
若不再踩这条路。

They are lonely
While we sleep, lonelier
For lack of the traveller
Who is now a dream only.

From dawn's twilight
And all the clouds like sheep
On the mountains of sleep
They wind into the night.

The next turn may reveal
Heaven: upon the crest
The close pine clump, at rest
And black, may Hell conceal.

Often footsore, never
Yet of the road I weary,
Though long and steep and dreary
As it winds on for ever.

Helen of the roads,
The mountain ways of Wales
And the Mabinogion tales,
Is one of the true gods,

他们显得孤寂
当我们睡时，更加孤寂，
因为缺少游子，
如今只是一场梦思。

披着黎明晨曦，
朵朵云彩如羊，
在沉睡的山坡上，
他们蜿蜒至夜里。

下个转弯会显露
天堂：山之巅，
茂密的松树丛，安眠，
黑暗，或许隐藏地狱。

我经常脚痛，但是
从不厌恶这条路，
尽管又长又陡又艰苦，
仿佛蜿蜒得一望无际。

威尔士的山路，
那阡陌中的海伦仙女，
据《马比诺吉昂》[1]所述，
是其中一位真神，

[1] 《马比诺吉昂》是一部中世纪威尔士文学作品，收录了 11 篇有关威尔士的故事，主要围绕神话、民间传说和英雄传奇等主题。——译者注

Abiding in the trees,
The threes and fours so wise,
The larger companies,
That by the roadside be,

And beneath the rafter
Else uninhabited
Excepting by the dead;
And it is her laughter

At morn and night I hear
When the thrush cock sings
Bright irrelevant things,
And when the chanticleer

Calls back to their own night
Troops that make loneliness
With their light footsteps' press,
As Helen's own are light.

Now all roads lead to France
And heavy is the tread
Of the living; but the dead
Returning lightly dance:

Whatever the road bring

诸神在树中安住，
三四成群，伶俐聪鉴，
更多的同伴，
在路边驻足，

屋椽下面
无人住着
除了死者；
她的笑言

我早晚听得见，
这时画眉鸟在歌吟
欢快无关的事情，
同时雄鸡在召唤

回归自己的夜营，
而营中孤寂萦怀，
他们的步履轻踩，
像海伦的一样轻盈。

如今，条条道路通法兰西
沉重是生者
的步履；而死者
归来时跳着轻盈的舞姿：

无论路带我

To me or take from me,
They keep me company
With their pattering,

Crowding the solitude
Of the loops over the downs,
Hushing the roar of towns
And their brief multitude.

何去何从，
他们伴我始终，
带着轻快的拍搏，

去挤那重重孤独
的环路，翻过丘陵，
让喧嚣的城镇肃静，
让短暂的人群静穆。

The Ash Grove

4–9 February, 1916

Half of the grove stood dead, and those that yet lived made
Little more than the dead ones made of shade.
If they led to a house, long before they had seen its fall:
But they welcomed me; I was glad without cause and delayed.

Scarce a hundred paces under the trees was the interval —
Paces each sweeter than the sweetest miles — but nothing at all,
Not even the spirits of memory and fear with restless wing,
Could climb down in to molest me over the wall

That I passed through at either end without noticing.
And now an ash grove far from those hills can bring
The same tranquillity in which I wander a ghost
With a ghostly gladness, as if I heard a girl sing

The song of the Ash Grove soft as love uncrossed,
And then in a crowd or in distance it were lost,
But the moment unveiled something unwilling to die
And I had what most I desired, without search or desert or cost.

白蜡林

1916年2月4—9日

一半的白腊林已枯死，那些还活着的树
无非形同那些荫蔽的枯树。
如若用来建房，早在此前他们便已消亡：
但他们向我致意；我无故欢笑，倍感迟木。

树下留有难得的百步之距空地——
每步距之地比最美的英里之地更美——但仅此而已，
甚至连记忆的神灵或带着焦虑羽翼的恐惧，
也不会爬下来折磨我逾墙而弃，

无意间我穿透了墙的两端。
如今那片远山的白腊林能带来同样
的宁静，在那儿，我游荡得像一个幽灵，
并带着幽灵般的喜悦，仿佛听见一位女孩儿在吟唱

白腊林之歌，轻柔如未传达的爱意，
不久在人群中或远方消逝，
但那片刻时光揭示了某些不愿消亡之事，
而我不费吹灰之力获得了所欲之物，不离不弃。

February Afternoon

7, 8 February, 1916

Men heard this roar of parleying starlings, saw,
A thousand years ago even as now,
Black rooks with white gulls following the plough
So that the first are last until a caw
Commands that last are first again, — a law
Which was of old when one, like me, dreamed how
A thousand years might dust lie on his brow
Yet thus would birds do between hedge and shaw.

Time swims before me, making as a day
A thousand years, while the broad ploughland oak
Roars mill-like and men strike and bear the stroke
Of war as ever, audacious or resigned,
And God still sits aloft in the array
That we have wrought him, stone-deaf and stone-blind.

二月午后

1916 年 2 月 7—8 日

人类听过椋鸟争论时的咆哮，也曾见过，
一千年前如此，甚至如今也一样，
乌鸦、白鸥成群结队地随着耕犁翱翔，
故此前队变为后队直到一声喊唆
命令后队再变为前队，—— 一个亘古不变
的法则，当一个人，像我一样，梦见
粉尘如何会落在他的眉间已千年，
而鸟儿经常在树篱和灌木之间穿梭。

时光从我身前游过，让千年仿若
一日，而那棵广阔田野上的橡树
发出磨坊般的咆哮，人们击打，忍负
战争的打击，勇猛向前或退缩回家，
上帝却依旧在队列中高悬而坐，
耳聋眼瞎，尽管我们造就了他。

I May Come Near Loving You

8 February, 1916

I may come near loving you
When you are dead
And there is nothing to do
And much to be said.

To repent that day will be
Impossible
For you and vain for me
The truth to tell.

I shall be sorry for
Your impotence:
You can do and undo no more
When you go hence,

Cannot even forgive
The funeral.
But not so long as you live
Can I love you at all.

我可能会爱上您

1916 年 2 月 8 日

我可能会爱上您
当您离世了，
似乎无能为力，
却有很多话要说。

忏悔那日之事将
无法使您
和我互吐真相，
互表心思。

您虚弱无力，
我深表惋惜：
您离去时，
您将再也无法攻守，

甚至无法赦免
自己的葬礼。
但只要您尚在人间，
我绝不会爱您。

Those Things That Poets Said

9 February, 1916

These things that poets said
Of love seemed true to me
When I loved and I fed
On love and poetry equally.

But now I wish I knew
If theirs were love indeed,
Or if mine were the true
And theirs some other lovely weed:

For certainly not thus,
Then or thereafter, I
Loved ever. Between us
Decide, good Love, before I die.

Only, that once I loved
By this one argument
Is very plainly proved:
I, loving not, am different.

诗人物语

1916年2月9日

诗人所说之事
关乎爱情，像是真理，
当我爱过，并以爱和诗
为食，不分彼此之时。

如今我想知道
他们是否是真爱，
或我们是否是真爱，
而他们的爱情是否像迷人的水草：

当然并非如此这般，
当时或后来，我虽然
曾经爱过。你我之间
抉择，真爱，在我离世之前。

我只爱过那一次，
如此便旗帜鲜明
应验了此番见地：
我，无爱，特立独行。

No One so Much as You

11 February, 1916

No one so much as you
Loves this my clay,
Or would lament as you
Its dying day.

You know me through and through
Though I have not told,
And though with what you know
You are not bold.

None ever was so fair
As I thought you:
Not a word can I bear
Spoken against you.

All that I ever did
For you seemed coarse
Compared with what I hid
Nor put in force.

My eyes scarce dare meet you
Lest they should prove

没人像你一样

1916 年 2 月 11 日

没人像你一样
深爱我的黏泥，
或像你一样哀叹
它垂死的样子。

你历来非常懂我，
虽然我未曾告知，
但你也未直言表露
你所知之事。

无人像你一样，我觉得，
曾如此美丽：
我无法忍受任何
诋毁你的言辞。

我曾为你所做的
一切看似粗纵，
相比我所隐藏的
和未付诸的行动。

我双眼不敢直视你，
生怕它们会泄露

I but respond to you
And do not love.

We look and understand,
We cannot speak
Except in trifles and
Words the most weak.

For I at most accept
Your love, regretting
That is all: I have kept
Only a fretting

That I could not return
All that you gave
And could not ever burn
With the love you have,

Till sometimes it did seem
Better it were
Never to see you more
Than linger here

With only gratitude
Instead of love —
A pine in solitude
Cradling a dove.

我除了回应你
却不爱你的思绪。

你我面面相觑、肚明心知，
却默默不语，
除非琐碎之事，
迸发极弱的言语。

因为我顶多接受
你的爱，却悔懊
一切：我所保守
的仅是烦恼

我无法回报
你给予的一切，
也无法激情燃烧
你所有的爱藉，

直到有时顿感：
不如从此
永不相见，
相比徘徊于此

仅仅带着感激
而不是爱意——
一棵松树孤独地
抚育着一只鸽子。

The Unknown

14 February, 1916

She is most fair,
And when they see her pass
The poets' ladies
Look no more in the glass
But after her.

On a bleak moor
Running under the moon
She lures a poet,
Once proud or happy, soon
Far from his door.

Beside a train,
Because they saw her go,
Or failed to see her,
Travellers and watchers know
Another pain.

The simple lack
Of her is more to me

佚名

1916 年 2 月 14 日

她非常优雅，
所有诗人们的贵妇
见她路过，
再也不在玻璃内窥睃，
转而跟随她。

荒野之上、
明月之下奔驰，
一旦傲娇或欣喜，
她便引诱诗人，霎时
远离他的门房。

火车附近，
因为见她远离，
或未能相见，
游客和看客心知
另一番苦境。

我更在意
她的缺席，

Than others' presence,
Whether life splendid be
Or utter black.

I have not seen,
I have no news of her;
I can tell only
She is not here, but there
She might have been.

She is to be kissed
Only perhaps by me;
She may be seeking
Me and no other; she
May not exist.

而非他者的存在，
不管生活绚丽，
还是廖光黑漆。

她，我未曾见过，
她的音信，我亦茫然；
唯能分享：
她不在此地，而在彼岸
她或曾去过。

或许只有我来
亲她、吻她；
她也许在追寻
我，而非他人；她
也许不存在。

Celandine

4 March, 1916

Thinking of her had saddened me at first,
Until I saw the sun on the celandines lie
Redoubled, and she stood up like a flame,
A living thing, not what before I nursed,
The shadow I was growing to love almost,
The phantom, not the creature with bright eye
That I had thought never to see, once lost.

She found the celandines of February
Always before us all. Her nature and name
Were like those flowers, and now immediately
For a short swift eternity back she came,
Beautiful, happy, simply as when she wore
Her brightest bloom among the winter hues
Of all the world; and I was happy too,
Seeing the blossoms and the maiden who
Had seen them with me Februarys before,
Bending to them as in and out she trod
And laughed, with locks sweeping the mossy sod.

黄罂花

1916 年 3 月 4 日

一想起她，起初我感到忧伤，
直到看见黄罂花上阳光显露
熠熠光彩，她如火焰一般跃起，
栩栩如生，非先前所培育的那样，
我逐渐爱上了这魔幻般的影子，
并非带着明亮单眼的生物，
我早想过永不相见，一旦消失。

她寻找到了二月的黄罂花簇，
总赶在我们前面。她的性情、名字
皆与那些花无异，如今她急速
归来，为了那稍纵即逝的来世，
美丽、幸福，仅仅当她穿上
最绚丽的盛装，脱颖于全世界
冬季的色调；而我也心怡神悦，
望着花朵绽放，忆起之前每逢二月
曾一同赏花的那位少女，向
它们弯腰，她曾踏进踏出，悦颜
欢笑，在苔藓地上拖扫着发辫。

But this was a dream; the flowers were not true,
Until I stooped to pluck from the grass there
One of five petals and I smelt its juice
Which made me sigh, remembering she was no more,
Gone like a never perfectly recalled air.

1916 年

但这是一场梦；花朵并非真确，
直到我弯下腰从草丛中拔起
五花瓣中的一瓣，闻着花汁液，
感慨万千，想起她已不再芬芳，
消逝如一阵永难追忆的空气。

Home (Fair Was the Morning)

7 and 10 March, 1916

Fair was the morning, fair our tempers, and
We had seen nothing fairer than that land,
Though strange, and the untrodden snow that made
Wild of the tame, casting out all that was
Not wild and rustic and old; and we were glad.

Fair, too, was afternoon, and first to pass
Were we that league of snow, next the north wind.
There was nothing to return for, except need,
And yet we sang nor ever stopped for speed,
As we did often with the start behind.
Faster still strode we when we came in sight
Of the cold roofs where we must spend the night.
Happy we had not been there, nor could be,
Though we had tasted sleep and food and fellowship
Together long.

"How quick" to someone's lip
The words came, "will the beaten horse run home!"

家园（美好清晨）

1916年3月7—10日

清新的早晨，美好的心情，
印象中那土地最具风情，
尽管陌生，雪地杳无人迹，
所驯服的变得狂野，摒弃
温顺、粗俗、陈旧；我们欣喜。

午后也美好，我们最先穿
过那片雪地，接着是北风。
我们无以为报，除了需求，
我们歌唱，不因速度逗留，
像常常不顾开始的行程。
迈着更快的步伐直到见着
冰冷的屋顶，须在此过夜。
在这儿，未曾觉得幸福，也不会，
尽管我们尝试同睡同食，
长久共处。
　　　　有人突然提起：
“策马扬鞭很快就可到家！”

The word "home" raised a smile in us all three,
And one repeated it, smiling just so
That all knew what he meant and none would say.
Between three counties far apart that lay
We were divided and looked strangely each
At the other, and we knew we were not friends
But fellows in a union that ends
With the necessity for it, as it ought.

Never a word was spoken, not a thought
Was thought, of what the look meant with the word
"Home" as we walked and watched the sunset blurred.
And then to me the word, only the word,
"Homesick", as it were playfully occurred:
No more.

If I should ever more admit
Than the mere word I could not endure it
For a day longer: this captivity
Must somehow come to an end, else I should be
Another man, as often now I seem,
Or this life be only an evil dream.

听到“家”，我们仨会心一笑，
一人笑着重复一遍，故此
大家心知肚明，嘴上不提。
我们来自三个郡县，彼此
相隔，面面相觑，不可思议，
心里清楚大家并非朋友，
而是情况所迫、顺应潮流、
最终团结在一起的同胞。

大家一语不发，不再思考，
不知何种表情由“家”引起，
边散步边望着晚霞直到模糊不清之时。
于我，这词，就这词，意味着
“乡愁”，像玩笑间提及罢了：
仅此而已。

倘若要我承认
“家”有多重含义，我很难容忍
它超过一天：这犹如囚禁
必须结束，否则我将不禁
变成——正如我经常看起来像另一人，
否则，此生就是一场噩梦。

Thaw

10 March, 1916

Over the land freckled with snow half-thawed
The speculating rooks at their nests cawed
And saw from elm-tops, delicate as flowers of grass,
What we below could not see, Winter pass.

融化

1916 年 3 月 10 日

雪地白花萦，凝融相伴行，
寒鸦巢中立，思索并啼鸣，
花草还精致，榆枝俯瞰倾，
身低难望眼，冬逝迹无影。

If I Should Ever by Chance

29 March–6 April, 1916

If I should ever by chance grow rich
I'll buy Codham, Cockridden, and Childerditch,
Roses, Pyrgo, and Lapwater,
And let them all to my elder daughter.
The rent I shall ask of her will be only
Each year's first violets, white and lonely,
The first primroses and orchises —
She must find them before I do, that is.
But if she finds a blossom on furze
Without rent they shall all for ever be hers,
Whenever I am sufficiently rich:
Codham, Cockridden, and Childerditch,
Roses, Pyrgo and Lapwater, —
I shall give them all to my elder daughter.

倘若我碰巧

1916 年 3 月 29 日—4 月 6 日

倘若我碰巧变得富足，
我将买下考德翰、考克里登、切德迪渠、
罗塞斯、派果和莱泊华特，
然后把它们全部租给我的大女儿。
我向她索要的租金将仅仅是
每年初开的紫罗兰，洁白、孤寂，
初开的报春花和兰花 ——
她必须比我先找到这些花。
然而她若找到盛开的金雀花，
无须付租金，它们将全部归她，
每当我的生活变得富足：
考德翰、考克里登、切德迪渠、
罗塞斯、派果和莱泊华特，——
我将把它们全部赠给我的大女儿。

If I Were to Own

1–7 April, 1916

If I were to own this countryside
As far as a man in a day could ride,
And the Tyes were mine for giving or letting, —
Wingle Tye and Margaretting
Tye, — and Skreens, Gooshays, and Cockerells,
Shellow, Rochetts, Bandish, and Pickerells,
Martins, Lambkins, and Lillyputs,
Their copses, ponds, roads, and ruts,
Fields where plough-horses steam and plovers
Fling and whimper, hedges that lovers
Love, and orchards, shrubberies, walls
Where the sun untroubled by north wind falls,
And single trees where the thrush sings well
His proverbs untranslatable,
I would give them all to my son
If he would let me any one
For a song, a blackbird's song, at dawn.
He should have no more, till on my lawn
Never a one was left, because I
Had shot them to put them into a pie, —

倘若我拥有

1916 年 4 月 1—7 日

倘若我拥有这乡间
远至一天内人所能驰骋过的乡壤：
泰氏宅邸归我，或赠人，或租赁——
温格尔·泰，玛格丽特婷·泰，
——斯科林一家、顾赛一家、考克热一家、
谢罗、罗切特一家、班迪斯、皮克热尔一家、
马丁一家、朗姆金一家、莉莉普特一家等宅邸，
以及他们的小树林、池塘、道路和辙迹，
田野上耕犁的马儿，怒气鸣嘶，
猛冲啜泣的千鸟，还有恋人们喜爱的藩篱、
一座座果园、一排排灌木、一道道墙垣，
夕阳沉落，任凭北风扰enhance，
单棵树上，一只画眉深情歌唱
他的条条谚语，难以译传，
那么我将把这一切赠给我的儿子，
倘若他愿意出租给我任何一个
只为清晨一曲，那乌鸫的歌吟。
他应该会一无所有，直到我的草坪
没留下任何一个，因为我早已
将他们射死，做成了饼食，——

His Essex blackbirds, every one,
And I was left old and alone.

Then unless I could pay, for rent, a song
As sweet as a blackbird's, and as long —
No more — he should have the house, not I:
Margaretting or Wingle Tye,
Or it might be Skreens, Gooshays, or Cockerells,
Shellow, Rochetts, Bandish, or Pickerells,
Martins, Lambkins, or Lillyputs,
Should be his till the cart tracks had no ruts.

他的艾塞克斯乌鸫，每一只，
最后只剩下我孤老终死。

除非我能，用作租金，支付得起一首歌
如乌鸫一样甜美、一样长久的歌——
仅此而已——他而不是我，应拥有一栋房子：
玛格丽特婷或温格尔·泰的房子，
或斯科林一家、顾赛一家、考克热一家、
谢罗、罗切特一家、班迪斯、皮克热尔一家、
马丁一家、朗姆金一家或莉莉普特一家的宅邸
应属于他，直到车道不见车辙为止。

What Shall I Give

2–8 April, 1916

What shall I give my daughter the younger
More than will keep her from cold and hunger?
I shall not give her anything.
If she shared South Weald and Havering,
Their acres, the two brooks running between,
Paine's Brook and Weald Brook,
With pewit, woodpecker, swan, and rook,
She would be no richer than the queen
Who once on a time sat in Havering Bower
Alone, with the shadows, pleasure and power.
She could do no more with Samarcand,
Or the mountains of a mountain land
And its far white house above cottages
Like Venus above the Pleiades.
Her small hands I would not cumber
With so many acres and their lumber,
But leave her Steep and her own world
And her spectacled self with hair uncurled,
Wanting a thousand little things
That time without contentment brings.

何为我所予

1916 年 4 月 2—8 日

我还将给予我小女何物，
除了让她免受饥寒苦楚？
我不会给她任何东西了。
她若与田凫、啄木鸟、天鹅、
白嘴鸦共享南林、哈韦林，
大片地产，两条小溪流淌
于佩恩斯河与林地河间，
那她将和女王一样清贫：
曾独坐在哈韦林凉亭里，
享受着树荫、快乐与权力。
她不会再觊觎撒马尔罕，
或一块山地，位于群山间，
及村舍上方远处的白房
如金星在昴宿星团[1]上方。
我不会让她的一双小手
牵累于诸多地产与木头，
仅留给她斯迪坡村和她
的世界：戴着眼镜，散着发，
渴望得到无数小玩意儿，
为时间所赋予，毫不吝啬。

[1] 在希腊神话中指阿特拉斯（Atlas）的七个女儿，后变成天上七星。——译者注

And You, Helen

9 April, 1916

And you, Helen, what should I give you?
So many things I would give you
Had I an infinite great store
Offered me and I stood before
To choose. I would give you youth,
All kinds of loveliness and truth,
A clear eye as good as mine,
Lands, waters, flowers, wine,
As many children as your heart
Might wish for, a far better art
Than mine can be, all you have lost
Upon the travelling waters tossed,
Or given to me. If I could choose
Freely in that great treasure-house
Anything from any shelf,
I would give you back yourself,
And power to discriminate
What you want and want it not too late,
Many fair days free from care
And heart to enjoy both foul and fair,
And myself, too, if I could find
Where it lay hidden and it proved kind.

致海伦

1916 年 4 月 9 日

至爱海伦，何物予你？
琳琅物品，我想予你，
倘若拥有：浩大商店，
应有尽有，立于货前，
任意选取。予你青春、
真善甜美，千类万群，
眼眸清澈，如我一样，
土地与水、花与酒香，
儿女满堂，如你所愿，
典雅艺作，远胜我鉴，
你之所失，过往一切，
或抛水中，随波翻跌，
或赠与我。假如允许：
宝藏财库，自由出入，
货架之上，任取东西，
我必将你，归还于你，
予你力量，供你辨析，
所恋之物，愿来得及，
愿你开心，无忧无虑，
尽情享受，实实虚虚，
我亦如此，若能发现：
它藏何处，必证其善。

The Wind's Song

22–30 April, 1916

Dull-thoughted, walking among the nunneries
Of many a myriad anemones
In the close copses, I grew weary of Spring
Till I emerged and in my wandering
I climbed the down up to a lone pine clump
Of six, the tallest dead, one a mere stump.
On one long stem, branchless and flayed and prone,
I sat in the sun listening to the wind alone,
Thinking there could be no old song so sad
As the wind's song; but later none so glad
Could I remember as that same wind's song
All the time blowing the pine boughs among.
My heart that had been still as the dead tree
Awakened by the West wind was made free.

风之歌

1916 年 4 月 22—30 日

思绪迟钝，我行走在修道院间，
望见不计其数的海葵花生长
在茂密丛林中，渐渐讨厌春天，
直到我出来到外面四处闲逛，
爬上丘原来到孤独的松林里：
共六棵，最高的已死，其中一颗仅剩下树墩而已。
阳光下，我坐在横卧、无枝、脱皮
的长树干上，独自聆听着风息，
心想可能没有一首老歌如此忧愁
像风之歌；但不久没有一首
我记得，像风之歌如此欢喜，
时时刻刻吹拂松枝，无休无止。
我的心曾经如枯树一样滞静，
被西风吹醒，重获悠然的心境。

Like the Touch of Rain

23–30 April, 1916

Like the touch of rain she was
On a man's flesh and hair and eyes
When the joy of walking thus
Has taken him by surprise:

With the love of the storm he burns,
He sings, he laughs, well I know how,
But forgets when he returns
As I shall not forget her "Go now".

Those two words shut a door
Between me and the blessed rain
That was never shut before
And will not open again.

像雨的触摸

1916 年 4 月 23—30 日

像雨的触摸，她滴
在人的肉体、毛发和双眸上，
信步的欢喜，因此，
已让他惊愕张惶：

带着对暴风雨的热爱，他燃烧着、
唱着、笑着，我深知其意，
归来时，他忘了
而我没忘记她说的“走起”。

那两个字封闭
我和甘霖之间的一扇门：
此前，从未被关闭，
此后，便不再开启。

When We Two Walked

23 April – 1 May, 1916

When we two walked in Lent
We imagined that happiness
Was something different
And this was something less.

But happy were we to hide
Our happiness, not as they were
Who acted in their pride
Juno and Jupiter:

For the Gods in their jealousy
Murdered that wife and man,
And we that were wise live free
To recall our happiness then.

当我们俩漫步时

1916 年 4 月 23 日—5 月 1 日

四旬斋时，我们俩散步，
心里想着幸福
是别具一格之物，
此乃不可多得之物。

而我们欣于藏着
自己的幸福，不像
朱诺与朱庇特
般傲慢，装模作样：

因为诸神心生妒忌，
将那位妻子和男人隐戮，
而明智的我们自由地
生活，追忆往日的幸福。

Tall Nettles

24 April – 1 May, 1916

Tall nettles cover up, as they have done
These many springs, the rusty harrow, the plough
Long worn out, and the roller made of stone:
Only the elm butt tops the nettles now.

This corner of the farmyard I like most:
As well as any bloom upon a flower
I like the dust on the nettles, never lost
Except to prove the sweetness of a shower.

高荨麻

1916 年 4 月 24 日—5 月 1 日

荨麻高大，几度春妍，
苍苍依旧，覆蔽锈耙，
吞没残犁，遮掩石碾：
唯有榆树，高过荨麻。

农场一隅，深得吾心：
繁花绽放，撩动心扉，
荨麻粉尘，吾甚幽欣，
从未消逝，唯证雨美。

The Watchers

24 April – 1 May, 1916

By the ford at the town's edge
Horse and carter rest:
The carter smokes on the bridge
Watching the water press in swathes about his horse's chest.

From the inn one watches, too,
In the room for visitors
That has no fire, but a view
And many cases of stuffed fish, vermin, and kingfishers.

守望者

1916 年 4 月 24 日—5 月 1 日

津渡城郭边缘，
马儿车夫歇待：
车夫桥上抽烟，
望着马胸水袋。

一人栈中凝望，
客房无火照耀，
唯有窗外景象，
箱装鱼虫翠鸟。

I Never Saw That Land Before

5 May, 1916

I never saw that land before,
And now can never see it again;
Yet, as if by acquaintance hoar
Endeared, by gladness and by pain,
Great was the affection that I bore

To the valley and the river small,
The cattle, the grass, the bare ash trees,
The chickens from the farmsteads, all
Elm-hidden, and the tributaries
Descending at equal interval;

The blackthorns down along the brook
With wounds yellow as crocuses
Where yesterday the labourer's hook
Had sliced them cleanly; and the breeze
That hinted all and nothing spoke.

I neither expected anything
Nor yet remembered: but some goal

我未曾见过那片土地

1916 年 5 月 5 日

我未曾见过那片土地，
如今却恐难再次相见；
然而，仿佛这片土地
曾因欢愉、痛苦、白霜
而惹人痴迷，深得我意：

恋上这座山谷、小溪、
牛、草及裸露的白腊树，
还有数不尽的农舍鸡
和所有榆树遮盖之物，
以及等距递降的支流水溪；

黑刺花顺着溪流而下，
带着伤痕，黄如番红花
因为昨日工匠的钩叉
将它们削净；微风飒飒
暗示一切，而万籁寂哑。

我不曾有过任何预期，
也未曾记得：却曾触及

I touched then; and if I could sing
What would not even whisper my soul
As I went on my journeying,

I should use, as the trees and birds did,
A language not to be betrayed;
And what was hid should still be hid
Excepting from those like me made
Who answer when such whispers bid.

某个目标；若我能唱起
未曾与心灵私语之事，
当自己继续旅行之时，

像树、鸟一样，我应行使
一种未被背叛的语言；
所被遮蔽的仍应被遮蔽，
仅向我一样的群类显现，
只因回应了私语的致意。

The Cherry Trees

7, 8 May, 1916

The cherry trees bend over and are shedding
On the old road where all that passed are dead,
Their petals, strewing the grass as for a wedding
This early May morn when there is none to wed.

樱桃树

1916 年 5 月 7—8 日

古道万物逝，唯剩樱桃树，
枝干俯身姿，叶叶正凋零，
花瓣满地延，宛若婚毯路，
五月清晨中，婚礼无人迎。

It Rains

11–13 May, 1916

It rains, and nothing stirs within the fence
Anywhere through the orchard's untrodden, dense
Forest of parsley. The great diamonds
Of rain on the grassblades there is none to break,
Or the fallen petals further down to shake.

And I am nearly as happy as possible
To search the wilderness in vain though well,
To think of two walking, kissing there,
Drenched, yet forgetting the kisses of the rain:
Sad, too, to think that never, never again,

Unless alone, so happy shall I walk
In the rain. When I turn away, on its fine stalk
Twilight has fined to naught, the parsley flower
Figures, suspended still and ghostly white,
The past hovering as it revisits the light.

下雨

1916 年 5 月 11—13 日

下雨，篱笆之内，万物沉寂
穿过那座未被踏足的、茂密
的芹菜林园。落在草叶上，
雨滴大如钻石，未被打碎，
已落的花瓣亦未被摇坠。

我尽可能快乐地去寻找
那片荒野，虽努力，却徒劳，
心想二者在那儿散步、亲吻，
被淋湿，却忘了雨滴之吻：
想到已难重现，倍感悲闷，

除非独自一人，我欣喜步行
于雨中。我转身时，欧芹花茎
精细，黄昏下模糊不清，芹花
形态，静止悬浮，白如幽灵，
它重访光明时，往事旋行。

Some Eyes Condemn

13, 14 May, 1916

Some eyes condemn the earth they gaze upon:
Some wait patiently till they know far more
Than earth can tell them: some laugh at the whole
As folly of another's making: one
I knew that laughed because he saw, from core
To rind, not one thing worth the laugh his soul
Had ready at waking: some eyes have begun
With laughing; some stand startled at the door.

Others, too, I have seen rest, question, roll,
Dance, shoot. And many I have loved watching. Some
I could not take my eyes from till they turned
And loving died. I had not found my goal.
But thinking of your eyes, dear, I become
Dumb: for they flamed, and it was me they burned.

有些眼睛谴责

1916 年 5 月 13—14 日

有些眼睛谴责他们所凝视的大地：
有些耐心等待，直到他们知道远超
大地所告知的信息：有些嘲笑万物，
像另一造物主所创造的蠢货：我知悉
一个嘲笑之物，因为他从内到外瞧
见过，而不是一个值得嘲笑的事物，
他灵魂整装待醒：有些眼睛已开始
发笑；有些人在门口感到惊愕忧焦。

其他人，我也看见，在休息、质疑、滚碌、
跳舞、射击，以及诸多我爱看的事情。
我无法从一些人的身上移开目光，
直到他们转身，深情死去。我的意图
未曾实现。然而想到您的双眸，啊，我不禁
哑口：因为它们曾燃起，将我灼伤。

The Sun Used to Shine

22 May, 1916

The sun used to shine while we two walked
Slowly together, paused and started
Again, and sometimes mused, sometimes talked
As either pleased, and cheerfully parted

Each night. We never disagreed
Which gate to rest on. The to be
And the late past we gave small heed.
We turned from men or poetry

To rumours of the war remote
Only till both stood disinclined
For aught but the yellow flavorous coat
Of an apple wasps had undermined;

Or a sentry of dark betonies,
The stateliest of small flowers on earth,
At the forest verge; or crocuses
Pale purple as if they had their birth

日曾闪耀

1916 年 5 月 22 日

日曾闪耀，你我二人散步，
步履缓缓，或停歇，或继续
前行，时而沉思，时而倾诉，
直至你我心满意足而离去，

夜夜如此。你我从未有分歧
经由哪扇门去休息。往事
和将来，我们略不在意。
你我不曾谈论男人与诗，

却谈远方战争的谣传，
直到你我皆无动于衷，
除了黄苹果诱人外裳，
虽被黄蜂破坏留下洞；

或黑暗水苏的岗哨，
或森林边缘世间最肃穆
的小花朵；或番红花貌，
紫中带白，像刚刚破土，

In sunless Hades fields. The war
Came back to mind with the moonrise
Which soldiers in the east afar
Beheld then. Nevertheless, our eyes

Could as well imagine the Crusades
Or Caesar's battles. Everything
To faintness like those rumours fades —
Like the brook's water glittering

Under the moonlight — like those walks
Now — like us two that took them, and
The fallen apples, all the talks
And silences — like memory's sand

When the tide covers it late or soon,
And other men through other flowers
In those fields under the same moon
Go talking and have easy hours.

来自无光的冥界。战争
回到脑海之中，月亮升起，
远在东边的战士都能
望见。然而，我们的双眸还是

能清晰地想象十字军、
凯撒的战役。一切暗淡
不清，像那些传闻消陨——
如溪流水，微微亮闪，

月光之下——如以往一样散步
如今——你我两位行者，
如落地苹果，所有倾诉
与寂静——像记忆的沙子，

迟早被那潮浪所没垮，
在那片土地的花丛中，
人们在同一轮明月下
闲谈，尽享时光的从容。

No One Cares Less than I

25, 26 May, 1916

"No one cares less than I,
Nobody knows but God,
Whether I am destined to lie
Under a foreign clod,"
Were the words I made to the bugle call in the morning.

But laughing, storming, scorning,
Only the bugles know
What the bugles say in the morning,
And they do not care, when they blow
The call that I heard and made words to early this morning.

百感交集

1916 年 5 月 25—26 日

清晨军号嘹亮，脑中闪现疑语：
“百感交集，人人欲知，
无人知晓，唯神能预，
是否注定命里
吾将客死他乡？”

号声咆哮，轻蔑激荡，
唯有军号知晓
清晨军号所嚷，
无情号角，
阵阵吹响，吾应清晨号响。

As the Team's Head-Brass

27 May, 1916

As the team's head-brass flashed out on the turn
The lovers disappeared into the wood.
I sat among the boughs of the fallen elm
That strewed the angle of the fallow, and
Watched the plough narrowing a yellow square
Of charlock. Every time the horses turned
Instead of treading me down, the ploughman leaned
Upon the handles to say or ask a word,
About the weather, next about the war.
Scraping the share he faced towards the wood,
And screwed along the furrow till the brass flashed
Once more.
                    The blizzard felled the elm whose crest
I sat in, by a woodpecker's round hole,
The ploughman said. "When will they take it away?"
"When the war's over." So the talk began —
One minute and an interval of ten,
A minute more and the same interval.
"Have you been out?" "No." "And don't want to, perhaps?"
"If I could only come back again, I should.

马队头戴黄铜挽具

1916 年 5 月 27 日

马队头戴黄铜挽具扭转时闪闪发亮，
此刻一对恋人消失在林中。
我坐在倒地的榆树枝间，
倒地的树占据了休耕地一角，
望着犁具逐渐缩小田芥
的黄色地盘。马儿每次转身
都没将我踩倒，农夫拽着
犁具上的套绳，时而搭话，
时而谈论天气，之后聊到战争。
面朝树林，犁着他的地，
顺着梨沟犁地直到黄铜挽具
再次闪耀。
　　　　　暴风雪吹倒了榆树，我坐在
树冠上，旁边有啄木鸟啄过的圆孔，
农夫问道：“他们何时将它拿走？”
“战争结束时。”话匣子就这样开启——
聊了一分钟，歇了十分钟，
又聊一分钟，又歇了十分钟。
“你出去过吗？”“没有。”“难道不想去吗？”
“要是我能再回来，我应该会。

I could spare an arm, I shouldn't want to lose
A leg. If I should lose my head, why, so,
I should want nothing more...Have many gone
From here?" "Yes." "Many lost?" "Yes: a good few.
Only two teams work on the farm this year.
One of my mates is dead. The second day
In France they killed him. It was back in March,
The very night of the blizzard, too. Now if
He had stayed here we should have moved the tree."
"And I should not have sat here. Everything
Would have been different. For it would have been
Another world." "Ay, and a better, though
If we could see all all might seem good." Then
The lovers came out of the wood again:
The horses started and for the last time
I watched the clods crumble and topple over
After the ploughshare and the stumbling team.

我可以牺牲一只胳膊，但我不想失去
一条腿。倘若我掉了脑袋，为何，如此，
我心应再无所恋……很多人从这儿
离开吗？”“是的。”“死了很多？”“是的，还挺多。
今年就只有两个马队在农场干活儿。
我有一个伙伴死了。他在法国
第二天就被杀了。那是三月的事儿了，
那晚正好也是狂风暴雪。假如现在
他仍待在这儿，我们应该会一起挪走这棵树。”
“我也不会坐在这儿。一切将会
变得不一样。因为那将是
另一番景象。”“哎，或许会更加美好，
如若我们能明白一切，或许万事顺意。”不久，
那对恋人再次走出树林：
马队复工，最后一次，
我望着土块被粉碎、倒塌
在犁耕和跌跌撞撞的马队后面。

After You Speak

3 June, 1916

After you speak
And what you meant
Is plain,
My eyes
Meet yours that mean —
With your cheeks and hair —
Something more wise,
More dark,
And far different.
Even so the lark
Loves dust
And nestles in it
The minute
Before he must
Soar in lone flight
So far,
Like a black star
He seems —
A mote
Of singing dust

你说之后

1916 年 6 月 3 日

你说之后，
你所指的
平淡直白，
我的双眼
直视你的双眼——
连同脸颊、头发——
暗含着更为聪慧、
更加幽玄、
不同寻常之事。
尽管如此，云雀
恋上尘埃
并筑巢其中，
不久
他必须
独自翱翔，
飞向遥远
如一颗玄星，
他看起来——
像一粒
歌吟的尘埃

Afloat
Above,
The dreams
And sheds no light.
I know your lust
Is love.

漂浮
上方，
梦想
毫无光亮。
我知道你的欲望
是爱。

Bright Clouds

4, 5 June, 1916

Bright clouds of may
Shade half the pond.
Beyond,
All but one bay
Of emerald
Tall reeds
Like criss-cross bayonets
Where a bird once called,
Lies bright as the sun.
No one heeds.
The light wind frets
And drifts the scum
Of may-blossom.
Till the moorhen calls
Again
Naught's to be done
By birds or men.
Still the may falls.

白云

1916 年 6 月 4—5 日

山楂花如簇簇白云，
遮蔽半塘。
远方，
只见江浔
高大芦苇，
苍翠绿翡，
交错如刀，
召唤栖鸟，
闪耀如日。
无人留意。
微风侵袭，
吹拂楂树
残花遍地。
未见松鸡
再鸣，
鸟未苏醒，
人未穿行。
山楂落英依然如故。

Early One Morning

8–11 June, 1916

Early one morning in May I set out,
And nobody I knew was about.
        I'm bound away for ever,
        Away somewhere, away for ever.

There was no wind to trouble the weathercocks.
I had burnt my letters and darned my socks.

No one knew I was going away,
I thought myself I should come back some day.

I heard the brook through the town gardens run.
O sweet was the mud turned to dust by the sun.

A gate banged in a fence and banged in my head.
"A fine morning, sir," a shepherd said.

I could not return from my liberty,
To my youth and my love and my misery.

清晨

1916 年 6 月 8—11 日

五月的一个清晨，我启程，
周围没有我熟悉的人。
　　我注定要离开，永不归来，
　　逃离某地，永不归来。

没有风来惹风向标。
我烧了信件，补了袜套。

没人知道我将要离开，
我想自己有朝一日终会归来。

我听见穿越小镇花园的溪流声。
噢，泥土芬芳，日照下化为粉尘。

篱笆大门嘣的一声，嘣响在我脑海里。
“清晨早安，先生”，一位牧羊人致意。

我无法从我的自由回到
我的青春、我的爱情和我的苦恼。

The past is the only dead thing that smells sweet,
The only sweet thing that is not also fleet.
    I'm bound away for ever,
    Away somewhere, away for ever.

过往仅是已死之物，却散发着芬芳，
而甜美芬芳之物亦不会好景不长。
　　我注定要离开，永不归来，
　　逃离某地，永不归来。

It Was upon

21 June, 1916

It was upon a July evening.
At a stile I stood, looking along a path
Over the country by a second Spring
Drenched perfect green again. "The lattermath
Will be a fine one." So the stranger said,
A wandering man. Albeit I stood at rest,
Flushed with desire I was. The earth outspread,
Like meadows of the future, I possessed.

And as an unaccomplished prophecy
The stranger's words, after the interval
Of a score years, when those fields are by me
Never to be recrossed, now I recall,
This July eve, and question, wondering,
What of the lattermath to this hoar Spring?

记得那是临近

1916 年 6 月 21 日

记得那是临近七月的一个夜晚，
我站在台阶上，顺道眺望
那乡村，挨着第二个清泉
再次透着纯绿色。“余波将
变美好。”陌生人如是诉言，
一位漫步者。我虽静静站着，
内心充满欲望。大地外延
像未来的草地，我拥有着。

作为一个未实现的预言，
那陌生人的话语，在时隔
二十年之后，当那些田园
我从未穿越时，如今忆着
这七月前夕，起疑，欲参悟：
白色清泉的余波为何物？

Bob's Lane

22 June, 1916

Women he liked, did shovel-bearded Bob,
Old Farmer Hayward of the Heath, but he
Loved horses. He himself was like a cob
And leather-coloured. Also he loved a tree.

For the life in them he loved most living things,
But a tree chiefly. All along the lane
He planted elms where now the stormcock sings
That travellers hear from the slow-climbing train.

Till then the track had never had a name
For all its thicket and the nightingales
That should have earned it. No one was to blame
To name a thing beloved man sometimes fails.

Many years since, Bob Hayward died, and now
None passes there because the mist and the rain
Out of the elms have turned the lane to slough
And gloom, the name alone survives, Bob's Lane.

鲍勃之道

1916年6月22日

他喜欢女人，胡须如铁锹般的鲍勃，
杜鹃花老农场主海沃德，爱慕
各种马。他自身就像一只矮脚马骡，
肤色如皮革。同时他也喜爱树木。

因热爱生命，他喜欢大多数的鲜活之物，
但主要是树。沿着那条小巷，两旁
他种满了榆树，如今，田鸫栖息吟诉，
匍匐前行的火车上，游人常听见。

在此之前，这小道从未有过名字，
尽管浓密的灌木，夜莺经常啼叫，
赋予它应有之名。没人会受申斥，
因命名心爱之物，虽然有时徒劳。

多年以后，鲍勃·海沃德离世，如今，
无人经过那里，因为榆树外的火车
与迷雾已将小道变成阴郁之境
和泥沼，仅名字“鲍勃之道”幸存着。[1]

---

[1] 诗人在此想表达的是文字或者确切地说地名是人类记忆的永恒存在方式，是自然生态和文化生态的载体。——译者注

There Was a Time

23 June, 1916

There was a time when this poor frame was whole
And I had youth and never another care,
Or none that should have troubled a strong soul.
Yet, except sometimes in a frosty air
When my heels hammered out a melody
From pavements of a city left behind,
I never would acknowledge my own glee
Because it was less mighty than my mind
Had dreamed of. Since I could not boast of strength
Great as I wished, weakness was all my boast.
I sought yet hated pity till at length
I earned it. Oh, too heavy was the cost.
But now that there is something I could use
My youth and strength for, I deny the age,
The care and weakness that I know — refuse
To admit I am unworthy of the wage
Paid to a man who gives up eyes and breath
For what would neither ask nor heed his death.

曾经

1916 年 6 月 23 日

曾经这可怜的躯体完好健全，
那时我拥有着青春，无虑无思，
从不被扰乱心神之事所牵缠。
但，除了偶尔遇到霜冷的气息，
我的脚后跟在被甩身后的城
中人行道上锤奏出一首妙曲，
我绝不会承认自己欣喜欢腾，
因为它比我内心所梦想之物
稍逊一筹。因我不会炫耀威力
如我所愿，软弱——我炫耀的身价。
我寻找却同时厌恶遗憾直至
最终获得。啊，多么惨重的代价！
然而，如今我却能为某事献出
自己的青春与力量，拒绝年事、
关心及自知之明的软弱——拒不
承认自己不值得那一份薪资，
若付给一位因不惧生死、奋身
不顾而放弃双眼与呼吸之人。

The Green Roads

28 June, 1916

The green roads that end in the forest
Are strewn with white goose feathers this June,

Life marks left behind by someone gone to the forest
To show his track. But he has never come back.

Down each green road a cottage looks at the forest.
Round one the nettle towers; two are bathed in flowers.

An old man along the green road to the forest
Strays from one, from another a child alone.

In the thicket bordering the forest,
All day long a thrush twiddles his song.

It is old, but the trees are young in the forest,
All but one like a castle keep, in the middle deep.

That oak saw the ages pass in the forest:
They were a host, but their memories are lost,

绿色之路

1916 年 6 月 28 日

条条绿色之路止于森林之中，
沿途零星点缀着六月白雁的羽毛，

前往森林的人留下生命的迹象，
以显示其足迹，然而一去不复返。

座座村舍顺着条条绿色之路俯瞰那座森林。
荨麻高耸覆盖其中一条；花丛沐浴着另外两条。

一位老者沿着一绿色之路前往森林，迷失
于其中一条，一个独行的孩童却迷失于另一条。

与森林接壤的灌木丛中，
一只画眉鸟整日在卖弄他的歌喉。

歌曲古老，而林中所有树木皆还年轻，
唯独正中央那棵城堡般的树已古邈穆清。

那棵橡树见证了林中所历经的岁月：
岁月主宰万物，其记忆却已消疏，

For the tree is dead: all things forget the forest
Excepting perhaps me, when now I see

The old man, the child, the goose feathers at the edge of the forest,
And hear all day long the thrush repeat his song.

因为那橡树已死：万物已忘记那片森林
或许除了我，因此刻我看见了

那位老人、那个孩童、那些白雁羽毛在森林边缘，
并听到了画眉鸟整日重复他的曲调。

The Gallows

3, 4 July, 1916

There was a weasel lived in the sun
With all his family,
Till a keeper shot him with his gun
And hung him up on a tree,
Where he swings in the wind and rain,
In the sun and in the snow,
Without pleasure, without pain,
On the dead oak tree bough.

There was a crow who was no sleeper,
But a thief and a murderer
Till a very late hour; and this keeper
Made him one of the things that were,
To hang and flap in rain and wind,
In the sun and in the snow.
There are no more sins to be sinned
On the dead oak tree bough.

There was a magpie, too,
Had a long tongue and a long tail;

绞刑架

1916 年 7 月 3—4 日

有只鼬鼠曾与家人一起
生活在阳光下，
直到一名猎手用枪将他击毙，
把他挂在枝丫，
任凭风吹雨打，
经历日晒雪蹂，
无痛无悦，
吊于枯橡枝头。

有只乌鸦曾不休不眠，
是一名小偷和凶手
直到最后一刻；这位猎手
同样将他吊于枝头，
任凭风雨拍敲，
经历日晒雪殄。
挂于枯橡树梢，
实属罪恶滔天。

还有只喜鹊曾长
长舌一个、长尾一条；

He could both talk and do —
But what did that avail?
He, too, flaps in the wind and rain
Alongside weasel and crow,
Without pleasue, without pain,
On the dead oak tree bough.

And many other beasts
And birds, skin, bone, and feather,
Have been taken from their feasts
And hung up there together,
To swing and have endless leisure
In the sun and in the snow,
Without pain, without pleasure,
On the dead oak tree bough.

他善行善言——
然而有何功效？
他同样任凭风雨摇曳，
与鼬鼠、乌鸦一道，
无痛无悦，
挂于枯橡树梢。

其他诸多鸟兽，
皮、骨、羽毛，
已迫离欢乐神守，
同样挂于树梢，
摇曳，无限悠闲
经历日晒雪蹂，
无痛无欢，
吊于枯橡枝头。

The Dark Forest

1, 5 and 10 July, 1916

Dark is the forest and deep, and overhead
Hang stars like seeds of light
In vain, though not since they were sown was bred
Anything more bright.

And evermore mighty multitudes ride
About, nor enter in;
Of the other multitudes that dwell inside
Never yet was one seen.

The forest foxglove is purple, the marguerite
Outside is gold and white,
Nor can those that pluck either blossom greet
The others, day or night.

幽林

1916 年 7 月 1、5、10 日

森林黑暗、幽深，繁星当空，
犹如光的种子
徒劳无益，但自从被播种
以来，万物明熠。

众神群仙经常林边驰骋，
却从来不进入；
而林中栖居的其他灵神，
芳容依旧难睹。

林中紫色的毛地黄，林外
金白色的雏菊，
而采花者只见花开采摘
却日夜难相聚。

When He Should Laugh

15 July, 1916

When he should laugh the wise man knows full well:
For he knows what is truly laughable.
But wiser is the man who laughs also,
Or holds his laughter, when the foolish do.

值得一笑时

1916 年 7 月 15 日

值得一笑时，智者全知晓：
心知且肚明，何事应欢笑。
更有聪慧者，或笑容依嘻，
或不苟言笑，愚者犹笑嗤。

How at Once

10 August, 1916

How at once should I know,
When stretched in the harvest blue
I saw the swift's black bow,
That I would not have that view
Another day
Until next May
Again it is due?

The same year after year —
But with the swift alone.
With other things I but fear
That they will be over and done
Suddenly
And I only see
Them to know them gone.

岂能马上

1916 年 8 月 10 日

我岂能马上知解
在丰收的蓝域中舒展时，
瞧见了雨燕的黑色蝴蝶结，
那景是否在其他的日子里
无法领略，
直至来年五月
它如期而至？

然而，年复一年——
与雨燕独自相处。
随同他物，我却惧惮
它们将会突然结束
并消藏；
我却睁眼
望着它们，心知其已远去。

Gone, Gone Again

3 September, 1916

Gone, gone again,
May, June, July,
And August gone,
Again gone by,

Not memorable
Save that I saw them go,
As past the empty quays
The rivers flow.

And now again,
In the harvest rain,
The Blenheim oranges
Fall grubby from the trees,

As when I was young —
And when the lost one was here —
And when the war began
To turn young men to dung.

流逝，再流逝

1916 年 9 月 3 日

流逝，再流逝，
五月、六月、七月、八月，
皆早已流逝，
并再次流逝，

孰忘孰顾？
唯有流逝，
如过空埠，
江水流逝。

而如今再次，
在丰收的雨季，
布伦海姆的柑橘
从树上坠落变脏，

当我年轻时——
当逝者埋葬于此——
当战争开始将
青年变为粪丸。

Look at the old house,
Outmoded, dignified,
Dark and untenanted,
With grass growing instead

Of the footsteps of life,
The friendliness, the strife;
In its beds have lain
Youth, love, age, and pain:

I am something like that;
Only I am not dead,
Still breathing and interested
In the house that is not dark: —

I am something like that:
Not one pane to reflect the sun,
For the schoolboys to throw at —
They have broken every one.

1916年

看那座旧房，
老式却庄严，
幽暗且空荡，
杂草正蔓延，

不见生活足迹，
友善、争吵难觅；
唯有床上曾经留住
青春、爱情、年老与痛苦：

我命亦如此；
只是今未死，
仍在呼吸，对明亮的房子
饶有兴致：——

我命亦如此：
无窗映阳曦，
供学童投掷——
他们已碎所有玻璃。

That Girl's Clear Eyes

10 September, 1916

That girl's clear eyes utterly concealed all
Except that there was something to reveal.
And what did mine say in the interval?
No more: no less. They are but as a seal
Not to be broken till after I am dead;
And then vainly. Every one of us
This morning at our tasks left nothing said,
In spite of many words. We were sealed thus,
Like tombs. Nor until now could I admit
That all I cared for was the pleasure and pain
I tasted in the stony square sunlit,
Or the dark cloisters, or shade of airy plane,
While music blazed and children, line after line,
Marched past, hiding the "Seventeen Thirty-Nine".

女孩双眸清澈

1916 年 9 月 10 日

女孩双眸清澈，彻底遮蔽
一切，不含已显现之物象。
间歇，我的双眼述说何事？
不多：不少。他们却如印章
不被损坏直到我死之后；
而后徒劳。我们每一个人，
今晨伏案工作，语不出口，
心中却千言万语。故此，我们
尘封如坟。如今，斗胆承认
我之所爱即欢乐与苦难，
曾体验过，在光照的寒石广场上，
在幽黑的回廊里，或在飞机的影子中，
当音乐奔放，孩童，一行又一行，
列队而过，遮住了“1739”字样。

What Will They Do

15 September, 1916

What will they do when I am gone? It is plain
That they will do without me as the rain
Can do without the flowers and the grass
That profit by it and must perish without.
I have but seen them in the loud street pass;
And I was naught to them. I turned about
To see them disappearing carelessly.
But what if I in them as they in me
Nourished what has great value and no price?
Almost I thought that rain thirsts for a draught
Which only in the blossom's chalice lies,
Until that one turned back and lightly laughed.

他们将何去何从

1916 年 9 月 15 日

我走后，他们将何去何从？
他们可以无我，正如雨散
可以无须花草一般，尽管
有雨百花盛，无雨千草枯。
只见他们穿过喧嚣马路；
对于他们，我如糠秕。转身
望着他们远逝，毫不在意。
若我们彼此心中孕育出
大爱却无价，将如何收场？
我顿悟：雨急需一场干旱，
而旱情仅存于花簇圣杯，
直到一方转身，微笑开眉。

The Trumpet

26–28? September, 1916

Rise up, rise up,
And, as the trumpet blowing
Chases the dreams of men,
As the dawn glowing
The stars that left unlit
The land and water,
Rise up and scatter
The dew that covers
The print of last night's lovers —
Scatter it, scatter it!

While you are listening
To the clear horn,
Forget, men, everything
On this earth newborn,
Except that it is lovelier
Than any mysteries.
Open your eyes to the air
That has washed the eyes of the stars
Through all the dewy night:
Up with the light,
To the old wars;
Arise, arise!

喇叭

1916年9月26—28日（不确定）

起床，起床，
号角吹起，
追逐士兵的梦，
黎明涌现，
繁星消逝，
山河明现，
起来，撩开
掩盖昨晚
恋人间印记的露珠——
拨开它，吹散它！

当你在聆听
清晰的号角时，
忘记人、世间
所有新生事物，
除了比神秘
更加美好的事物。
睁开你的双眼，看那空气
早已洗净繁星的双眸，
透过露水灵灵的夜幕：
随着晨曦升起，
走向古老的战争；
奋斗，奋斗！

When First

? October, 1916

When first I came here I had hope,
Hope for I knew not what. Fast beat
My heart at sight of the tall slope
Or grass and yews, as if my feet

Only by scaling its steps of chalk
Would see something no other hill
Ever disclosed. And now I walk
Down it the last time. Never will

My heart beat so again at sight
Of any hill although as fair
And loftier. For infinite
The change, late unperceived, this year,

The twelfth, suddenly, shows me plain.
Hope now, — not health nor cheerfulness,
Since they can come and go again,
As often one brief hour witnesses, —

初来乍到

1916 年 10 月某日

初来乍到，满怀希望，
而我不知何之所盼。
眺望高坡、草地、紫衫，
心跳加速，双脚好像

在白垩岩台阶踏行，
瞧见一些其他山坡
无法展现之物。如今，
我最后一次走下坡。

其他山峦，美丽依现，
愈加高耸，心潮不会
如初澎湃。因为无限
变化今年姗姗迟归，

十二月，突向我展露。
心愿——非健康，非欢喜，
因为他们匆匆来去，
如短暂时刻所证实，——

Just hope has gone forever. Perhaps
I may love other hills yet more
Than this: the future and the maps
Hide something I was waiting for.

One thing I know, that love with chance
And use and time and necessity
Will grow, and louder the heart's dance
At parting than at meeting be.

心愿早已永逝。或许
其他山峦，相比此处，
我会爱上：未来、地图
隐藏我所期待之物。

我深知爱随着需要、
用途、时间，还有时机，
会增长，心灵舞曲更妙，
离别之际，非见面时。

The Child in the Orchard

? October, 1916

"He rolls in the orchard: he is stained with moss
And with earth, the solitary old white horse.
Where is his father and where is his mother
Among all the brown horses? Has he a brother?
I know the swallow, the hawk, and the hern;
But there are two million things for me to learn.

"Who was the lady that rode the white horse
With rings and bells to Banbury Cross?
Was there no other lady in England beside

园中孩童

1916年10月某日

“他在果园中翻滚：沾满苔衣、
泥土，那匹老白马孤独无依。
在所有的棕色马群里，
父亲何在，母亲何在，有无兄弟？
我已知燕子、飞鹰和苍鹭，
仍有东西要研习，不可胜数。

“环铃白马前往班伯里十字碑[1]，
背上坐着的那位贵妇姓甚名谁？
难道英格兰附近无其他贵妇[2]

---

❶ 班伯里十字碑（Banbury Cross），是位于牛津郡班伯里集市小镇一条宽敞马路的十字路口。这座十字碑始建于中世纪，毁于17世纪初，重建于19世纪中期，以此来纪念1858年的一场皇家婚礼。英国一些儿歌经常传唱此碑，据传伊丽莎白一世曾经造访过此碑。——译者注

❷ 朗利教授查阅了《牛津儿歌词典》，据其所言，此处贵妇人或许指伊丽莎白一世或贵妇葛黛瓦。（LONGLEY E. Edward Thomas: the annotated collected poems[M]. Glasgow: Bell & Bain Limited, 2008: 314.）贵妇葛黛瓦（Lady Godiva）为一千年前生活在英格兰考文垂的一位伯爵夫人，因劝谏其伯爵丈夫减免苛捐杂税，而被伯爵挖苦，并建议她赤裸骑马绕城一圈，以此作为交换条件。贵妇欣然答应条件，游城一圈时，市民皆紧闭门窗，以示尊重。最终，伯爵被迫履行了诺言。英国不少艺术文学作品皆以这美丽的故事为创作源泉，例如，1898年约翰·柯里尔（John Collier）创作的一幅油画便叫作《马背上贵妇葛黛瓦》（“Lady Godiva”），以及托马斯这首诗歌。——译者注

That a nursery rhyme could take for a ride?
The swift, the swallow, the hawk, and the hern.
There are two million things for me to learn.

"Was there a man once who straddled across
The back of the Westbury White Horse
Over there on Salisbury Plain's green wall?
Was he bound for Westbury, or had he a fall?
The swift, the swallow, the hawk, and the hern.
There are two million things for me to learn.

"Out of all the white horses I know three,
At the age of six; and it seems to me
There is so much to learn, for men,
That I dare not go to bed again.
The swift, the swallow, the hawk, and the hern.
There are millions of things for me to learn."

供一首儿歌传唱其朝圣史录？
雨燕、家燕、飞鹰和苍鹭。
我仍有东西要研习，不可胜数。

“一匹威斯伯里白马跃然
索尔兹伯里平原绿墙上，
是否曾经有人跨坐过？
他去威斯伯里？可曾摔倒过？
雨燕、家燕、飞鹰和苍鹭。
我仍有东西要研习，不可胜数。

“所有白马中，我已知三匹，
时值六岁；依我看来，
人类有诸多东西要研习，
以至于我不敢再次就寝。
雨燕、家燕、飞鹰和苍鹭。
我仍有东西要研习，不可胜数。”

Lights Out

? November, 1916

I have come to the borders of sleep,
The unfathomable deep
Forest where all must lose
Their way, however straight,
Or winding, soon or late;
They cannot choose.

Many a road and track
That, since the dawn's first crack,
Up to the forest brink,
Deceived the travellers,
Suddenly now blurs,
And in they sink.

Here love ends,
Despair, ambition ends,
All pleasure and all trouble,
Although most sweet or bitter,
Here ends in sleep that is sweeter
Than tasks most noble.

灯熄

1916 年 11 月某日

我已至沉睡的边缘，
森林深不可探，
万物迟早会迷失
方向，无论笔直，
还是蜿蜒曲折；
他们无法选择。

许多道路小径，
自从晨曦初临，
延至森林边缘，
欺骗行人游子，
突然模糊升起，
然后他们沦陷。

此处爱终结，
绝望、雄心终结，
所有欢乐，所有烦膺，
无论苦或甜，
终结于更甜的睡眠，
不逊于神圣使命。

There is not any book
Or face of dearest look
That I would not turn from now
To go into the unknown
I must enter, and leave alone,
I know not how.

The tall forest towers;
Its cloudy foliage lowers
Ahead, shelf above shelf;
Its silence I hear and obey
That I may lose my way
And myself.

没有任何书本
或最慈祥的脸神，
如今令我无法转辙，
走进未知境地，
我须独自进入、别离，
但不知该如何。

森林高耸巍然；
叆叇的树叶向前
低垂，层层相叠；
聆听、遵循它的静谧
或许我会方向迷失，
自我迷邪。

The Long Small Room

? November, 1916

The long small room that showed willows in the west
Narrowed up to the end the fireplace filled,
Although not wide. I liked it. No one guessed
What need or accident made them so build.

Only the moon, the mouse, and the sparrow peeped
In from the ivy round the casement thick.
Of all they saw and heard there they shall keep
The tale for the old ivy and older brick.

When I look back I am like moon, sparrow, and mouse
That witnessed what they could never understand
Or alter or prevent in the dark house.
One thing remains the same — this my right hand

Crawling crab-like over the clean white page,
Resting awhile each morning on the pillow,
Then once more starting to crawl on towards age.
The hundred last leaves stream upon the willow.

长屋狭室

1916 年 11 月某日

西面杨柳栽，长屋狭室居，
逼仄至尽头，壁炉匠意巧，
尽管不宽敞。从不嫌其貌。
无人知其用，未晓其事故。

屋外青藤密，窗扉月徘徊，
鼠耗吱吱觑，麻雀唧唧窥。
双眼之所见，两耳之所闻，
倾诉古藤听，古砖音旋回。

顾首长相望，方觉已如月，
无异鼠与雀，唯有干瞪眼，
黑屋神秘显，无力变与防。
一物恒不变：右手拿书阅，

书页净且白，阅行如蟹爪，
清晨枕上卧，休憩养心静，
歇后继前行，无奈向终老。
柳树剩百叶，飘涌随风行。

The Sheiling

23 November, 1916

It stands alone
Up in a land of stone
All worn like ancient stairs,
A land of rocks and trees
Nourished on wind and stone.

And all within
Long delicate has been;
By arts and kindliness
Coloured, sweetened, and warmed
For many years has been.

Safe resting there
Men hear in the travelling air
But music, pictures see
In the same daily land

瑟聆居

1916 年 11 月 23 日 [1]

岩石属地，
独自屹立，
恰如古阶，风化腐蚀，
放眼望去，岩石树木
风石育滋。

村里万物，
柔和雅素；
艺术之作，不仁之功，
多年以来，斑斓色彩，
甜美气息，温暖情愫。

安心栖此，空气清婉，
每日天地之间，
聆听天籁之音，
观自然之图景，

[1] 托马斯前往湖区边坎福斯小镇（Carnforth）附近的锡尔弗代尔村庄（Silverdale），拜访好友诗人戈登·博顿利（Gordon Bottomley，1874—1948），并逗留其住所瑟聆居（The Sheiling）数日。此诗为托马斯回家后不久所作。——译者注

Painted by the wild air.

One maker's mind
Made both, and the house is kind
To the land that gave it peace,
And the stone has taken the house
To its cold heart and is kind.

自然之气造焉。

道之慧，天地之根：
土地屋舍不仁，
地赋恬和于屋，
屋舍寒石上，
却恬和不仁。

The Lane

? December, 1916

Some day, I think, there will be people enough
In Froxfield to pick all the blackberries
Out of the hedges of Green Lane, the straight
Broad lane where now September hides herself
In bracken and blackberry, harebell and dwarf gorse.
Today, where yesterday a hundred sheep
Were nibbling, halcyon bells shake to the sway
Of waters that no vessel ever sailed ...
It is a kind of spring: the chaffinch tries
His song. For heat it is like summer too.
This might be winter's quiet. While the glint
Of hollies dark in the swollen hedges lasts —
One mile — and those bells ring, little I know
Or heed if time be still the same, until
The lane ends and once more all is the same.

绿道

1916 年 12 月某日

思有朝一日，佛罗斯科地，
绿道宽且直，黑莓篱外延，
人头多攒动，意摘莓果归。
九月终来临，隐匿寻不见，
蕨莓蓝铃匿，矮雀花丛隐。
昔日百羊群，低头似嚼食，
而今太平铃，摇荡水波粼，
河流静寂寥，不曾舟舸行……
春景或如此：苍头燕雀啼，
清嗓试奏曲。暖热似夏季。
静如冬日谧。冬青幽暗立，
深藏胀篱中，荧华缝中透——
绵延一英里——铃儿声声脆，
启路前不知，光景如昔否？
直至路尽头，万物何其似！

Out in the Dark

24 December, 1916

Out in the dark over the snow
The fallow fawns invisible go
With the fallow doe;
And the winds blow
Fast as the stars are slow.

Stealthily the dark haunts round
And, when a lamp goes, without sound
At a swifter bound
Than the swiftest hound,
Arrives, and all else is drowned;

And star and I and wind and deer
Are in the dark together, — near,
Yet far, — and fear
Drums on my ear
In that sage company drear.

How weak and little is the light,
All the universe of sight,
Love and delight,
Before the might,
If you love it not, of night.

漆黑野甸

1916 年 12 月 24 日

茫茫大雪，漆黑野甸，
黄褐小鹿，若隐若现，
母鹿同迁，
风急狂掀，
繁星迟至，点缀天边。

夜幕潜伏，绵延万里，
灯火无声，极速跃熄，
猎犬虽驰，
其速不及，
抵达之际，万物淹溺。

星辰与我，狂风与鹿，
似近实远，共享黑幕，
闻听恐惧，
声如击鼓，
智鹿为伴，犹生阴郁。

放眼望去，光暗微小，
宇宙乾坤，无穷浩邈，
爱薄欢寥，
夜道玄妙，
不仁与君，爱若稀少。

The Year 1917

1917 年

The Sorrow of True Love

13 January, 1917

The sorrow of true love is a great sorrow
And true love parting blackens a bright morrow.
Yet almost they equal joys, since their despair
Is but hope blinded by its tears, and clear
Above the storm the heavens wait to be seen.
But greater sorrow from less love has been
That can mistake lack of despair for hope
And knows not tempest or the perfect scope
Of summer, but a frozen drizzle perpetual
Of drops that from remorse and pity fall
And cannot ever shine in the sun or thaw,
Removed eternally from the sun's law.

真爱之哀

1917 年 1 月 13 日

倘若真爱只堪哀，世间凄怆恰如斯，
两情相爱伤离别，明媚翌日亦悲嘶。
忆昔欢愉情意绵，无奈终须道别离，
绝望无缘盼相逢，泪水遮蔽前路迷，
穹顶之下风雨至，穹顶之上晴空现。
那堪真爱方渐少，满腹心酸更漪涟，
悲情不知晴何处，错把无惘作希望，
怅惋不知风雨怒，不觉夏日犹晴朗，
只记冰雨滴滴坠，不知何时是方休，
意恐悔恨无尽时，可怜遗憾不绝休，
乌阳未曾见闪耀，烈日不曾闻融泣，
渐行渐远离日道，此后绵绵无绝期。

Afterword

Edward Thomas, who was born in London and graduated from the University of Oxford, was a reknowned Anglophone Welsh poet of the early 20th century. Before morphing into a poet, he had been quite an established literary critic and essayist in England. He was a close friend of Robert Frost, an eminent American poet. They had a literary friendship that could not be erased in the history of British and American literatures. Initially, Frost's future as a poet in the United States was unforeseeable, and he was so dismayed that he decided to set foot on the road to Britain, to start a new life. When the American poet came to England in 1912, he was still unknown. Thomas, by contrast, was then quite a prominent figure. After the two men met for the first time, both felt mutually like-minded. With the deepening of their personal relationship, the two naturally realized that they could support each other in literature. Thomas aimed to make Frost well-known in the circle of English poets[1], while the latter returned the favor by inspiring the former's poetic talent[2], meanwhile encouraging and suggesting that his prose

---

❶ SPENCER M (ed.). Elected friends: Robert Frost and Edward Thomas to one another[M]. New York: Handsel Books, 2003: xi.

❷ SMITH S. Edward Thomas[M]. London and Boston: Faber and Faber,1986: 167.

译后记

爱德华·托马斯，生于伦敦，毕业于牛津大学，为20世纪初著名的盎格鲁—威尔士诗人。成为诗人之前，其在英国便已是小有名气的文学评论家和散文家。他与美国著名诗人罗伯特·佛罗斯特互为挚友，有着一段在英美文学史上难以抹去的文学友谊。当初，佛罗斯特在美国诗界的前途渺茫，一筹莫展，故而决定踏上前往英国之路，寻找新的生机。这位美国诗人于1912年来到英国，仍旧默默无名；相反，托马斯彼时已是一名响当当的人物。二人初次见面后，均感志趣相投，相见恨晚。随着私交的不断深入，双方自然而然地意识到在文学上彼此可以相互帮助与提携。托马斯帮助佛罗斯特在英国诗界扬名，后者则激发前者的诗歌创作才能，鼓励并建议其将所写的散文作品

be rewritten in poetic forms[1]. Therefore, Thomas was heartened and grew more confident in poetry writing. In October 1914, he began to write poems formally.

Absorbing the essence from his own earlier prose works, Thomas modified and polished them into poems, which rendered him increasingly adept in poetic art. Despite his short life, his great talent and increasing inspiration during the less than three years prior to his death led him to compose 142 poems (144 poems by a different scholarship) in total which have widely spread in later generations. His poems vary in theme, including war, love, family, flora and fauna, landscape, nature, and folklore. Generally, they are gloomy and heavy in tone but restrained in emotion, reflective and philosophical in thought, and pure, simple, vigorous, and forceful in language; some lyrical like prose, some critical like literary criticism, some finely-rhymed and some free in scansion. Unfortunately, however, his poems were not widely accepted by the academia of English poetry at that time when he published his works sporadically. For example, in 1915, Thomas embedded two of his own poems when editing the anthology entitled ***This England*** for Oxford University Press. Another seven were published in some small literary magazines such as ***Root and Branch*** and ***Form and Poetry***. In 1916, the poet published six poems under the pen name Edward Eastaway in what was then called The Pear Tree Press, a small private London publisher.

---

[1] LONGLEY E. Introduction[M]// LONGLEY E. Edward Thomas: the annotated collected poems. Glasgow: Bell & Bain Limited, 2008: 11-27 (14-15).

修改成诗。故此，托马斯备受鼓舞，写诗的自信心倍增，于1914年10月开始正式进行诗歌创作。

托马斯从早期的散文作品中吸取精华，并将其修改润色成诗，且技艺不断娴熟。尽管英年早逝，在逝世前近三年的时光里，托马斯才思泉涌，诗兴大发，共创作了142首诗歌（亦有144首之说），流传于后世。诗歌涵盖战争、爱情、家庭、动植物生态、乡村风景、自然、民俗风情等丰富的主题；诗风沉郁隐忍，善于反思，富含哲理，语言质朴纯净，苍劲有力，既有散文的抒情性笔调，亦有文艺批评的犀利笔锋；格律上，既有韵律诗，亦有自由诗。然而，不幸的是生前其诗作并未得到当时英国诗坛的广泛认同，且只是零星发表，如1915年，托马斯为牛津大学出版社编撰的《此英格兰》诗集中即收入了两首其自创作品。另有7首作品分别发表在《根与枝》《形与诗》等文学小杂志上。1916年，他以笔名爱德华·伊斯特威在伦敦一家名叫梨树出版社的私人小出版社出版了6首诗歌作品。

The depression that plagued the poet worsened after marriage: Thomas's pressure came not only from his lofty ideals and unyielding rigidity for literary creative writing and poetry criticism, but also from his high sense of family responsibility. He enlisted in the British army in July 1915 as a map reader, in hopes that joining in the First World War in France could serve as a means of both achieving his high-minded ambitions and dealing with the depression issue. In early 1917, as a second lieutenant in the Royal Artillery, he was sent to the battlefield in France. However, something unexpected ensued shortly: on the April 9th of the same year, he was killed in action by a 77 mm. shell in the Battle of Arras. He died at age 39.

In October 1917 and December 1918, his two collections *Poems* and *Last Poems* came out successively. In 1920, *Selected Poems*, containing his 135 poems, was published with a preface by his friend Walter de la Mare. It is a pity, however, that Thomas would never be able to witness all those glorious moments himself.

After his demise, Thomas's poetry attracted an increasing attention from the field of British poetry and literary academia. Thomas's reputation as a poet was not formally established until his quietus. This "posthumous reputation" view has also been firmly held by British literary academia.[1] Later, through the tireless efforts of a number of British scholars and poets, Thomas eventually was enshrined as a "war poet" in the poets' corner of Westminster Abbey in London in 1985. Officiating the ceremony of unveiling the War

---

[1] WISNIEWSKI J. Edward Thomas: a mirror of England[M]. Newcastle upon Tyne: Cambridge Scholars Publishing, 2009: 207.

托马斯婚后一直深受抑郁症困扰。压力源自其自身对文学创作和诗评有着崇高的理想与严格的要求，同时也源自其高度的家庭责任感。他于 1915 年 7 月应征入伍，成为一名英国陆军地图观察员，希望通过参军，前往法国加入第一次世界大战，一方面意在实现建功立业的远大理想，另一方面企图以此来解决自身的抑郁症问题。1917 年，作为皇家炮队少尉，诗人被派往法国战地。然而，天有不测风云：同年 4 月 9 日，托马斯在阿拉斯战役中不幸被 77 毫米弹片击中当场身亡，年仅 39 岁。

其诗集《诗歌》《最后诗篇》在诗人逝世之后同年 10 月和翌年 12 月，相继问世。1920 年，《诗选集》也正式出版，该诗集收入了 135 首诗，由诗人好友沃尔特·德·拉·梅尔为其作序。只可惜托马斯永远无法亲眼见证这些光荣的时刻了。

诗人死后，其诗歌才逐渐引起了英国诗界和学界的重视。托马斯的诗人身份，死后才被正式确立起来。这“垂诗名于身后”之观点也是英国学界一直以来所持有的比较稳妥的看法。后来，通过一些英国学者和诗人的不懈努力，1985 年托马斯最终以“战争诗人”的身份，位列伦敦威斯敏斯特教堂“诗人角”。在当时“战争诗人纪念活动”的揭幕仪式上，英国已逝的著名桂冠

Poets Memorial, Ted Hughes, a late British poet laureate, hailed Thomas as "the father of us all" [1]. This suggests that Thomas's poetics has been a profound effect on later British poets. By Jacek Wisniewski's statistics, the influenced poets include W. H. Auden, Alun Lewis, Geoffrey Hill, R. S. Thomas, Philip Larkin, Gavin Ewart, David Harsent, Andrew Motion, Seamus Heaney, Michael Longley, Derek Mahon, Tom Paulin as well as Ted Hughes.[2] In the process of translating the third National Poet of Wales Gillian Clarke into Chinese contexts, I found traces of Thomas's poetic influence in her works.[3] A review of *The Irish Times* also informs that Clarke loves Thomas's poetry so much that her poems are naturally embedded with a Thomas-like angle.[4] She even wrote a poem entitled "Nettles: for Edward Thomas" to pay tribute

---

❶ LONGLEY E. Under the same moon: Edward Thomas and the English lyric[M]. London: Enitharmon Press, 2017: 263, 291.

❷ WISNIEWSKI J. Edward Thomas: a mirror of England[M]. Newcastle upon Tyne: Cambridge Scholars Publishing, 2009: 225.

❸ For details about Clarke's poetics, see: XU J. Gillian Clarke: writing for the tribe and Welsh ecology[J]. Foreign literature and art. 2016, 6: 38-50.

❹ As for her collection *The Sundial*, a review of *The Irish Times* points out the relationship between Clarke and Thomas: it 'remains at a proper emotional distance from her Welsh scenes, allowing them to speak for themselves··· beautifully achieves an Edward Thomas-like perspective'. The Irish times [J/OL]. [2017-02-06]. http://www.gillianclarke.co.uk/gc2017/reviews/.

诗人泰德·休斯曾高度赞誉托马斯为“我们所有诗人之父”。由此可见，托马斯的诗风对其后世诗人有着深远的影响。据亚切克·维什涅夫斯基统计，深受托马斯影响的英国著名诗人除了休斯之外，还有其他十几位，比如W. H. 奥登、阿伦·刘易斯、杰弗里·希尔、R. S. 托马斯、菲利普·拉金、加文·伊沃特、大卫·哈森、安德鲁·姆辛、谢默斯·希尼、迈克尔·朗利、德里克·马洪、汤姆·保林等。在汉译和引介第三任威尔士民族诗人吉莲·克拉克的过程中，笔者发现其作品亦有托马斯的诗风痕迹。❶ 据《爱尔兰时报》的一篇诗评所言，诗人吉莲如此喜爱托马斯诗歌以至于其诗自然而然地流露出托马斯式的视角。❷ 她甚至还写了一首题为《荨麻：致爱德华·托马斯》的诗致敬托马斯，回应其诗作《高荨麻》。另一位崇拜托马斯的威尔士诗人便是第一任威尔士民族诗人格温妮丝·刘易斯。2017年，因一次偶然的机会，笔者有幸在托马斯曾经走过的

---

❶ 欲知克拉克诗学理念，详见拙文：许景城. 吉莲·克拉克：为族群发声、为生态言说的威尔士民族诗人 [J]. 外国文艺, 2016, 6: 38–50.

❷ 《爱尔兰时报》的一篇诗评就吉莲的诗集《日晷》指出了吉莲与托马斯的关系：此诗集在情感上与威尔士风景保持适当的距离，以便它们能为自己言说……完美地获得了爱德华·托马斯式的视角。The Irish times [J/OL]. [2017–02–06]. http://www.gillianclarke.co.uk/gc2017/reviews/.

to Thomas in response to his poem "Tall Nettles".[1] Another Welsh poet who admires Thomas is Gwyneth Lewis, the first National Poet of Wales. By chance, I was lucky enough to have a face-to-face encounter in 2017 with her in a picturesque countryside of South Wales where Thomas once walked. Asked if she was impacted by Thomas, she responded frankly with a positive yes and upheld the eulogization on Thomas for his unique poetics. From all this it fellows that Thomas has been influential one way or another among generations of British poets, enjoying a tremendous increase in prestige in the history of British poetry.

Why does Thomas's reputation as a poet come on the rise after his death and remain so enduring? Probably the answer can be found from the preface written by Andrew Motion, the Britain's Poet Laureate from 1999 to 2009, for the book ***Branch-Lines: Edward Thomas and Contemporary Poetry***:

> Thomas's overall vigilance, his attention to neglectable details, his sympathetic quiet-speaking, his genius for producing poems which appear to think aloud rather than be a means of delivering finished thoughts: all these things make this work [referring to

[1] Cf. A short history of poetry in Wales[J]. Welsh writers' trust. July 12, 2014. [2017-02-06]. https://welshwriterstrust.wordpress.com/2014/07/12/a-short-history-of-poetry-in-wales/.

2017 年 4 月 21 日与诗人格温妮丝在布雷肯比肯斯国家公园（Brecon Beacons National Park）

风景宜人的威尔士南部乡村与她进行了面对面的交谈。被问及是否深受托马斯影响之时，她坦诚相告，给予了肯定的回答，并高度赞扬了托马斯独特的诗风。可见，托马斯影响了一代又一代的英国诗人，在英国诗坛拥有崇高的地位。

为什么作为诗人的托马斯死后却名声鹊起，影响力经久不衰？英国桂冠诗人（1999—2009）安德鲁·姆辛在为《支线：爱德华·托马斯与当代诗歌》一书作序时给出了答案：

> 托马斯周身的警惕性，对易被忽略之物的关注，他同情的低语述说，及其在诗歌创作时所展示的深度思考过程而非传达思考成型的思想这一天赋才华：正是这些要素促使这部作品（即《支线》一书）活灵活现，甚至不言而喻

> *Branch-Lines*] intensively alive, even as they prove it to be a storehouse of qualities identified with the "English line" which runs back to the Romantics (Wordsworth and Clare especially) and forward to Larkin and other more recent poets who are interested in what we now call "environmental issues".[1]

Motion's acknowledgement above of Thomas's unique poetics and his important position in the development of English poetry is actually an echo of the claim by Edna Longley, a prestigious Thomas Studies scholar and an Irish literary critic from the Queen's University in Belfast, Northern Ireland. Longley has been digging into the poet's works, arguing that Thomas who inherited the strong tradition of English poetry could be enshrined somewhere between romanticism and modernism, in the line from William Wordsworth, John Clare, all through Thomas Hardy, Ted Hughes, Philip Larkin to R. S. Thomas. In her view, Thomas is undoubtedly a significant "missing link between Hardy and Larkin"[2]. Thus it can be concluded that Thomas is indeed a great poet in the history of British poetry.

---

[1] MOTION A. Foreword[M]// CUTHBERSON G and NEWLYN L. Branch-lines: Edward Thomas and contemporary poetry. London: Enitharmon Press, 2007: 11-12 (11).

[2] LONGLEY E. Poetry in the wars[M]. Newcastle: Bloodaxe, 1986: 113.

> 地让它成了各种诗艺的汇集地，汇聚了“英格兰诗歌传统”，上可追溯到浪漫主义诗人（尤其是华兹华斯和克莱尔），下可延伸到拉金或者其他诸多当下所谓的“环境议题”诗人。

从上可知，姆辛指出了托马斯独特的诗学理念并高度肯定了托马斯在英国诗歌发展中所处的重要地位。这其实呼应了北爱尔兰贝尔法斯特女王大学文艺批评教授、著名的托马斯研究专家埃德娜·朗利的相关主张。她一直致力于研究托马斯的文学作品，为其立论言说，论证了托马斯继承了浓厚的英格兰诗歌传统，肯定了他的文学地位是介于浪漫主义与现代主义之间，上承华兹华斯、约翰·克莱尔、哈代，下启泰德·休斯、菲利普·拉金和R. S. 托马斯。正如朗利所言，“倘若哈代与拉金之间缺少重要一环的话，毫无疑问那一环便是爱德华·托马斯”。由此可见，托马斯在英国诗歌史上的确是一位承上启下的伟大诗人。

The Poster of the Edward Thomas Centenary Conference 2017

The Thomas scholarship has in recent decades been increasing and unfolding with the enriching and deepening of his identity. Because of certain poems' insinuation about the First World War and of his sacrifice in the war, he is widely known as a "war poet". Due to the depiction of English landscape in his verses, he is also regarded as a "nature poet", or an "ecological poet" by some school of Thomas studies spearheaded by Longley who also encourages and motivates scholars of interest to conduct further research into Thomas's works. By virtue of the unceasing support from Longley and of the professional arrangement led by Professor Katie Gramich and Dr Jamie Castell from the School of English, Communication and Philosophy, Cardiff University, Wales, the Edward Thomas Centenary Conference was successfully held at Cardiff University from 19th to

2017 年 4 月 20 日在朗利教授新书发布会上 (At Longley's Book Launch)

托马斯研究近几十年来一直方兴未艾，诗人的身份名片也一直在不断丰富与深化。因其诗影射一战情形，并且其本人战死沙场，托马斯普遍被英国学界视为“战争诗人”，又因其诗中涉及英格兰自然风景描写，而被以朗利为首的托马斯研究学派称为“生态诗人”或“自然诗人”。朗利还鼓励学界继续深入研究托马斯作品。在她的大力支持和威尔士卡迪夫大学英语交际哲学学院凯蒂·格拉米琪教授和杰米·卡斯特尔博士的共同筹备下，2017 年 4 月 19 日至 21 日期间，卡迪夫大学成功举办了“爱德华·托马斯逝世百年学术研讨会”，以纪念托马斯去世 100 周年。会议期间，朗利还召开了新书发布会，签售最新力作《明月共此时：爱德华·托马斯与英语抒情诗》。此学术盛宴与会者近百人，笔者亦在此

21st April, 2017 to commemorate the 100th anniversary of Thomas's death. During the conference, a book launch was organized for Longley's latest book entitled ***Under the Same Moon: Edward Thomas and the English Lyric***. This academic feast was attended by nearly 100 participants, including me who shared my own research with the experts and scholars present. My presented paper discusses how Thomas offers insight into the "kin(d)ship" between humans and the non-human natural world in his poetry from the perspective of the "Non-mercy" ("Buren") Daoist ecology. On a related note, the case study of my doctoral thesis titled ***Early Daoism, Ecocriticism, and the Anthropocene: The Case of Edward Thomas*** also pivots around Thomas's poetry by lending the ecocritical prism to the review and interpretation of his works within the framework of early Daoist ecology.[1]

Presented at the Conference in Cardiff University, 19th April, 2017

[1] For details, please see XU J. Early Daoism, ecocriticism and the Anthropocene: the case of Edward Thomas[D]. Bangor: Prifysgol Bangor University, 2018.

列，与参会专家学者分享了自己的研究成果。笔者的参会文章重在从中国道家“不仁”生态视角探析托马斯诗歌作品中人与非人世界的“友善”关系。笔者的博士论文《早期道家、生态批评、人类世：爱德华·托马斯案例研究》的相关案例研究章节关注对象亦是托马斯的诗歌作品，主要在生态批评视域下将其作品放在早期道家生态理论框架下进行观照和阐释。

2017 年 4 月 21 日循着诗人托马斯曾经留下的足迹，徒步来到威尔士南部布雷肯国家公园的 Llyn-y-Fan Fach 小湖旁，与参会的诗人、学者托马斯 · 泰瑞尔博士（Dr Thomas Tyrrell）和 BBC 威尔士电台记者黛娜 · 琼斯女士（Ms Dinah Jones）共同演绎托马斯的诗歌作品

During my doctoral study, I translated into Chinese the whole range of Thomas's poetry. This translation work is published for three reasons.

Firstly, my later archival search informs that there has been no Chinese translation in complete spectrum of Thomas's poetry ever published in printed form in China, although some sporadic or relatively epic scale of Chinese translations can be seen online as well as two pieces — "Cherry Trees" and "The Owl" translated by Professor Zuoliang Wang in his monograph *A History of English Poetry*, and some short poems by Thomas quoted in some domestic texbooks of British and American poetry for Chinese university students. It should be noted that my enterprise of translating Thomas's poems into Chinese which was in sync with my doctoral study initiated in North Wales from September 2013 was aimed at facilitating the later writing-up of my doctoral thesis. Before, during and after the translation, I have never referred to any rendition available online. In this sense, my translation is original. In other words, this translation work is both a catalyser to and a derivative from the translator's doctoral dissertation. It principally adopts both literal and free translation approaches to faithfully represent at their full wings Thomas's poetic techniques and ideas.

Secondly, Thomas's works are strongly imbued with ecological insights. Unravelling them in the framework of early Daoist ecology, my doctoral research finds that although Thomas and early Daoists across time and space share a large variety of unexpected affinities in ecological wisdom. It is guided by the experimental thought of probing into "the unexpected affinities" and by my own translation

笔者在读博期间，曾汉译了托马斯诗歌作品全集。出版此译著，原因有三。

第一，据笔者后期检索发现目前国内尚未有托马斯诗歌全集汉译出版，尽管有一些零星或较为完整的译作散落于网络，以及王佐良教授的著作《英国诗史》中提及了《樱桃树》和《枭》（即本译集中的《猫头鹰》）两首诗，还有一些英美诗歌选集教材中涉及部分托马斯短诗。需要申明的是，笔者从 2013 年 9 月北威尔士读博开始，便着手汉译托马斯诗歌全集，以便开展博士论文研究与后期写作，始终未参考网上任何已有的译作，故此，译笔彰显原创性。换句话说，此译著是译者博士论文的催化剂和衍生品。译文主要采用直译和意译相结合的翻译方法，尽最大努力忠实地再现托马斯的诗艺和诗学理念。

忧郁的诗人爱德华·托马斯

第二，托马斯作品具有浓厚的生态韵味，笔者博士论文将其放在中国早期道家生态思想框架下进行对比关照解读，发现了二者所处时空虽不同却在生态思想方面有着诸多异曲同工之处。正是带着这种探寻“异曲同工之处”的实验思想，秉承自己长期诗歌翻译实践而总结出来的译诗理

belief firmly grounded on my long practice of poetic translation (i.e. "The way of poetic translation acknowledges poetic translation through philosophical underpinning, and philosophical ideas through poetic interpretation in pursuit of the mutual echoing and integration of poetry and philosophy.") that I occasionally and unconsciously adopted Aligned Meanings[1] as one of the translation approaches used to display Thomas's Daoist-like ideas in a deeper and better manner during the translation of his poems such as "The Other", "Lob" "The Glory" "July" "The Word" "For These" "The Sheiling" "Out in the Dark" "The Sorrow of True Love" to name but a few. Noted that the "unexpected affinities" expressed in the Chinese translations are occasioned not simply by my benevolent behaviour of "violent translation" but more significantly by the echoing ideas conveyed in Thomas's poems themselves. That is to say, in addition to maintaining the fidelity to the original texts, my volume also harnesses Aligned Meanings as a translation strategy by lending the angles and insights from traditional Daoist ecological poetics to the interpretation of

[1] This translation approach was primarily adopted by ancient Chinese translators and scholars when translating Indian Buddhist scriptures by resorting to traditional Chinese Daoist and Confucian thoughts and concepts. Nonetheless, the approach I use here to translate Western poems like Thomas's to some extent can be regarded as a bold attempt, an experimental and creative practice in the contemporary age. For details about the history and the method of Aligned Meanings, please see: SAUSSY H. Translation as citation: Zhuangzi inside out[M]. New York: Oxford University Press, 2017: 61-94; XU J. Review of Haun Saussy, *translation as citation: Zhuangzi inside out*[J]. Modern language review, 114.2(2019):341-343; GAO S, LIU Y. Aligned Meanings: an approach of integrating thoughts[J]. Foreign languages research. (4)2006: 52-56; QIU H. A textual research of Geyi (Aligned Meanings) in strategy evolution of translating Buddhism into Chinese[J]. Foreign language learning theory and practice. (4)2009: 71-75.

念"以哲译诗，以诗释哲，诗哲相融，译诗之道"，笔者在翻译托马斯作品时，偶尔不知不觉地会采用"格义"策略❶作为其中一种翻译方法，使某些译作更好地、更深层次地展示出托马斯的"道家思想"，比如《他者》《罗勃》《荣耀》《七月》《言道》《心之所盼》《瑟聆居》《漆黑野甸》《真爱之哀》等作品，不一而足。当然，需要申明的是译作中这种看似有意的"异曲同工之处"并非笔者纯粹的"暴力翻译"之善举，而是诗人诗歌本身所具有的类似思想使然。换言之，在忠实于原作思想的基础上，拙著还采用了"格义"策略，借用传统道家生态诗学视角译介托马斯诗学，与笔者博士论文相互照应，力图有理有据地为托马斯构建一张新的身份名片，即"类道家诗人"，以期丰富

❶ "格义"策略多为中国古代译者、学者汉译印度佛经时所采用的方法，即用中国传统儒道概念与思想来进行阐释。尽管如此，本译著将其用于汉译西方诗歌的翻译行为从某种程度上可被视为一种当代实验性和创新性的大胆尝试与实践。欲知"格义"翻译策略及其历史，详见 SAUSSY H. Translation as citation: Zhuangzi inside out[M]. New York: Oxford University Press, 2017: 61–94; XU J. Review of Haun Saussy, *translation as citation: Zhuangzi inside out*[J]. Modern language review, (114.2)2019: 341–343; 高圣兵，刘莺．"格义"：思想杂合之途[J]. 外语研究．(4)2006: 52–56; 裘禾敏．从格义看佛教中国化过程中翻译策略的演进[J]. 外语教学理论与实践．(4)2009: 71–75.

Thomas's poetics. By so doing, echoing what the doctoral thesis does, it aims to enrich Thomas studies by virtue of the well-grounded construction of a new title, i.e., "Daoist-like poet" for Thomas, and meanwhile contributes to boosting the enterprise of traditional Chinese culture and literature "going global" in response to the "Belt and Road Initiative" and the call of "telling China's story well" by integrating Chinese elements into the interpretation of Thomas's poetry through a Chinese prism. It is my sincere and ultimate hope that it will offer both readers and scholars home and abroad a platform of transcultural and transtextual communication across time and space.

Thirdly, upon the centenary year (2017) of Thomas's death, the timely publication of the Chinese translation of Thomas's poetry in entire body is of great significance, which will not only further promote the cultural and literary exchanges between China and Britain, but also deepen Thomas studies by comprehensively introducing Thomas to Chinese readers, and inspiriting more Chinese scholars to study and interpret him and his poetry from different angles.

At the Edward Thomas Exhibition, Special Collections and Archives, Arts and Social Studies Library of Cardiff University, 19th April, 2017

My Chinese translation is based on *Edward Thomas: The Annotated Collected Poems* edited

托马斯研究，同时加入中国的元素，从中国视角阐发托马斯诗歌，也有助于中国传统文化文学“走出去”，响应“一带一路”倡议和“讲好中国故事”号召，最终真挚地希冀为中西学人搭建跨时空、跨文化、跨文本的交流平台。

《爱德华·托马斯：诗集详注》

第三，正值2017年托马斯逝世100周年之际，乘势出版其诗歌汉译集，意义非同凡响，既能进一步推动中英文化文学交流，同时也能丰富深化托马斯研究；向中国读者全面译介托马斯，有益于更多的中国学者从不同角度对托马斯及其诗歌进行阐释研究。

此次汉译所依据的英诗蓝本是埃德娜·朗利教授所编撰的《爱德华·托马斯：诗集详注》。该版本由英国著名非营利性文学出版社

by Professor Longley and published in 2008 by Bloodaxe Books, a leading non-profit literary British publisher. The annotated version, an updated one of Longley's 1973 collection of Thomas's poems, details the composition date for each poem and offers intertextual notes. The annotation section includes the quotes of similar themes or ideas from the poet's prose and personal letters, and also relevant arguments from Thomas scholarship (mainly in the UK) over the past decades. It should be stated that my Chinese version is not a word-for-word translation of Longley's updated edition from cover to cover; rather it is based simply on the section of Thomas's poetry edited by Longley and excludes the explanatory notes. Surely, it is a common practice to present Thomas's poems chronologically by composition date in my translation book in the same manner the Longley version presents.

Before publishing my translation, I have contacted some relevant board members of the Edward Thomas Fellowship Committee for the copyright issue of Thomas's works, such as Mr Jeremy Mitchell, who offered positive response and strong support. My attempts to approach by various means Ms Lucy Milner, the poet's great-granddaughter who is alleged to own the rights to Thomas's works have not given rise to something fruitful: she has not replied yet. However, it is my hope and belief that she will offer endorsement as well. Of interesting note is that since Thomas has been dead for over a hundred years, and his works have already entered the public domain, there is no copyright dispute whatsoever. In any case, I am grateful to the Edward Thomas Fellowship Committee and to the poet's descendants for their support.

血斧出版社于2008年出版。该详注诗集为朗利1973年汇编托马斯诗集的升级版，详实记录了每首诗的创作时间，并对每首诗进行了互文性的注释。注释内容涉及诗人的散文、个人信函中类似的主题或观点，以及过去几十年英国学界托马斯作品研究的相关论点。需要强调的是此汉译本仅以郎利教授汇编的诗歌作品为蓝本，并非逐字逐句地汉译其作品，其注释部分不在汉译之列。此汉译本诗歌排序类似于郎利版本的诗歌排序，皆按诗歌创作时间先后排序。此乃惯例。

译作出版之前，笔者曾与爱德华·托马斯研究机构委员会相关理事会成员如杰拉米·米切尔先生联系过，询问相关作品版权问题，得到了其正面回应和大力支持。也曾多渠道尝试与托马斯作品的版权持有者——（据说是）诗人托马斯的曾孙女露西·米尔纳女士进行联系沟通，却始终未能如愿。然而，笔者相信并希望，她也会给予大力支持。由于托马斯已逝世百年，其作品早已进入公版期，故此，并无任何版权争议问题。无论如何，笔者对爱德华·托马斯研究机构委员会和诗人的后代子孙所（要）给予的支持深表感谢。

My wholehearted gratitude primarily goes to China Scholarship Council and Bangor University for co-funding my PhD program from where this translation book originated. During the doctoral study, my PhD supervisor, Dr Andrew Webb, Dean of the School of Linguistics, Languages and Literatures, Bangor University, Wales, and an Edward Thomas scholar, gave careful and professional guidance, and were always ready to help contact and introduce Thomas experts to me when needed. As his first PhD student, I have always been sincerely respectful and deeply indebted to him. Great thanks also goes to Professor Longley for contributing a preface and an endorsement, and to Ms Lucy Newlyn, a poet, a Thomas Studies scholar, and an Emerita Professor of English Literature at St Edmund Hall, the University of Oxford for her endorsement that affirms my contribution to the global acceptance of Thomas. Gratitude should also be given to the scholars and poets such as Ms Sioned Puw Rowlands, former Head of Wales Literature Exchange, Professor Katie Gramich, Dr Jamie Castell and Dr Thomas Tyrrell, all from the School of English, Communication and Philosophy, Cardiff University, and Ms Dinah Jones, a BBC Wales reporter, for offering concern, encouragement and feedback to my translation and doctoral research before, when or after I attended the Edward Thomas Centenary Conference at Cardiff University in late April 2017.

Special thanks to Professor Helen Wilcox, ex-Dean of the School of English Literature, Bangor University, who guided me to analyze and read some of Thomas's poems, so that I could better understand the way that native English speakers interpret English poetry. Thanks

特别感谢国家留学基金委和班戈大学联合资助笔者的博士项目，正因为有此资助，才会有这部译著的诞生。读博期间，笔者的博士生导师威尔士班戈大学语言学语言文学学院院长、托马斯研究学者安德鲁·韦伯博士给予了悉心专业的指导，并在需要时帮忙联系和引荐托马斯研究专家与笔者相识。作为开门弟子，笔者在此真诚地向导师致以最崇高的敬意与谢意。朗利教授对拙译给予大力支持并撰写了序言和推荐语。牛津大学圣艾德蒙学院英语文学退休教授、托马斯研究专家、诗人露西·纽琳女士对笔者就推动托马斯国际接受度进程所做的贡献给予了高度的评价，并欣然为本书撰写了推荐语。威尔士文学交流中心前负责人萧德·普·罗兰兹女士，以及卡迪夫大学英语交流哲学学院凯蒂·格拉米琪教授、杰米·卡斯特尔博士、托马斯·泰瑞尔博士和BBC威尔士电台记者黛娜·琼斯女士等学者与诗人，在笔者2017年4月底参加由卡迪夫大学举办的“爱德华·托马斯逝世百年纪念学术会议”时或在此前后，对拙译和博士论文研究给予了关注、鼓励和反馈。对以上诸位的认可与帮助，笔者深表感谢。

班戈大学英语文学院前院长海伦·威尔考克斯教授曾在百忙之中与笔者一起解析并朗读了托马斯部分诗作，让笔者能更好地领悟到英语为母语的本土人士诠释英诗的方式。曾执教于班

to Dr Yan Ying, who taught at the School of Modern Languages at Bangor University, and currently lectures at the University of Leicester, and to Dr Samuel Rogers, currently senior lecturer in English Literature at the University of the West of England, Bristol for their constructive feedback for my doctoral program, and also for Sam's endorsement for this book. Furthermore, I feel greatly grateful to Professor James Miller, a world prestigious Daoist scholar and currently Co-Director for the Humanities Research Centre in Duke Kunshan University, who as the external examiner for my viva spoke highly of my doctoral thesis and my translation work. Gratitude is also registered to my best friends such as Mr Stephen Rowlands, Mr Cecil Condron, Ms Elizabeth Vipond, Dr Daniel Hughes, Dr Joanna Melville-Richards, and Dr Sven Greitschus. When I was confused about some culture-loaded words in Thomas's poetry, they kindly and patiently offered explanations and spiritual encouragements.

Thanks should also be recorded to Dr Dhaifallah Alotaibi, a good friend from Saudi Arabia, who used to accompany me days and nights in our PhD research office of humanities at Bangor University. When I felt low in mood, he was always revitalizing me by brewing Arabic coffee for me to drink. I would like to show my gratitude to the visiting scholars at Bangor, such as Professor Yangquan Li from the School of Literature, Southwest University, and Associate Professor Lizhong Sun, from the School of Foreign Languages, Zhejiang Gongshang University, who, in addition to giving spiritual encouragement, shared with me their knowledge of Western literary theories and traditional Chinese poetics, which has strengthened

戈大学现代语言学院、如今任教于莱斯特大学的应雁博士，西英格兰大学（布里斯托）英国文学高级讲师萨缪尔·罗杰斯博士都曾或多或少地为笔者的博士项目给予一些意见与建议，后者还为此书撰写了推荐语。全球知名道学专家、昆山杜克大学人文研究中心联合主任苗建时教授作为答辩外审专家对笔者的博士论文及译著给予了充分的肯定。威尔士挚友斯蒂芬·罗兰兹先生、塞西尔·康德伦先生、伊丽莎白·维庞德女士、丹尼尔·休斯博士、乔安娜·梅尔维尔—理查兹博士、斯文·格雷楚斯博士在笔者对托马斯诗歌中的一些文化负载词倍感困惑之时，耐心地给予解答和精神鼓励。对以上诸位，笔者深表感激。

感谢来自沙特阿拉伯的博士好友大卫阿拉·阿罗泰比在班戈大学人文学科博士研究室陪笔者日夜奋战，在笔者情绪低落时，给予鼓励，并熬煮阿拉伯咖啡与笔者共饮，让笔者精神重振。感谢曾在班戈大学访学的诸位好友，比如西南大学文学院黎杨全教授、浙江工商大学外国语学院孙礼中副教授，除了给予精神鼓励，还一起探讨西方文论和中国传统诗学，不断强化笔者的知识体系。感谢曾在班戈大学法学院访学的好友上海交通大学范进学教授、曾在班戈大学孔子学院就职的好友中国海洋大学刘华义教授、曾在班戈大

my knowledge system. Thanks is also vented to Professor Jinxue Fan from Shanghai Jiaotong University who visited as a scholar the School of Law, Bangor University, Professor Huayi Liu from the Ocean University of China who used to work in the Confucius Institute at Bangor University, and Professor Hui Chen from Zhejiang Agriculture and Forestry University who visited the School of Linguistics and English Language at Bangor University. In our spare time, we travelled together across the UK, exploring local customs and scenery. With that experience, I became more confident when translating the relevant topics mentioned in Thomas's poems into Chinese. I also feel indebted to Ms Kun Jiao, the first headmaster and founder of Bangor Chinese School, and her husband Professor James Zengbo Wang, from the School of Computer Science and Electronic Engineering, Bangor University, my good Chinese friends in North Wales who used to invite me for dinner at their home where cultural and philosophical issues were debated. With all those experiences, my understanding of the commonalities and differences between Chinese and Western thinking has ever since been undoubtedly enhanced.

Furthermore, I would like to express my thanks to the following friends who worked, visited and studied at Bangor University: Dr Jianmin Fang, Associate Professor Lin Shen, Associate Professor Tong Xie, Associate Professor Shan Gao, Ms Xiaoling Wang, Dr Ping Zhang, Professor Dong Li, Dr Yuying Shi, Dr Zhizhou Kong, Mr Derui Kong, Associate Professor Tao Zeng, Dr Fengxian Yang, Mr Ruihua He, Professor Jiehui Hu, Associate Professor Yujuan Feng, Professor Lihua Yang, Professor Yalian Zhang, Professor

李健教授、黄晓玉教授、李芝副教授、武立红副教授、朱红梅副教授、苏静副教授、常青副教授、祝葵副教授、范婷婷副教授、陈莉莎副教授、陶嘉玮副教授、高月琴副教授、李兵副教授、祖国霞副教授、李欣副教授、刘玮副教授、陈晓颖副教授、吕丽塔副教授、罗灿副教授、杨海龙副教授、杨文澈先生、郑涛博士、代琦先生、杨丹女士、覃艳茜女士、谭晓妮女士、姜玉丹女士、黄娟女士、刘翠琼女士、韩琳琳女士、蓝瞻瞻博士、孔祥彬先生、刘瑞光先生、吴凡女士、向羽女士、吴琼贤女士、李莹女士、陈宇先生、曾巾力女士、万里先生等（以上排名不分先后）。

从班戈大学主楼休息台俯瞰班戈城与远处的梅奈海峡（Menai Strait）

衷心感谢广东外语外贸大学给予的科研出版经费支持。感谢刘岩教授、张欣教授、陈开举教授、张保红教授、李明教授、刘茂生教授、方开瑞教授、黄忠廉教授、董金伟教授、杨满珍教授、刘胡敏教授、吴庄教授、李成团教授、赵一农教授、潘莉教授、张平功教授、欧阳护华教授、邱小轻教授、杨静教授、李元教

Zhang, Professor Kaiju Chen, Professor Baohong Zhang, Professor Ming Li, Professor Maosheng Liu, Professor Kairui Fang, Professor Zhonglian Huang, Professor Jinwei Dong, Professor Manzhen Yang, Professor Humin Liu, Professor Zhuang Wu, Professor Chengtuan Li, Professor Yinong Zhao, Professor Li Pan, Professor Pinggong Zhang, Professor Huhua Ouyang, Professor Xiaoqing Qiu, Professor Jing Yang, Professor Yuan Li, Professor Min Jiao, Professor Feng Ding, Professor Jie Zheng, Associate Professor Rui Han, Associate Professor Jingjing Fu, Associate Professor Xiaoyan Cai, Associate Professor Dongqing Wang, Associate Professor Zhuyu Jiang, Associate Professor Qunying Huang, Associate Professor Qiuming Lin, Associate Professor Weichao Wang, Associate Professor Jing Shi, Dr Yunfeng Wang, Dr Wei Feng, Dr Tie Zheng, Dr Zirong Li, Ms Chunmei Pan, Mr Licheng Lu, Mr Shaoxiong Lin, Mr Zetang Wang, Ms Xiaomei Huang, Ms Yukun Xia, Mr Changqing Zheng, Dr Zhanping Wang, Ms Li Yang, Ms Yujie Xie, Dr Lei Yu, Ms Liyun Chen, Mr Li Yang, Mr Dong Wang, Ms Leling Li, Mr Yunnan Hou, Ms Hong Yang, Dr Yiting Qiu, and Ms Liu Wu (listed in no particular order).

No less significantly, my sincere gratitutde also goes to Dr Feng Robin Wang, associate professor and PhD supervisor of the School of Foreign Studies, Jilin University for generously sharing academic and publishing experience. It is a great honor to publish my book with the Intellectual Property Publishing House, one of the Top 100 Presses in China. Therefore, I would like to display my warm thanks to my editor Ms Jingjing Chen for her hard work along the way. Particular thanks to Mr Xiangzhan Cheng, a distinguished professor of Changjiang Scholars Program of the Ministry of Education, Deputy

授、焦敏教授、丁凤教授、郑杰教授、韩锐副教授、付晶晶副教授、蔡晓燕副教授、王冬青副教授、蒋竹雨副教授、黄群英副教授、林秋茗副教授、汪谓超副教授、石静副教授、王蕴峰博士、冯蔚博士、郑铁博士、李子容博士、潘春梅女士、卢立程先生、林邵雄先生、王则唐先生、黄晓梅女士、夏玉坤女士、郑常青先生、王战平博士、杨丽女士、解育洁女士、余蕾博士、陈丽韵女士、杨励先生、王栋先生、李乐玲女士、侯运男先生、杨宏女士、邱依婷博士、吴柳女士等广东外语外贸大学同事好友（以上排名不分先后），百忙之中抽暇在科研经费申请和相关学术问题等方面无私地分享经验和给予帮助。

译者于班戈大学不远处的
罗斯柯林（Rhoscolyn）岛上面朝大海

感谢挚友吉林大学外国语学院副教授、博士生导师王峰博士细心与笔者交流学术心得，分享出版经验。拙著能在全国百佳图书出版单位知识产权出版社出版，倍感荣幸，故此，特别感谢编辑陈晶晶女士一路的辛苦付出。同时，还感谢教育部长江学者特聘教授、现任山东大学文学院副院长和博士生导师程相占先生，广州大学英语文学教授、广东省外国文学学会会长、中国英语诗歌研究会副会长兼秘书长、诗人黎志敏博士，暨南大学外国语学院教师、R. S. 托马斯诗歌全译者、诗人程佳女

Dean and PhD Supervisor of the School of Literature of Shandong University; meanwhile to Dr Zhimin Li, a poet, Professor in English Literature of Guangzhou University, Director of Guangdong Society of Foreign Literature, and Deputy Director and Secretary General of English Poetry Studies Association of China (EPSAC); and furthermore to Ms Jia Cheng, a poet, a Chinese translator of R. S. Thomas's poetry in nearly entire range, and a lecturer from the College of Foreign Studies, Jinan University, for their respective endorsements for this book.

Additionally, my appreciation should be given to Mr Zhiwu Xu, Mr Wude Xu, Ms Meiyan Huang, Mr Yizhang Tu, Ms Shufan Lin, Mr Zhengzhao Xu (listed in no particular order), etc. for offering an amicable mentorship in one way or another, and their tacit and selfless support all the way. Last but not least, my deepest debt is of course owed to my beloved Dr Ying Yuan and kinfolks for their consistent support, selfless love, and full understanding of my little time to return my care and love while I was deciphering Thomas's poetry. Without the encouragement and assistance of the aforementioned institutions, colleagues, peers, friends and relatives, I would not be able whatsoever, I am afraid, to stand constantly optimistic and persevere in accomplishing such a difficult task.

My Chinese translation has journeyed many years of winds, rains, storms and sunshines, from autumn to spring and from winter to summer. The underlying difficulties go self-manifested, as Mr Zhongshu Qian in his monograph ***Patchwork: Seven Essays on***

士为本书撰写了推荐语。特此感谢。

译者于班戈大学文科主楼前

此外，非常感谢许志武先生、许武德先生、黄梅燕女士、涂义樟先生、林舒帆女士、许政钊先生等良师益友（以上排名不分先后）一直以来所给予的默默支持和无私帮助。当然，最需要致谢的是笔者的爱人袁莹博士和家人，感谢他们一直以来对笔者的支持，付出无私的爱，以及充分理解笔者在汉译托马斯诗歌时无法回报他们对笔者所付出的关心和爱。倘若没有以上机构、同事、同仁以及亲朋师友的鼓励、支持与帮助，恐怕笔者无法迎难而上、锲而不舍地顺利完成如此艰巨的任务。

汉译此诗集历经多个春秋，冬去春来，夏去秋来，译旅艰程。翻译之苦旅，正如钱钟书先生在《七缀集》中所言，翻译是一段从源语言至目标语的艰辛之旅，从开始到结束，期间总会遇见各种风险，出现遗失，甚至

Art and Literature[1] articulates that translation which always travels from the original language to the target language is a hard journey of ups and downs from the beginning to the end, during which there are inevitably risks, losses and even damages. Therefore, I dare not moan about the difficulties that have plagued my journey. Rather by my limited knowledge and ability, I aspire to present readers a faithful, smooth and elegant translation to the extent that it demonstrates Thomas's poetics sufficiently. Due to the limitation to my capability and knowledge bank, nor dare I deny that the book has never been speckled by errors or mistakes. It is my sincere hope, thereupon, that readers, experts, scholars and colleagues of inquisitivenesss could offer criticism and feedback if any, for which my deepest gratitude is vented.

Ultimately, I would like to end this epilogue with a poem written during my doctoral study in the UK as a tonic and encouragement for readers as well as for myself:

---

[1] The English title was borrowed from Duncan Campbell's beautiful translation of Qian's collection of his own seven essays, the work originally entitled *Qi Zhui Ji* 七缀集 (literally "Seven Stitched-together Collection"). The English translation was published by a famous Leiden publisher called Brill. QIAN Z. Patchwork: seven essays on art and literature [M]. CAMPBELL D, translated. Leiden: Brill Publishers, 2014.

蒙受损害。[1]故此，译路艰辛自不敢怨，笔者尽己所能呈现给读者较为忠实、顺达、雅致的译本，希冀能较为充分地展示出托马斯的诗艺特点和诗学理念。由于笔者知识能力水平有限，书中瑕疵亦在所难免，恳望广大读者、专家、学者和同仁批评指正，不胜感激。

2018 年 7 月 19 日，博士毕业典礼上译者与导师 Andy 和博士论文答辩内审专家 Helen 合照

最后，笔者以一首创作于英伦读博期间的诗结尾，以飨读者，同时共勉：

❶ 钱钟书．七缀集 [M]. 北京：三联书店，2007: 83.

Self Encouragement

By Peter Jingcheng Xu

Seagulls soar over the cold sea in morning light;
Cold jackdaws swoop trembling on the moors in twilight.
I alone surf the murk mist sweeping and swerving,
And climb over the wild hills 'n mountains unswerving.
Day and night, I've been drafting a long arcane tune,
When will it be done leaving me in triumphant croon?
Strong and sanguine we should be, yielding to no funk;
Ne'er on our first choice should we regret or debunk!

Initially written at Menai View Terrace, Bangor
01/01/2017-08/01/2018
Revised by White Clouds Mountain, Guangzhou
01/06/2019-28/03/2020

自 勉

许景城 作

掠鸟朝寒海，
寒鸦暮瑟泽。
独乘迷雾漫，
勇越险山隔。
终日谱玄韵，
何时奏凯歌？
自当行志强，
应不怨初择。

初作于班戈梅奈观海楼
2017/01/01–2018/01/08
修改于白云山麓
2019/06/01–2020/03/28

图书在版编目（CIP）数据

爱德华·托马斯诗歌全集译介：基于道家生态诗学视角：英汉对照 /（英）爱德华·托马斯著；许景城译．— 北京：知识产权出版社，2022.8

ISBN 978-7-5130-8309-6

Ⅰ．①爱…　Ⅱ．①爱…②许…　Ⅲ．①诗集—英国—近代—英、汉　Ⅳ．① I561.24

中国版本图书馆 CIP 数据核字（2022）第 155670 号

责任编辑：陈晶晶　　**责任校对：**谷　洋

封面设计：邵建文　马倬麟　　**责任印制：**孙婷婷

爱德华·托马斯诗歌全集译介

——基于道家生态诗学视角（英汉对照）

［英］爱德华·托马斯　著　许景城　译

出版发行：知识产权出版社有限责任公司	**网　址：**http：//www.ipph.cn
社　址：北京市海淀区气象路 50 号院	**邮　编：**100081
责编电话：010-82000860 转 8391	**责编邮箱：**shiny-chjj@163.com
发行电话：010-82000860 转 8101/8102	**发行传真：**010-82000893/82005070/82000270
印　刷：北京九州迅驰传媒文化有限公司	**经　销：**新华书店、各大网上书店及相关专业书店
开　本：787mm × 1092mm　1/32	**印　张：**16.875
版　次：2022 年 8 月第 1 版	**印　次：**2022 年 8 月第 1 次印刷
字　数：310 千字	**定　价：**89.00 元

ISBN 978-7-5130-8309-6